8

PARAFFIN

ALLEY

CATHIE MELLING

"Something wicked this way comes."

William Shakespeare,
Macbeth Act 4, scene 1

ISBN: 9798375533889

PART ONE
NORTH WEST ENGLAND

CHAPTER 1

David Phillips looked up from his desk at the young woman entering his estate agency.

She wore a brown gabardine mackintosh buttoned up to the neck. Her hair was mousy, pulled severely away from a heart shaped face scrubbed clean of make-up. Nervous fingers plucked at the handles of a shopping bag. His gaze dropped lower. Her legs were encased in thick brown stockings, her feet in sensible brogues.

He summed her up in two words. Time waster. He breathed away irritation and formed his mouth into a polite smile. "Good morning, Madam. Can I help you?"

She stepped forward shyly. "You've got a house in the window. Stockport. A three bed semi. South facing rear garden."

"Ah, yes. One of our recent instructions. I'll get the details. Please take a seat."

She bit her lip. When she visited estate agencies, she would select the sales sheets she wanted then go, but this man was so handsome she didn't want to. She set her shoulders, walked over and perched on the chair he indicated.

He leafed through the top drawer of a filing cabinet and emerged with the details, which he brought over and placed on the desk. He took the seat opposite. "This is a very desirable residence, madam."

Desirable. A nervous giggle escaped her.

"Sorry, is something wrong?"

She shook her head and fixed her eyes on the sheet as he turned it to face her. "Bit of wind."

He smiled vaguely. "Do you have a property to sell, Madam?"

"Iris."

"What?"

"Iris. My name's Iris. Iris Ferguson."

"So, do you?"

"What?"

David clicked his tongue. "Have a property to sell or are you a first time buyer?"

Iris's heart was thudding. She took a deep breath to explain. "What it is, I live with my grandmother. She's very old and in poor health but I won't inherit her house until she dies, not that I'm waiting for her to die." She paused then rushed to finish, her face burning, "So I collect these to cheer myself up but I'm wasting your time so thank you but I'd better go."

She gulped in air, grabbed her bag and headed for the door. As she reached it, he spoke. "Miss Ferguson. you're not wasting my time. Please, come back and sit down."

Iris hesitated then walked back.

He waited until she was seated again. "I think you're wise to plan ahead. Be prepared. In case the worst happens. How about I pull together some home portraits."

"What?"

"Sales particulars..."

"Right."

"...for houses similar to this one and post them to you?"

Iris brightened. "That's a super idea."

"Good. Your address is?"

"Surprise View, Paraffin Alley." She smiled shyly. "That's number eight in numerical terms."

An eyebrow lifted. "Didsbury?"

"Yes."

He leaned forward suddenly. She would have happily drowned in the blue ocean of his eyes. "Actually, Iris, perhaps I could come to the house and value it for you. Then you could focus on properties in your price range. Would you like that?"

"Oh. Yes, Mr..."

"Phillips. I own this Estate Agency."

She felt that required an acknowledgement. "That's nice."

"But please, call me David."

"David. When would that be? You must be very busy."

"Oh, I'm sure I can squeeze you in."

Iris let out a sigh.

David's lips parted as he opened his Filofax.

She imagined kissing him.

"I have a cancellation tomorrow at..."

"Perfect."

"...eleven." He stood and held out his hand. She realised he was inviting her to go. She shook it. His grip was firm, his hand soft and warm. "I'll see you then, Iris."

"You will, David." Her smile stretched from ear to ear.

He led her to the door and placed a hand lightly on her back as he opened it. She said goodbye and set off down the street, her stomach somersaulting with excitement.

David. Impossibly handsome. Piercing blue eyes. Chiselled jaw. Dimpled smile. Tall. Broad of shoulder, long of limb. She sighed expressively.

David. Manly. Gentle, yet strong.

David. She rolled his name around in her mouth, tasting each letter.

¤

Dorothea Ferguson scowled into Iris's shoulder as the young woman arranged the pillows behind her. "You took your time. I could have died of starvation while you were swanning around doing who knows what."

"I only nipped into Bramhall, Gran."

"Why? What do you need there that you can't buy round the corner at the Coop?"

"A walk and some fresh air and I thought I'd look for a dress for my thirtieth birthday."

"Don't know why you're bothering. Not like you have anywhere to go." She broke off and gnarled fingers raised a handkerchief to dab at rheumy eyes. "Who'd look at you anyway?" Gran pressed her lips together until they were white, then opened her mouth again. "None of the Ferguson genes in you, that's for sure. You take after your mother. Short and tubby."

Iris straightened and held her anger back. She'd heard this a thousand times. Gran enjoyed needling her. It was pointless responding. She set a luncheon tray of ham sandwiches and a beaker of milk on Gran's lap and walked back downstairs, through the dark oak-panelled hallway and into the kitchen, tucked at the rear of the house like an afterthought.

She sat at the big oak table and stared at her own plate of sandwiches and cooling mug of tea. With a sigh, she began to eat.

¤

After settling Dorothea that night, Iris turned on the television in the living room and curled up on the sofa with a contented sigh. This was her time now. She tuned in to Coronation Street and picked up her Babycham glass. It was full of sweet Pomagne, golden in the light from the screen, little bubbles popping on the surface. It was as delicious as a fine champagne. These were some of her special moments. Another was browsing in charity shops. She'd bought the Babycham glass from one, as she did her clothes, all paid for from a small allowance Gran gave her each week.

Her favourite thing of all was looking through

her collection of house sales particulars, imagining the day when she would have her own home.

It was a year since her last visit to Bramhall. Today was the first time she'd seen David Phillips Estate Agency. From the moment she set eyes on David, her past had paled into insignificance and her future sparkled with promise.

Because she was in love and it was the most beautiful feeling in the world.

CHAPTER 2

David's assistant returned from lunch and stopped when she closed the door, noticing a smug expression on his face. She hung her coat on the rack and sat on the edge of his desk. "Come on, what's tickled you?"

David picked up his Parker pen and tapped it casually on the desktop. "Suze, what comes to mind when I say Paraffin Alley?"

"Keswick or Didsbury?"

"Didsbury."

Her eyes widened. "Ridiculously expensive Victorian terraces. Why?"

"Because," he replied, "A girl was here while you were out. She lives there with her grandmother. Her very old grandmother. Her very old, sick grandmother."

"She's selling?"

"Not until the old dear pops her clogs but, by the sound of it, that could be any time soon."

"What's going on in that scheming little mind of yours?"

"Just keeping a finger on the pulse. I'm going there tomorrow morning to value it."

"You're going to value it? When she's not in a

position to sell?"

"Pays to be prepared."

"You're a devious git, Phillips."

He smiled. "Never pretend to be anything else, my love."

¤

At eleven o'clock next morning, David pulled up outside 'Surprise View'. As he applied the brakes, the door of the house opened and Iris ran down three steps that led onto a tiny garden. She was breathless when she reached the car and hurried round to the driver's side where David was sorting papers.

He rolled the window down and smiled up at her. "Good morning, Iris."

"Hello, David. You need to put this on the dashboard. It's a parking permit." She panted. "There are no driveways, you see. All the houses have two permits. One for the homeowner and one for visitors," She added unnecessarily, "Like you."

David's fingers brushed hers as he took it. "What happens if a householder owns two cars? Aren't they allowed visitors?"

Iris blushed at his touch. "They borrow ours. We never have any."

"I can't believe that. You must have a boyfriend, surely?"

Iris's colour deepened. Did he really think that? She hoped so. She'd spent all morning getting ready. After a desperate search through her wardrobe, she'd eventually picked a pair of brown crimplene trousers and a cream blouse with an embroidered Peter Pan collar. She'd looked despairingly at her reflection in the mirror but cheered up after a liberal spray of her favourite perfume, Avon *Occur!*. Her neighbour, an Avon Lady, had let her have it at cost. She often wondered how you would say *Occur!* with an exclamation mark as opposed to *Occur* without one. She'd mentioned it to the Avon Lady once but she hadn't known either.

Iris couldn't let Gran find out about the valuation so when she'd heard her sluicing in the bathroom that morning, walking heavily on her heels back to bed and calling to Iris to make her breakfast, she had crushed one of Gran's Zopiclone tablets into her porridge and added an extra spoonful of syrup to disguise the taste. Luckily, Gran hadn't noticed. An hour later, her snoring was resonating through the bedroom walls.

David cleared his throat. "Shall we go in then?"

"Oh. Yes, of course." Iris led the way, aware of his closeness as she climbed the steps back into the house. She stood to one side. "Well, this is the hall. As you can see..."

David smiled. "Iris. I'm not a prospective buyer. Why don't you make us a nice cup of tea while I get to work?" He opened his case and took out a pencil, clipboard and tape measure.

"Of course." Iris glanced up the stairs. "Don't go in the room facing you at the top. Gran's asleep in there. She mustn't know what you're doing."

David winked and whispered, "Don't worry. I'll be as quiet as a church mouse."

She stared after him as he climbed them then walked quickly to the kitchen and brought her hand to her mouth. Yesterday he'd placed his hand on her back as she left the shop. This morning, he'd asked about a boyfriend. Hadn't he walked a little too closely up the steps just then? Now he'd winked at her. She knew she couldn't read anything into it but, conversely, wondered if perhaps there was a remote chance that he liked her? Before the thought settled, she banished it and laughed at its absurdity.

¤

David entered the first bedroom, closed the door quietly and busied himself measuring. This must be Iris's room. In a moment of curiosity, he opened the wardrobe door and a snort of laughter escaped. Were these her clothes? He shook his head as he picked out a hanger and held up a pleated tartan skirt with an elasticated waistband.

He shoved it back, closed the door then stopped to give the wardrobe a closer inspection. If he wasn't mistaken, it was solid mahogany. He glanced around the room and walked to a matching tallboy. He pulled open a drawer. Solid wooden base, dovetail joints. The dressing table in front of the bay window was of the same quality. So was the bed, with its intricately carved head and tail board.

He turned full circle. There were some

valuable antiques in here. If this was representative of the furniture in the rest of the house, there was a small fortune to be made.

He thought about his ambitions to open a second agency. How his accountant had explained that, despite the success of his first year, it would take many more to raise sufficient capital to expand.

He thought about the sick old lady in the room next door, the eager girl waiting downstairs.

As he measured, scribbled numbers and moved on to the next room, he was already outlining a plan. She would be a very rich girl when her grandmother died. A very rich girl who obviously had a crush on him.

He could wait.

¤

Iris wondered how long David would be. Was there time to make a batch of scones to have with their tea? That might impress him. She searched the cupboard and found some glacé cherries, always a bit special. She quickly pulled the ingredients together, humming along to the radio as she added eggs and milk. The trick, her mum had taught her, was to roll the dough out to a thickness of exactly an inch and a quarter, otherwise they wouldn't rise enough. Iris used a ruler every time and her scones were always perfect.

David entered the kitchen as they were cooling on a wire rack. "They smell delicious."

Iris smiled with pleasure. "Would you like one

with your tea?"

"Oh, would I?" Quickly, he measured the room dimensions, listed the fixtures, inspected the small yard beyond the window, then slipped the tape, pen and clipboard back inside his briefcase. "Well, that's that, Iris. I'll work out the valuation back at the office. Mind if I take my jacket off?"

"Please do." Iris smiled again. "Would you like English Breakfast or Earl Grey?"

"Earl Grey please."

"Lemon?"

"Milk please. Bit of a philistine when it comes to Earl Grey."

Iris nodded in agreement, "Me too." She measured leaf tea into a china teapot, filled it with hot water and placed it on the table with a strainer while she prepared the scones. She brought them over with cups, plates, knives, butter and a pot of strawberry jam. As she took the seat opposite, she leaned forward conspiratorially. "Actually, you're not supposed to put jam on a fruit scone but I always do."

He laughed, "That's something else we've got in common."

Iris poured the tea, rested back in her chair and brought the cup to her mouth.

David picked a scone and broke it carefully in half. A cherry fell onto his plate. He picked it up between finger and thumb, brought it to his lips and looked straight at her. "You know, Iris, there's nothing nicer than sucking a juicy red cherry."

Iris coughed out her tea. Eyes watering, she mopped the table with a serviette. "Sorry. Bit of scone went down the wrong way." She cleared her throat. "So what do you think about the house, then?"

She watched David licked his fingers. "Very impressive. These Victorian houses are highly sought after." He sat forward to rest his elbows on the table. "As for the furniture and some of the other contents, clocks, ornaments? Well, I'm no expert but I think you have some very expensive and collectable pieces here. If you like I could get a friend of mine, an antique dealer, to take a look?"

Iris frowned. "But the house won't go up for sale until Gran passes."

David jumped in. "No, no, of course not. You misunderstand me. I'm just saying that when the time comes, you could clear the house and make a substantial amount of money into the bargain. I'm sure that would be very welcome?"

Iris nodded, "Yes. I see what you mean."

David finished his tea and popped the rest of the scone into his mouth as he stood and reached for his jacket.

"Oh. You're going." She couldn't disguise her disappointment.

"I have to. I've got a valuation back in Bramhall. Listen, Iris, would you have dinner with me tomorrow night? I'll have the figures ready by then and we can discuss the way forward."

Iris couldn't speak. She blinked several times.

He added, "If it's convenient, that is?"

"I'd love to."

David donned his jacket. "That's great. I'll pick you up at seven thirty."

"I'll be ready."

"Perfect." David gave her a captivating smile and followed her into the hall. He paused as they reached the front door. The rays of the sun were shining through the stained glass panels and illuminated his face with a glow that made his perfect features almost god-like. Without warning, as she opened the door, he leaned forward, placed a kiss on her cheek that left a hint of aftershave and mint toothpaste then strode down the steps to his car and climbed in.

Stunned, she hurried after him and waved as he drove away. When the car disappeared round the corner, she didn't move, her arm still raised. He had kissed her cheek.

Iris did a half twirl that brought her back to face the house. She sighed happily, pushed open the gate, danced up the steps and inside the house.

"Who was that at the door? Where's my cup of tea?"

Gran was at the top of the stairs, one hand clutching the newel, the other, her cane. Iris thought quickly. "Jehovah Witness, Gran."

Gran yawned, stretching parchment thin cheeks. "Hope you showed them the sole of your shoe."

"I certainly did, Gran. Right. Are you getting up or staying in bed this morning?"

"Staying in bed. Don't know what's wrong with me today. I was alright when I woke up but after that porridge, I couldn't keep my eyes open. I'm going back to sleep so don't disturb me."

Iris shrugged innocently. "Maybe it's because it's nearly autumn. You know? Like hibernating?"

"Don't be so stupid. I'm not a bloody hedgehog."

Iris lowered her voice. "You're prickly enough."

"What? Speak up girl."

"I said I'll bring you a cuppa. I made some scones. D'you want one?"

"Don't mind. Butter and jam. Is there any clotted cream?"

"No."

"Psshhht." Gran turned laboriously and shuffled back into her room.

Iris walked into the kitchen with a wide smile. Nothing Gran could say or do today could dent her happiness. She was under no illusion that dinner with David was anything other than business. But what puzzled her was why? She was sure it wasn't common practice and he knew that her visit to his agency had been an indulgence, that the house wasn't hers to sell.

Iris shrugged. It was of no consequence. All that concerned her was that David Phillips was taking her out to dinner. She was going to pretend it was a real date. For that, she wanted something really special to wear.

She would show him that frumpy, dumpy, mousy Iris Ferguson was, in fact, all woman.

✳

After lunch, Iris decided to revisit Bramhall and have another look in the charity shops. She thought about walking past David's agency but batted it away. If she was spotted, he might think she was stalking him. Which, of course, she wasn't.

There was a new shop on the high street. Iris had seen it yesterday but it had been closed, its purpose unknown. However, this afternoon when her bus passed, she noticed signwriters clearing up and the door was open. Iris jumped off at the next stop and hurried back to it. The signage said 'Whiskers Galore' and had a kindle of kittens frolicking in and out of the lettering. It was a cat charity, which made Iris smile with pleasure.

She walked into a strong odour of fresh paint: the penetrating sharpness of white gloss woodwork infused with the powdery blandness of denim blue emulsion.

"Sorry, it's a mess in here, we're still unpacking, pricing and hanging!"

The voice came from a smartly dressed older lady who appeared from behind the counter.

Iris smiled at her. "Is it alright if I look around?"

"Of course it is!"

The lady talked like every sentence was an exclamation. Iris chuckled to herself. She bet she could say *Occur!* perfectly.

"Just have a rummage. If you fancy anything,

just shout!"

"Thank you." Iris began to walk round the
rails. Maybe she could look for some decent
daywear too, there were some lovely things on
display, but first things first. Tomorrow night's
outfit.

She turned to the lady and blurted, "I'm
looking for something really special. For a
dinner date tomorrow night. With a man."

"Ooh! First date?"

Iris blushed. "Kind of. He's very handsome.
Looks like Tony Hadley. You know? From
Spandau Ballet?"

"Oh, yes. I like him, he's very nice! Well
then..." The lady stood back, put her hands on
her hips and tilted her head, "...let's have a look
at you!" She walked around Iris slowly. "You've
got nice legs!"

"Have I?" Iris was surprised.

"You should show them off! What size are
you?"

"I've no idea. Biggish."

"Oh, honestly! Let's find out."

She vanished behind the counter and emerged
with a tape measure. Before Iris knew it, she
had reached her arms around her and pulled the
tape together over her bust. "Thirty six." She
measured again. "You're a 'B' cup, lucky you!"

"Am I?" Iris looked down at herself.

"Keep still! Right – waist 28. Gosh! I'd never
have guessed. You're petite but, forgive me, your
outfit is shapeless and it makes you look plump,
you're literally hiding your light under a

bushel!"

Iris opened her mouth to say no, that wasn't literal but the lady's cheek was pressed against her stomach as she brought the tape around her hips. "Thirty six inches!"

She stood back delightedly. "You have a perfect hourglass figure! Now, before I retired, I worked at Kendals in Manchester as a personal shopper in the ladies department so I'd love to help you. I'm Patricia, by the way but please call me Trish!"

"That would be absolutely brilliant!" Iris was beginning to sound like her but she was being bowled along by Trish's enthusiasm. She knew she would leave the shop with something sensational.

CHAPTER 3

The butterflies in her stomach woke Iris long before the alarm. Tonight was her date with David. She looked at the dress hanging from the wardrobe door. Trish had shown an endless supply of patience yesterday and when she'd shown this one to Iris, she fell in love with it.

"Iris, you look fabulous!" Trish had clapped her hands together with glee when Iris stepped out of the changing room. The dress could have been made for her. It was in figure hugging black jersey with a balcony bodice that emphasised her generous cleavage.

Trish said it was a Biba original but she only charged Iris three pounds and only another two for some flattering pieces of everyday wear. Iris announced that she was never going to wear any of her old clothes again so Trish suggested she donated them to the shop.

The best thing of all was that Iris had made a friend. Trish made them a cup of tea after Iris paid for her purchases and as they chatted, Iris found herself opening up about her life. Trish could tell that she was lonely and suggested that Iris might like to work one day a week in the shop, perhaps on Thursdays with her. Iris thought it was a grand idea, even though she didn't know how she would persuade Gran to let her.

¤

Back in the present, Iris glanced at her clock radio. It was nearly time to wake Gran for breakfast. She was hoping to invite David in for coffee when he dropped her off tonight. So that Gran wouldn't find out, Iris was going to slip another Zopiclone into her cocoa when she prepared her for bed. It would also mean she could get ready without raising suspicion.

That afternoon she walked the short distance into Didsbury Village, where a lovely assistant in Boots helped her choose some make-up, demonstrated how to apply it, persuaded her to buy a shampoo-in rinse to lighten her hair to honey blonde and gave her tips on styling it. On her way out, Iris stopped at the men's aftershave counter to see if she could identify the one David had been wearing. After many sprays, sniffs and sneezes, she found it on the Estee Lauder stand. It was *Aramis*. When she got home, she carefully washed off the other scents so that only his fragrance remained on her skin, bringing a smile to her face each time she sniffed it.

That evening, Iris attended to Gran then flew into her own room to get ready. Five minutes before David was due, she carefully pulled on sheer black tights, the Biba dress and stepped into a pair of black suede court shoes she'd spotted in a bargain bucket a long time ago.

Her eyes widened and her mouth fell open when she looked in the mirror. With her hair and her make-up and her dress and her legs and her shoes, she looked beautiful. She let out a bubble of laughter and hugged herself.

She felt dizzy with excitement and the conviction that tonight would change her life forever.

¤

The maître d' greeted David at the door of Le Petit Coco, gave Iris a charming smile and took her coat. David's eyes widened in amazement. This wasn't the same Iris, surely.

"You look lovely, Iris. You've got beautiful green eyes."

Iris's heart flipped at his compliment and a blush warmed her cheek as the maître d' reappeared with menus and balancing a small silver tray holding two glasses of champagne. They followed him to a table where he set down the menus and tray and moved Iris seamlessly into her seat.

In one fluid movement, he moved the glasses to the table. "A glass of Dom Perignon to welcome you, with the compliments of the house." He tucked the tray under his arm and curled his hands together. "Your waiter will be with you shortly to take your orders. I hope you enjoy your evening."

A swift bow and he vanished. Iris frowned as

she studied the menu.

David noticed her expression. "What's wrong? Is there nothing you fancy?"

"I don't know. I don't eat out so I don't know what some of these things are. Well, that is, I have gone out for meals before, obviously, but not recently."

"When was the last time?"

Iris closed one eye and looked up at the ceiling as she thought. "Um. Nineteen sixty eight."

David laughed then stopped. "You're serious."

"Yes." She pressed her lips together and looked back at the menu.

"How come?"

"Because my parents and Grumps had died by then and Gran never went out. So that was it, really." She tailed off and shrugged her shoulders.

"Grumps?"

"Grandad. I called him that because he wasn't. Grumpy, I mean. He was the loveliest, funniest man that ever lived. He's the one who named our house 'Surprise View'."

"But your house faces an eight foot brick wall."

"Yes, I know. That's the surprise. There's no view."

David smiled politely as Iris doubled up with laughter. She wiped her eyes and straightened when their waiter approached.

"Are you ready to order, Sir? Madam?"

David inspected the menu. "Yes. I'll have the Chateaubriand with Duchesse potatoes."

"Certainly, Sir. Would you like beurre Maître

d'Hotel?"

"Yes, thank you..." David passed the menu to him. "...and I'll have a small glass of Cabernet Sauvignon please. Do you have Napa Valley?"

Of course, Sir. Madam?"

Iris bit her lip as he turned to her. "I'm not sure. I don't usually eat meat."

The waiter said kindly, "Can I recommend the creamy mushroom tagliatelle?"

Iris smiled at him gratefully. "That sounds lovely. Thank you."

The waiter smiled back. Iris smiled. The waiter continued to smile. David leaned forward. "Iris, he's waiting for you to tell him what you want to drink."

"Oh. Sorry. Could I have another glass of that champagne, please."

David turned to the waiter, "Will you bring a fillette for the lady, please?"

¤

The champagne loosened Iris's tongue and it was easy for David to find out more about her. She explained that her parents had died in the Stockport plane crash of 1967 and Grumps had died the following year. "Gran made me leave school at sixteen to be her full time carer. That's what I've done ever since." She gave a little apologetic smile. "She hates me going out, especially in the evening, so I slipped a sleeping tablet into her cocoa tonight. It was naughty of me but it won't do her any harm."

David frowned. "But what do you do when

you're not caring for her?"

"Well, I'm never not caring for her."

"What do you do for entertainment then?"

"Well, Gran doesn't like noise. We've got a telly but I can't watch it until I've settled her down after tea. We don't have a video player. Or a record player. We've got a radio though, in the kitchen, at the back of house, where it won't disturb her."

David sat back in shock. "It sounds dreadful. How do you stand it?"

"I'm used to it, I suppose." Iris stopped and dug her fork into her pasta. Why would someone like David be remotely interested in a life coloured in a palette of grey?

"That's about the saddest thing I've ever heard, I mean, it's nineteen eighty five, for god's sake. Can't you put her in a home or something?"

Iris looked at him in horror. "I couldn't do that." It was true. She had a sense of duty, an obligation to look after Gran. However much she hated the old woman, she was the only family Iris had left.

"So what's wrong with her?"

"It's her heart. She's on lots of different tablets and almost bed ridden. She's in her late eighties now. She had my dad late in life." Iris pulled her shoulders back and shrugged expressively. Her breasts lifted and pressed against the low bodice.

David felt his loins tighten. He looked away. "Well, I'm sure you're doing the best by her. Now." Pushing his plate to one side, he extracted a manilla envelope from inside his jacket. He leaned over and placed it by her glass.

"What's this?" She looked at it curiously.

"It's your house valuation. I told you we'd look at it tonight."

"Oh yes." Iris had almost forgotten. She opened it, read the contents, folded it and placed it down, her palm pressed lightly on top. "Are you serious?"

"Deadly." He sat back and took a sip from his glass, studying her reaction. "Is it not what you expected?"

"One hundred thousand pounds?"

"As an opening price, yes. To invite interest."

"You mean people might pay more?"

"Probably, if it's marketed well. These houses are highly sought after, especially by property developers. They're perfect for apartment conversions."

"Gosh." Iris's brows lifted and her eyes widened.

"So, there's not much else I can do at the present. Until your grandmother dies and you come into your inheritance."

"I suppose not."

"I assume, when you do, you'll still want me to handle the sale?"

She couldn't recall that conversation. "Yes, of course."

"I'll add the cost of the valuation to the sales commission then."

She hadn't realised he was charging for it.

"Well, I think that just about winds up the

evening."

"Oh. Right." Crestfallen, Iris finished her champagne and set the glass gently down.

"I'll just settle the bill." He beckoned their waiter.

Iris collected her bag from under her chair and waited quietly.

¤

Surprise View was in darkness when David pulled up. He smiled at Iris, the engine still running, his hand resting on the gear lever.

Iris had to ask him now, before she lost her nerve. "Would you like to come in for a drink?"

"I can't, I'm afraid. It's a school night."

Iris looked puzzled then realised it was a joke.

"Well, do get in touch once you're ready to sell. In the meantime, I'll put you on our mailing list."

She nodded. "Thank you David. For dinner and everything."

Then she was standing outside the car and watching as it drove away.

¤

Iris closed the front door quietly and crept up to her room. In the bathroom, she rushed through her ablutions. In the bedroom, she put her underwear in the laundry basket, her dress on a padded hanger in the wardrobe and pulled on a cotton nightie. When she climbed into bed, she laid her head on the pillows and relived the evening in her mind. But her imagination invented a new ending, one in which David accepted her invitation to come in. As the scene unfolded, she pushed her covers away, pulled up her nightdress, closed her eyes and began to touch herself.

David follows me into the living room, catches my hands and guides me to the sofa. He sits me down and faces me, one hand curling round my neck, then he kisses me.

I move away slightly. "David, I need to tell you something."

David takes my hands again and smiles. "You're a virgin?"

I am surprised. "You know?"

"I guessed. Look," He sits closer and drops his hands to my thighs. "Do you trust me not to hurt you?"

I pause then nod, my heart thudding.

He murmurs in my ear, "Then will you let me make love to you? I want to so, so much. Your body is incredible. I've thought about nothing else since we first met."

David slowly undresses me, his fingers and lips caressing my breasts, tongue circling my nipples. My excitement mounts, my breath shortens until each inhalation ends with an upward gasp.

With his hand, he begins to touch me. I push

against it and my rhythm becomes fluid, fast, urgent.
David carefully enters me. It feels incredible. I match each thrust. I am riding a lightening bolt, clinging on for dear life as something sweet and unstoppable floods through me.

On the bed, Iris orgasmed with a loud cry, then lay exhausted, breathing heavily, sweat glistening, heart pounding. There was a click. The door opened.

"What's that noise? What on earth are you doing?" Gran strode into the room, the thump of her cane preceding each step. She towered over Iris and stared down at the nightie ruched around her waist, the hand between her thighs. "You filthy girl. Is this what you do in your bedroom?"

Iris dived out of bed, her face burning with embarrassment and shame. She dragged her gown down.

"You little whore. You're just like your mother."

Iris clenched her fists by her side and dug her nails into her palms. "I've not done anything. I've only been out for a meal." She stopped abruptly.

Gran tipped her head sideways and looked at Iris from that angle. "A meal? Tonight? When? Who with?"

Iris mumbled a reply.

Gran moved nearer. "It was a man, wasn't it?"

Her eyes narrowed. "You put a sleeping pill in my cocoa, didn't you? I thought it tasted funny. I threw it away. You've just proved you're the devious little bitch I always knew you were. You tried to drug me so you could sneak out behind my back. What if I'd had a heart attack? You're supposed to care for me. I've not seen much evidence of that these days. My God but you're your mother's child and no mistake. Well, go and shack up with your boyfriend before you get pregnant. I'll not have another bastard child under my roof. Now, get out of my house."

Iris held her arms out. "Please, Gran. I'm sorry."

"I said get out. Now. This minute. And first thing in the morning, I'm ringing my solicitor to change my will. You're not getting a penny off me now. I'd rather give it a tramp on the street." She turned, stamped her cane and headed for the door.

In panic, Iris rushed after her, struggling to find the words to appease her. "Gran, please, you can't throw me out. I'm your granddaughter."

Gran reached her bedroom but stopped at the door to face Iris. "If you ever were, you're not any more. I'm disowning you." She spat the next words out. "I only let you stay here out of charity after Peter and your mother died. Even after the shock killed your grandfather. Are you grateful? No! This is how you repay me."

Iris cut through the vitriol. "What do you mean, you let me stay here? This is my home."

31

"This isn't your home. It never was. I've always suspected you're another man's child. It was your mother's fault that Peter and your grandfather died."

"No, it wasn't. You're a liar." Iris was crying openly now, heaving sobs that made her words hiccup.

Gran ignored her. "If your grandfather hadn't paid for that holiday in Majorca, Peter wouldn't have been on that plane and his father wouldn't have died of a broken heart."

Iris dragged the back of her hand across her streaming nose. "Grumps paid for that holiday to give them a break from you. Mum and Dad hated you. You were horrible to them, especially Mum. They only stayed because of Grumps. You started on me as soon as Grumps died and you've made my life hell ever since. If you weren't such an evil old cow, they'd have never been on that flight. It's your fault they died."

"How dare you."

Iris shouted over her. "The only people I ever loved are dead and it's your fault. And who do I have left?" Her voice rose. "You! The person I hate most in the world."

Iris stopped to draw ragged breaths and the air turned rancid and heavy in the space between them.

Gran narrowed her eyes, bared her teeth and shoved her face into Iris's. "When that plane crashed only twelve souls survived and I prayed to God my son was one of them. My world ended when I found out he wasn't. Not a day

PARAFFIN ALLEY

has passed since then that I haven't wished that you'd been on that plane with your mother, instead of him."

Iris veered back in shock. Gran's words lit a furnace inside her. She felt the heat rising, burning her face and yelled, "I've wanted you dead all my life and I wish you would die now."

A rumble sounded deep in Gran's throat. It swelled until she opened her mouth to expel it. "How dare you. You ungrateful bitch."

The cane rose in the air. Iris screamed, squeezed her eyes shut and curled her arm protectively over her head. With her other, she pushed Gran away.

There was another scream but this time it wasn't Iris.

A body falling.

Landing.

Silence.

Iris dropped her arms, lowered her shoulders and opened her eyes.

She stared at Gran lying motionless at the foot of the stairs.

She closed and reopened her eyes but Gran was still lying there.

She saw blood pooling around her skull.

Iris screamed again.

CHAPTER 4

The phone was ringing when David arrived next morning. He switched off the alarm, dropped his briefcase, perched on the edge of the desk and picked up the receiver. He nodded to Suzanna as she walked in. "David Phillips Estate Agency. David speaking."

There was nothing from the other end so he added, "Hello? Can I help you?"

A sob. Two more sobs. Then a small wobbly voice. "David, it's me."

"Sorry, who?"

"It's me. Iris. Iris Ferguson." Her voice broke and all he could hear were more sobs, louder this time. He stood and spoke urgently into the mouthpiece. "Iris. What's happened? Tell me. Are you ill?"

Suzanna stopped in the act of hanging her coat and stared at him. He glanced at her, shoulders and eyebrows lifting. "Iris, talk to me."

"It's Gran."

"Your gran? What's wrong with her?"

A fresh outbreak of sobs. David pressed his palm against his brow. "Iris. Sit down, take some deep breaths and calm down. Now, are you OK?"

"Yes. No. I'm not hurt but Gran."

"Jesus, Iris, what's wrong with her?" He looked helplessly at Suzanna and mouthed an expletive.

The answer was charged with emotion. "She's dead."

It didn't register. David stared down at his shoes, across to the window display, up at the fluorescent light and down again. "What?"

"Dead. Gran's dead. She fell downstairs last night." She broke off and wailed. "It's all my fault."

"Where are you?"

"At home."

Right. Stay there. I'm coming straight over. Don't move. OK?"

"OK. Thank you, David."

His voice was like warm honey. "Not a problem. I'll be there before you know it."

He put the phone down and looked at Suzanna.

She stared back. "What was that about?"

He smiled. "Ding dong. The witch is dead." His smile widened and he folded his arms. "Kerching."

¤

The curtains were drawn. David rang the doorbell and waited. After a moment, he rang it again. There was no sound from within. He put his mouth to the letter box and shouted her name. When he looked through it, he saw a dark stain in front of the bottom stair but nothing else.

David stood back and scratched his chin. Where was she? It hadn't taken long to get here and he'd told her to stay put. He hoped she hadn't done anything stupid. Now he'd have to go back to the shop and ring her.

He cursed and walked away. As he reached the car, he heard his name called. He looked around.

"David. Up here!"

He looked wildly to left and right.

"David, It's Iris. Look up at the roof."

He obeyed and, sure enough, the top of Iris's head was visible above a parapet. He panicked and began waving his hands in the air. "Iris. Oh my God, Iris! Step away from the edge. Everything will be alright, I promise."

"I'm coming down."

His voice pitched. "No! Don't! Please Iris, don't jump. You have so much to live for. It'll be OK. Don't jump. For the love of God, please don't jump!"

"I'm not jumping. I'm coming downstairs to let you in."

"Oh. Right." He smoothed his jacket into place and walked back to the front door. Moments later, he heard a key turn in the lock.

Iris was out of breath when she opened the door. She threw herself at him. "Oh, David, thank you for coming so quickly."

He moved away in surprise and held her arms as he looked worriedly into her face. "What were you doing on the roof?"

"It's terraced. It's where Grumps kept his homing pigeons. I used to spend a lot of time up there with him. After I rang you, I felt the need to feel close to him." She smiled a sigh then brightened. "Please come in, David. I'm sorry, I think I'm still in shock. It was dreadful."

"Of course you are. It must have been. Yes. Put the kettle on. When you're ready, you can tell me what happened." He put his arm around her shoulder as they passed though the hall. "So, she's definitely dead then?"

Iris walked on into the kitchen and flicked the kettle on. She turned to get two cups from the cupboard. "Of course she is."

"Of course she is. Sorry."

Iris spooned ground coffee in a cafetière, added hot water and brought it over to the breakfast table with two cups and a jug of single cream. They sat facing each other and he studied her as she pressed down on the plunger. Her eyes were red and bloodshot, puffy from crying but her hair was all mussed up in a sexy way. David felt a sudden mixture of lust and affection. He listened while she poured the coffee and explained, in a flat voice, the events of the previous night. At one point, he took her hand and stroked it with his thumb, nodding and punctuating her story with sympathetic noises.

"Gran was still alive when the ambulance got here but she suffered a massive heart attack and died at the hospital. They were marvellous

though. Did everything they could to save her."
Iris sniffed and pulled a tissue from her sleeve.
"I didn't get back until this morning. She's in
the mortuary. The hospital staff were wonderful
too. I saw a really kind gentleman who took me
into his office and explained the procedures."

David nodded and patted her hand. "So, what
happens now?"

"Well, they've put the cause of death as
myocardial infarction. A heart attack," She
explained at his blank look, "She was under the
doctor with her heart and as she didn't die at
home, there won't be an autopsy or an inquest.
The death certificate was signed off this
morning. Gran had an account with the Co-op
so they're arranging for the undertaker to collect
her and take her to the Chapel of Rest." She
made a little noise in her throat and her voice
broke. "Oh. I'll have to arrange the funeral and
tell people. Then there's the Will and
everything. I don't know where to start."

David stood, walked round to her side of the
table and crouched by her chair. "Why don't you
let me worry about all that."

"It's my fault she fell."

No. No. No. Hush now." He reached for her
hand and patted it again. "You were only
defending yourself."

Iris sniffed. "I know that. I mean I caused the
row."

"Why?"

She buried her head in his shoulder to muffle
her voice. "She came into my bedroom when she

38

heard me cry out."

"Why did you cry out?"

"I'd rather not say." She tailed off then went on, "I don't want to stay here now. This was the reason I rang you. I wondered if you could sort out somewhere for me to rent, until 'Surprise View' is sold and I can buy a place of my own."

"Haven't you any family you can stay with?"

"There is no other family."

"Friends?"

"I don't have any." She kept her head down. Despite her grief, being this close to him was wonderful. She held her breath in case the spell was broken.

David thought quickly. "Iris. Look, why don't you come and stay with me for now? I've got a spare room. It's yours for as long as you need it. I'll help with the funeral and after, I can get the house on the market and arrange to have the contents collected and sold for you."

Iris lifted her head slowly and looked at him rapturously. She gave a little quiver. "You want me to move in with you?"

"Yes, temporarily. As long as you're happy with..."

"I'm happy."

"But if you want time to think?"

"Don't need to."

"Well then. No time like the..."

"I'll pack now."

David watched as Iris hurried out of the kitchen. Thoughtfully, he refilled his cup and added a dash of cream.

Once she was under his roof, he would wait for the right moment to move the relationship along. That would be easy.

He could already see his second agency. In fact, a gold encrusted path to the third was already beckoning.

CHAPTER 5

Attendance at Gran's funeral was sparse. It was composed only of Iris, David, the family doctor and the Pastor of Dorothea's church, who conducted the service and read the liturgy. It had been brief, the last of the day, and as they emerged into the late afternoon the clouds that had been threatening rain cleared and they were greeted with a cornflower blue sky.

To Iris, it was a symbol of a bright new future. Her grief at Gran's passing had been fleeting. Two weeks living at David's had highlighted how miserable her life had been before. Now her pallet of grey was replaced with every colour of the rainbow.

The small procession followed behind the coffin, borne aloft on the shoulders of hired pall bearers. At the graveside, Iris dabbed her eyes politely, the only mark of respect she could muster for the woman whose death had given Iris a new life.

David had booked an Italian restaurant in Didsbury for the wake but as the tiny party left the grave, they melted away with excuses and goodbyes, leaving David and Iris to make their way to the venue on their own. He was secretly pleased. It was all over now. The reading of the will last week had confirmed Iris as sole beneficiary of the house, the contents and Gran's savings of £5,000. The latter was an unexpected bonus. With Iris's fortune guaranteed and the old girl six feet under, David could begin his plans in earnest.

Once Iris had moved in and been established in the guest room, David had been pleasantly surprised at the benefits it brought to his quality of life. Iris was used to being a carer. David became her focus.

He had also noticed a change in Iris's appearance. No longer restricted by the demands of her grandmother and removed from the dark Victorian heap, she had blossomed into a pretty girl, with flattering clothes, hair and make-up.

Now it was time to move their relationship on. David was looking forward to initiating sex. The restaurant presented the perfect opportunity to start reeling her in. He stretched his arm across the table and laid his hand flat on the linen cloth. "Iris, you were so brave today. I really admire your resilience." He turned his palm upwards.

Iris stared at it then at him. "That's nice of you to say, David. It wasn't easy, I must admit."

He cupped his palm and wiggled his fingers. Iris cautiously lowered her hand inside. He smiled gently. "You know, Iris, it's hard to believe that we've only known each other a couple of weeks. In that short space of time, I've grown very fond of you."

Iris blinked. Did he mean that the way it sounded?

He continued, voice buttery smooth. "I'm so glad you agreed to move in. I don't know if you feel the same?"

The same? Did he mean the suitability of their living arrangements or was he expanding on his sentient declaration? She thought carefully and decided to take the middle ground. "I'm very happy staying with you, David and grateful for everything you've done since Gran died."

He sat back and smiled. She was trying to be coy but those emerald eyes held a glimmer of hope and expectation. "Well, you'll be pleased to know that I have someone interested in the property and I'm confident I can get you a really good price."

Iris's face lit up, "That's wonderful. How much are you hoping for?"

David arranged his features. "I'll tell you when the deal's done. Is that OK? Wouldn't want to disappoint you."

"Oh, you could never do that, David." She gave him a beatific smile. "I trust you completely."

His hand closed over hers. "It means so much to hear you say that, Iris."

¤

The atmosphere was charged. Iris felt it when they arrived home in the early evening. On the way, David had suggested they skip dinner and open a bottle of champagne.

While he was in the kitchen, Iris showered and changed into a flimsy black satin chemise. She'd got it from the shop last Thursday, her first day volunteering with Trish and had stored it away, just in case. If David's words, back at the restaurant, meant what she hoped they meant, it was time and the chemise would send a clear message back that she was ready and waiting.

Iris hurried downstairs, her heart racing. She was tingling inside and in the pit of her body she could feel the sweet ache of lust. She reached the foot of the stairs as David walked though the hall with champagne and glasses. He stopped and his eyes lit up. "Is that for my benefit?"

Iris blushed. "Perhaps."

He nodded appreciatively and ushered her ahead of him into the lounge. David poured, handed her a glass and patted the seat beside him as he settled on the sofa. She joined him and clutched her glass tightly to stop it shaking.

The bubbles skittered into her nostrils and she sneezed. David laughed as he refill her glass. "Bless you!"

She threw back the second glass. This time the little bubbles worked their magic. She smiled.

David moved nearer. Seconds later he was kissing her, forcing her back onto the seat of the sofa, his hands pulling down her straps, dragging at the bodice, body shifting over hers, heavy, unapologetic.

What happened next was too fast for Iris to

take in. She realised her breasts were exposed and her chemise had ruched up around her waist. One of David's hands was undoing his trousers, the other moving roughly over her skin. Lips closed around her nipples, sucking, tongue prodding. A knee between her legs forced them apart.

Then she felt a pain, like nothing she'd felt before, as he forced himself inside. She cried out as he began to thrust, each one stabbing, making her wince. She squeezed her eyes shut. He was relentless, piston-like, intense and unstoppable. His hip bones were banging hard against hers, making her breasts jiggle and the back of her head bounce against the wing of the sofa.

Suddenly he juddered, grunted and became still.

Iris lay under him, tears pooling at the corner of her eyes.

David threw out a heavy breath. "That was fantastic." He raised himself on his arms until he was looking down at her. He stopped. "What's the matter? Didn't you enjoy it?"

Iris stayed motionless until he manoeuvre himself upright. He quickly pulled off a condom and knotted it.

Iris tugged her chemise in place and sat up. "I was a virgin, David. That really hurt."

"Why didn't you tell me?"

"I'm sorry."

"You better not have bled on my sofa." He pulled her up and swore at a bud of red where she'd lain. "Jesus, Iris. Get this cleaned up."

Iris stood, walked gingerly into the hall and locked herself in the cloakroom. She went to the toilet then carefully soaped herself clean.

She allowed herself a little cry before washing her face. This wasn't how it was supposed to be, was it? She thought it would be romantic. She thought she would be transported to heaven.

With a final sob, she unlocked the door and walked slowly into the kitchen for the upholstery cleaner.

CHAPTER 6

David stood outside and stared up at the imposing frontage of 8 Paraffin Alley. Next to him stood the purchaser, Bill Byrne, a local builder. They made an odd couple. David, tall, slim, immaculately attired in black trousers and a knee length, single breasted Edwardian jacket, in the New Romantic style. Bill, short and stocky in faded denim jeans, grey hair poking out from a cement dusted green beanie hat.

"How about it then, Bill? One hundred and fifteen thousand and we'll shake on it." David faked a spit on his hand.

Bill thrust his hands deep into the pockets of an old herringbone coat and turned. "One hundred and five and the deal's done."

"No chance. You're robbing me. Three two double-bedroom flats, the top one a penthouse with a private roof garden? One-o-five? I'm not Santa Claus, Bill."

"Neither am I. Tell you what, I'll meet you halfway. One hundred and ten grand. Middle for diddle. Cash up front. I can have the money in your account on Friday."

David twisted his mouth to one side while he

considered. "Alright. Offer accepted. Don't forget. It's a hundred G to my business account, ten to my personal one and I want your agreement to sell the apartments through my agency."

Bill regarded him for a moment then nodded. "OK."

They shook hands. Bill looked up at number 8 and grinned. "It's a job and a half but it'll be feckin' worth it. Road like this, one of the most expensive in Didsbury. I'm keeping my eye out for any more. I reckon there'll be more old-timers popping their clogs at some point."

David laughed. "When will you start?"

Bill lifted his hat and scratched his head before replacing it. "Early Spring, probably. Got a new build of flats to finish in Chorlton first. Can I leave you to get the locks changed?"

They parted company and David drove home, charged with adrenaline. His contact in the antiques trade had cleared the house the day after the funeral and auctioned everything shortly after. It had netted an incredible £42,500, thanks to the discovery of two extremely rare and valuable pieces of porcelain that his friend passed to Sotherbys. Iris was only too grateful to let David deal with everything. When he told her the auction had produced a net sum of £25,000, she accepted his word. He paid the remaining £17,500 into his account. This added to the ten grand he'd pocketed from the sale of 8 Paraffin Alley was enough to fund his second agency.

Iris had never had so much money in her life. She knew she'd be getting the proceeds from the house soon, so the £25,000 was an unexpected bonus. As soon as it was paid into her bank, she bought David a brand new Porsche, which he'd mentioned was his dream car. It was a thank you for everything he had done for her. She paid a year's comprehensive insurance and road tax and had it delivered to the house.

David had been overwhelmed and Iris waved away his polite show of resistance. She put aside Gran's £5,000 savings for a rainy day.

Iris was blissfully happy with David. After her first disastrous experience of sex, he had moved her into his bed. Sex had improved and although he took his pleasures selfishly, he sometimes made the effort to satisfy her first. He never brought up the subject of her buying her own house and she was beginning to hope that he could see a permanency in their relationship.

She was discovering though that David had a short fuse which was easily lit. She put it down to him being busy with the agency and to the huge amount of time and effort he had put into supporting and guiding her through the financial and emotional minefield following Gran's death. She loved his sumptuous four bedroomed house in Poynton, a prestigious part of Cheshire, and she was grateful beyond words for him giving her such a beautiful home when she needed one. She owed him more than she could ever repay. She loved him. She never wanted to let him go.

¤

David arrived home from Paraffin Alley, still on a high. Iris was waiting. "Hi, David. How was your day?" She handed him a glass of scotch, took his briefcase and kissed the cheek he offered. "Dinner will be ready when you've had your shower."

"Thanks Iris." David walked past her into the lounge to warm himself in front of the fire.

She followed him in, stood behind him, wrapped her arms around his waist and clasped her hands together at the front. Her cheek rested against his back. "Ooh, I've missed you."

David downed his scotch, unlocked her hands and walked to the drinks cabinet for another. "You want one?"

Iris glanced at her watch. "No thanks, It's only half six. I'll wait a bit longer."

"What for? Your Pomagne?" He laughed.

Iris's brows knitted. "You won't let me buy it."

"Too right. It's cheap shite. Why don't you buy Champagne? God knows you can afford it."

"Yes, but I can drink Pomagne without any ill effects. I love Champagne but I get drunk too quickly."

David laughed again. "That might not be such a bad thing. Might liven things up in the bedroom."

Iris's face dropped and she inhaled sharply. She didn't know how to reply.

David didn't give her a chance. "I'm going for

my shower."

With puzzled eyes, she watched him walk out. Was he bored with her already? Was he tired? Maybe he needed a holiday. She reminded herself again how hard he had been working. Perhaps she could use some of her money to book a holiday. Spain? Or a cruise maybe?

For now, she could make his evening special. She hurried upstairs and took a dress from her wardrobe. Trish had put it aside for her as soon as it had been donated to Whiskers Galore. It was a duck egg blue halter neck dress that was a perfect fit. She had kept it for an occasion. Why not make that tonight?

She grabbed a towel from the heated rail in the bathroom and showered quickly with her favourite Body Shop shower gel. Once she was dry, she rubbed the matching body oil into her skin and hurried downstairs into the kitchen with the dress. Minutes later, she heard David coming out of the bedroom. She stepped into the dress, tied the halter behind her neck, lifted a chicken casserole out of the oven and carried it quickly into the dining room.

David appeared a minute later and took his seat, reaching for the napkin folded by his plate. Iris served up.

David noticed. "Is that a new dress?"

Iris did a little pirouette. "Sort of. You like?"

"I like." He stood. "Come here, you."

"Why?"

"Because, my sexy little Iris..." He waltzed her over to the fire, "...I'm going to make love to

51

you."

He unfastened the halter and let the dress drop to the floor. "You're not wearing any underwear, you little minx."

Iris laughed happily. "No I'm not."

He knelt on the sheepskin rug and pulled her down to face him. She sighed with pleasure as he began to plant feathery kisses on her face, her neck, her shoulders.

"Dinner will get cold." It was a gasp.

David chuckled as he pushed her onto her back. "You're dinner."

Iris felt a rush of happiness as he entered her. There was nothing wrong. They were fine. Everything was fine.

¤

David woke after a refreshing night's sleep. The money for number 8 was nearly in his hands. The proceeds paid into the client account would go to Iris, after deduction of solicitor's costs and David's valuation and commission. The money paid into his own account would be transferred to a new investment account. He'd earn good interest with rates being as high as they were. At last, he could start seriously looking for premises in Didsbury, ready for next Spring.

He kicked himself for the way he'd treated Iris last night. He had to keep her sweet. He'd need her money for the third agency. When interest rates eventually fell and the housing market showed an upturn, he wanted to be ready.

His criticism of Iris's lovemaking had been

unfair. He'd wanted to hurt her. She irritated him. Always hovering around in that goofy loved-up way she had and so bloody grateful all the time. But he had to learn to be more patient. If he pissed her off once too often, she might do the unthinkable: buy her own place and move out.

¤

On Friday, as promised, Bill's money was in both accounts. David took Suzanna out to lunch to celebrate and by the time the shop closed at six pm, he was giddy with euphoria. He left the Porsche at the shop and Suzanna dropped him home.

He was planning to have a few more drinks when he got in. Saturday was his day off. He'd brought the keys to the Fiesta home so he'd tell Iris to take a taxi to the shop with them tomorrow and drive the Fiesta back. On Sunday he'd drive it back and pick up the Porsche. Iris had recently passed her test after an intensive course of lessons. He had given her his old VW Golf to reduce her dependence on him.

When he walked up the driveway he was surprised that she was not in her usual spot by the front door. He let himself in, dropped his briefcase by the hall table and walked into the lounge. He grinned when he saw her standing by the fireplace. "Iris, I got your money today for the house. You are now officially a very, very rich lady."

Iris said nothing. Her face was set and her

arms tightly folded. Her whole body was closed. He walked up, put his hands on her shoulders and peered into her face. "What's wrong?"

"Who dropped you off just then?"

"What?"

"I couldn't see properly but it looked like a woman. Who is she?"

Dave let go and jerked his head back in puzzlement. "It's Suzanna."

"Why was she giving you a lift home? What's wrong with your car?"

"Nothing. I had a few drinks today so she dropped me off."

"Why did you have a few drinks?"

David arranged his feet to balance himself. This wasn't like her. "We went to the Fairmont for lunch. I had wine with the meal."

"Who's we?"

"Me and Suzanna."

"You took Suzanna out for a meal."

"It was to celebrate your money coming through. That's all."

"Liar."

The tone of David's voice changed. "What did you just call me?"

"A liar." Iris's face was pinched. Her chin trembled as she took a step nearer. "Are you having an affair with her?"

"Don't be so bloody stupid. When do I have time for an affair?"

"Any time. Just pop the closed sign up and nip in the back room. It wouldn't take long, knowing you."

She could see his facial muscles twitching but she didn't care. "Go on, deny it. I dare you."

"I don't have to."

Iris inhaled sharply. "I think you do, David. After all, I am your girlfriend."

David slapped her hard across her face.

Iris fell back against the fire surround, eyes wide and glistening with shock. Her hand flew to her reddening cheek. He stepped closer and moved his face to hers. "Let's get things straight, Iris. You're not my girlfriend. You never were and you never will be."

She burst into noisy tears. "What am I then? Tell me. What am I to you?"

He stepped back. "Most of the time, a bloody pain in the arse."

Iris hiccuped more tears, pushed past him and out of the room. Sobbing loudly, she ran up stairs to the bedroom and slammed the door behind her.

The elation David had felt since the morning was being replaced by a hangover. He needed a hair of the dog. He walked to the cabinet, poured a generous measure of scotch into a tumbler and wandered over to the window as he sipped it. The security light had been triggered by a dog walker and the harshness cast the front garden into sharp relief. An early frost was settling on the lawn and the branches of the conifers. He stood for a while before turning back to face the room and the stupidity of what he had done.

He refilled his glass and returned to the

fireplace, a stagger in his step. After all his resolutions that morning he'd fucked up again. All that talk about affairs was crazy. But she could be up there packing right now. He knew he had to go and smooth things over.

¤

Iris curled into herself on the bed and sobbed into a tissue. She'd pulled the silk counterpane over her head to block out the room but she couldn't blot out what had happened. David had hit her. He had actually hit her. And called her a pain in the arse. He must have been so angry with her accusation that he wanted to hurt her. It hadn't been fair of her to accuse him. She could see that now. All he had done was celebrate the house sale. Suzanna had probably helped him so it was a nice gesture to treat her. There was nothing wrong with getting a lift home from a colleague when you'd been drinking. It was the sensible thing to do. Thinking about it, the fact that he had slapped her demonstrated how much he cared.

Feeling better, she brushed the counterpane away and blew her nose. There was a tap on the door. She sat up nervously, praying he wasn't still angry.

It opened and David's contrite face appeared round it. "Can I come in?"

Iris wiped her eyes with a fresh tissue and forced a bright smile. She patted the bed by her side. He moved into the room and sat where she beckoned. He put his finger and thumb on her chin and tilted it to inspect her cheek. "I'm so, so sorry Iris. I didn't mean to do that to you. It's because you wound me up."

"I know and I'm sorry. I can't think what came over me."

"I didn't mean the stuff I said. I do care for you and I think you know our relationship has moved forward."

"That's what I'd hoped."

He reached and pulled her into his arms. "I'm just a stupid thoughtless man, babe. Can we forgive and forget?"

Iris smiled happily. "That's all I want to do."

David wrapped his arms around her and kissed her. "I'll get dinner finished and serve up. You just relax. Then we can open a bottle of champagne and celebrate. But first..."

He pushed her back on the bed and slowly unbuttoned her blouse. His fingers slipped inside and pulled her bra away from her breasts. As his lips sank to a nipple, her body arched in anticipation.

Their lovemaking was quick and frenzied. Afterwards, she fell back by his side and curled a leg around him. A few moments later, she lifted her face to his. He was asleep, mouth open, breath throwing out stale wine and scotch and the beginnings of heavy snoring. Iris shook him a few times but he didn't respond. She smiled. He was so tired, bless him. She would go down and put their dinner in the fridge to have tomorrow night.

Back upstairs, she got ready for bed. It was

only seven but she was tired after such an emotional evening. An early night would do her good. She crawled in next to David and turned her back, pressing it against the warmth of his body. In moments, she was asleep.

¤

Iris woke suddenly. It was dark and she stifled a giggle. David had an erection and it was pressing against her. She pushed against it and felt his hand guide it in. She glanced behind her but his eyes were tightly shut. She turned back with a smile.

His body went rigid as he approached climax. His breath became quicker and when he came, he mumbled something.

She froze.

He pulled out, turned his back on her and resumed his snoring. Iris felt her heart palpitate. It was like a second slap. David had mumbled a name. With three syllables. She couldn't make out the first but the second was 'an' and the third, 'a'.

'An-a'. Anna.

She pressed her fists to her mouth to stop herself crying out.

He'd said Suzanna.

CHAPTER 7

David woke with a grunt and thrust his palms into his eyes when Iris opened the curtains.

"Jesus H. Christ. How much did I have to drink yesterday?"

Iris walked back to where he lay. "Too much, I think. It's only nine. Why don't I make you a strong coffee then you can have a lie in."

"Ooh, that sounds great. Did I ever tell you you're an angel?" He moved his hand and grinned blearily up at her. "Can I have a bacon sarnie too?"

"Of course you can. D'you want a fried egg in it?"

He flopped back against the bed. "Even better – and brown sauce?"

"Coming up."

As she reached the door, David held his hand up. "Before I forget. When you've done that, can you get a taxi to the shop and pick up the car? The keys are in my briefcase."

"OK."

"It's the Fiesta."

She had already left the room. He shrugged. Suzanna would show her when she got there. He

59

intended doing absolutely nothing today but chill. He deserved it after such a busy week.

He pulled the covers up and slid down. He had his money, Iris had forgiven him and he was going to have breakfast in bed. He scratch himself contentedly. Life was good.

¤

Iris pushed open the door of David Phillips Estate Agents and the girl at the desk facing her lifted her head with a smile. "Good morning, Madam. Can I help you?"

Iris didn't answer straight away. She was examining her acutely. She had black curls tied back in a Fergie bow. Perfect make-up. Brown skin. Long black eyelashes. Probably of Caribbean extract. She stood and smiled with pearly white teeth. She was beautiful.

"Are you Suzanna?" The question was accusatory.

Suzanna kept her smile. "Yes, I am. Can I help you?"

"I'm Iris."

"Iris. Oh. David's Iris?" She came round the desk and held her hand out. Iris went to shake it but she was pulled into a hug. Suzanna's smile stretched. "It's so nice to meet you at last."

Iris looked up at her. She must be easily five foot eight. Slim. Long limbed. Tight skirt and cardigan. Iris felt a surge of jealousy that made her stomach contract. So this was her love rival.

She pulled away. "David's asked me to collect the car."

"Ah, yes. The Fiesta."

"No. It's the Porsche."

Suzanna pulled her brows together. "Are you sure?"

Iris pursed her lips and held up the keys.

"It is the Porsche." Suzanna looked up and smiled. "He must trust you."

"Shame it doesn't work both ways." Iris clutched the keys to her chest. "Where is it?"

"Round the back. I'll show you. You might need some help to get out."

"Don't bother. I'll manage." Iris spoke abruptly.

"Oh. OK then. Well, just turn right out the door and again at the corner. It's parked at the back. It's a tight three point turn though to face the right way. Are you sure..."

"Yes."

"Right then. Anyway, it was nice to meet you, Iris. Perhaps when you come into Bramhall again, we could have lunch?"

Iris couldn't resist it. "Why? So we can compare notes?"

"What?"

Iris continued without missing a beat. "Actually, I don't have time. You know? Busy with my volunteering work and then of course, there's David..." She tailed off with a shrug and followed it with a thin smile.

Suzanna nodded. "Yes. Of course. Though I suppose you'll be looking to buy your own house soon, now your money's come through. Obviously, I hope you'll let us help when you start looking."

Iris blinked. She stared at Suzanna in puzzlement for a few moments before replying curtly, "I'm not going anywhere, Suzanna. I'm not a lodger. David and I live together. We're a couple. Surely you knew that?"

Before she could answer, Iris turned on her heel and walked out. Suzanna fell back in her chair and let out a low whistle. What was that all about? She picked up the phone to tell David that Iris was on the way back and decided to keep her own council about the odd conversation they'd had. The way David spoke about Iris, it was apparent that the arrangement was temporary. Suzanna often listened to him as he bragged about the women he dated, used and discarded. If Iris thought they were in a serious relationship, she'd was sorely mistaken. Suzanna knew she would end up on the scrap heap like the others.

Suzanna corrected herself. There had been only one woman he seemed to care for and she had dumped him last Spring. It had taken a long time for him to bounce back.

Suzanna sighed and grasped the edge of the desk to pull her chair in. During that conversation with Iris, there had been an undercurrent of hostility, as if she was delivering a warning. Suzanna shook her head sadly. She couldn't blame Iris. Having a slippery customer like David as a boyfriend, it was understandable.

¤

Iris sat in the driving seat of the Porsche 911 and closed her eyes while she calmed herself. She was shaking from her talk with Suzanna. She had tried to convey a warning but now she felt sick because Suzanna genuinely thought that she and David weren't an item. Had David told her that? If he had, then Suzanna wasn't to blame if they were having an affair. But if they weren't, the fact that he breathed her name meant that he wished they were. Iris had chosen not to mention it to him this morning. It would have made her sound paranoid. Perhaps she was.

Iris stared down at the console. For now, she had a more pressing concern. She thought she'd be confident driving the Porsche home but now she was sitting in the driver's seat, she was petrified. She hadn't driven much since she passed her test and this flashy sports car, David's pride and joy, was a million steps too far. She swallowed and spoke sternly to herself. "It's only a car. I'm in control. As long as I know where the brake pedal is, I'll be fine. No problems. Come on, Iris. You can do this."

She inserted the key, turned it and jumped when the engine fired. With a deep breath, she glanced behind. The back of the shop looked quite far away. There should be plenty of room to reverse. She looked at the knob on top of the gear stick. There it was. Capital 'R' left and forward. She put her foot down on the clutch pedal, slipped the clutch into reverse, raised the pedal and pressed down on the accelerator. She took the handbrake off.

There was a sickening crunch as the Porsche shot forward into the wall.

CHAPTER 8

David's voice shook with fury. "Iris. This is not a Ford Fiesta 1000 cc. It is a 1985 Porsche 911 with a three point three litre engine. What's that in cc's?"

Iris didn't answer. She perched upright in the passenger seat, hands stiffly clutching her bag. Her face was cast down, her lower lip was wobbling and tears were falling onto the back of her hands.

He turned his head and snarled, "I asked you what three point three litres is in cc's. It's not that fucking difficult, even for you."

A sob escaped with her answer. "Three thousand three hundred."

"Correct. Three thousand three hundred cubic centimetres. And when you press down on the accelerator pedal of a Porsche 911 3.3 litre engine, what should you do?"

"Do it gently."

"Do it gently. That's right. You do it gently. Especially when..." He turned to her again and bellowed, "You've put it in the wrong fucking gear!"

Iris cringed.

"You're useless, you are. Why would you think for one nano-second that I would let you anywhere near the wheel of my Porsche?"

"They were the only keys I could see in your briefcase."

"I told you it was the Fiesta."

"I didn't hear you."

"Back to my previous question." He leaned over until his face was inches from hers. This time his voice was measured and low and delivered through clenched teeth. "Why would you think for one nano-second that I would let you anywhere near the wheel of my Porsche?"

She shrank against the passenger door. "Well, you'd had quite a lot to drink the day before. I thought maybe you trusted me."

"You know, Sometimes I wonder about you."

"I keep saying I'm sorry, what else can I do?"

"You've done enough. When we get home, I'll drop you off then I'll have to go to the Porsche dealer and book in to have the repairs done. All this on my day off."

"I'm sorry."

"Will you stop apologising?"

"I'll pay for it."

"Too right you will."

Iris cried the rest of the way home. When they reached the house, David pulled up outside and leaned across to open her door. "Now, get out and you'd better stay out of my sight for the rest of the day."

She stood by the gatepost as the car roared off

and stared after it miserably. She sniffed loudly, hugged her bag to her chest, walked slowly up the driveway and let herself in. God only knew what mood he'd be in when he came home. She wished she could hide away somewhere.

When the Porsche hit the wall, Iris had frozen in shock. Eventually she had climbed out and walked to the front to inspect the damage. The bumper had caved and both headlights were smashed. Her knees went weak. She had slumped against the side of the car, knowing that David would kill her.

Iris sighed, threw her coat over the bannister and walked into the kitchen. She clicked the kettle and took a mug from the cupboard. While she waited for it to boil, she leaned against the counter and thought back to when she'd returned to the shop. Suzanna had been marvellous. She'd sat Iris down, made her a cup of sweet tea and rang David again. Iris could hear his anger through the earpiece. The colour had drained from her face.

By the time Suzanna came off the phone, Iris was in tears. Suzanna had rushed over and flung her arms around her, not flinching at the snotty nose pressed against her cardigan. Her sympathy made Iris weep more. Eventually, Suzanna gently moved her away and handed her the tea and a tissue box.

When David arrived, he said nothing to Suzanna. He threw her the keys of the Fiesta then caught hold of Iris's arm, dragged her from the chair, marched her through the shop and out into the street, ignoring the shocked looks from passers-by as he pushed through them. Iris was flushed with embarrassment by the time he shoved her down the side of the shop to the Porsche.

Iris sighed, turned back to the counter and made herself a filter coffee. She added extra cream and carried it up to the bedroom. The dishevelled bed was testament to how quickly David had responded to Suzanna's call. Iris felt abashed, not only because of the car but also because of the hatred she had spawned for Suzanna, who had been so kind.

She reached into the drawer for some paracetamol. She had another headache. When she moved in with David, she'd stopped taking her antidepressants. Was this a side effect? Her forehead wrinkled as she sat on the bed and nursed her coffee. The events of the last two days were scaring her. David was scaring her. He was changing. Was it her fault? Did he want something she couldn't give him? Was he tiring of her? Maybe she should go and see her family doctor and go back on her medication while she navigated this rough patch.

¤

The sound of the front door slamming jerked Iris awake.

The light had faded. Her eyes flashed to the clock radio. It was seven pm. She'd been asleep for hours. Why was David back so late? She shot out of bed and ran downstairs, running her fingers through her hair. She stopped short when she entered the kitchen. David was standing by the cooker, inspecting it with exaggerated care. He half turned at her entrance. "Ah. There you are. You know, when I get home this time of the evening, I expect dinner, if not on the table then somewhere between it and the oven. So where is it, Iris?"

Iris pressed her hands together nervously. "I'm sorry, David. I had a headache. I took some tablets. I fell asleep. I only woke up when I heard the door just now."

"You had a headache. You fell asleep."

She blinked into the silence that followed.

"I had a headache too, Iris. But I didn't have the luxury of having a nice long sleep. Although that was what I'd been hoping to do today. On my day off. Before you decided to smash my car." His eyes alighted on her. "It's going to cost over a thousand pounds to put it right. You'll transfer that to my account on Monday."

"Yes, of course I will." Iris nodded furiously. "First thing."

"Yes, you will. Now, what about dinner?"

She moved towards the fridge. "I can warm up last night's. It won't take long."

As she passed, he caught her arm and pulled her against him. She could smell whisky on his breath. She tried to wrest his hand away but his grip was too tight.

There was a cold look in his eye. An expression on his face. Suddenly she was frightened.

His other hand grasped her arm and he

smiled. "Am I hurting you, Iris? I don't mean to. Can't you see how much you upset me today? My Porsche: What you did to it?"

With almost superhuman strength, Iris stiffened her arms and broke his hold. She pushed him against the fridge and suddenly her fear was subsumed by an explosion of anger. "You and that car. I didn't do it on purpose. It was an accident. That's all. An accident. Have you forgotten that I bought it for you in the first place? You wouldn't have it, if it wasn't for me. Just remember that."

The silence that followed was palpable. It stretched. David didn't move. His lips parted and he frowned, eyes narrowing. He was looking at a woman he didn't know. Iris knew she had crossed the line but she didn't care. Her chin lifted in defiance.

"You're quite the bitch, when you want to be." David grabbed her wrists and forced her arms up behind her back. His breath was sour. "Let me give you something to remember as well."

He headbutted her.

¤

Iris turned in bed and winced. A hand flew to her forehead. She raised herself on one elbow to look at the clock. It was nearly nine. What had happened? Where was David? As she fell back against the pillow, she remembered an argument but nothing else. She switched on the bedside light and glanced around. A sound on the stairs made her turn anxiously towards the door. It opened. David walked in with a tray and sat on the bed by her side. He smiled sadly. "Oh Iris, my poor little girl. Your head."

She touched it again and sucked her breath in. "It's sore."

David tutted sympathetically. "Come on. I reheated dinner. Eat it while it's hot."

She wasn't hungry but with his eyes watching her, she picked up the fork. She forced down each mouthful until her plate was clear.

"That's my girl." He smiled. "Now drink your wine."

She took the glass. It was large, easily holding half a bottle. He held the bottom of the stem, forcing her to keep drinking until she had finished it, then he put it back on the tray and set the tray on the floor.

"Now, let's not think about our little falling-out. I'm taking the car in on Monday to be fixed and it should be ready by Wednesday. So no lasting damage, eh?"

Iris was already feeling the effects of the wine. She nodded, feeling her lip trembling again. David shook his head, a tender smile on his face. He pushed her back gently until her head was resting on the pillows. "You know the best thing about falling out?"

She shook her head.

"Making up." He bent to kiss her. "We could be really good together if you'd stop winding me up."

When he lifted his head, she touched his cheek. "I'll try harder, David. I promise. I hate upsetting you. I want it to be like it was when we first met."

"It can be, if only you'd let it." David's mouth dropped to hers.

A buzz of wine and happiness washed over her. She cast aside the detritus of the day and sank into the pleasure of the man she loved.

CHAPTER 9

"How's Iris?"

David hooked his scarf over a peg, unfastened his cashmere coat, hung it on a wooden hanger, walked to his desk, sat down, straightened his wide striped tie, smoothed his dark hair and turned on his computer.

Suzanna waited patiently, crossing her legs as she watched him. "Well?"

David rested his palms on his desk and leaned forward to inspect his nails. He replied slowly, without looking at her. "She's fine. Why?"

"You know why. You were well out of order yesterday."

"She smashed my Porsche."

"It was an accident. Why did you give her the keys in the first place?"

"I didn't. She took the wrong ones."

Suzanna shrugged. "It was a misunderstanding. She was hysterical yesterday. Absolutely terrified of what you'd do."

David looked over at her. A pulse was

throbbing in his neck, just above the starched white collar. "Keep your nose out, Suze."

She wasn't deterred. "And why does she think you're a couple? You told me she was only lodging until her house was sold. Are you two sleeping together? "

"Is that any of your business?"

"Yes, actually. I think it is because yesterday was the first time I'd met her and it was embarrassing for both of us, me having completely the wrong end of the stick."

"Just ignore her next time. She's off her head. Seems to think we're an item."

"So you are sleeping with her. Well, what came over very clearly is that she's in love with you and you're treating her like shit. If you want some friendly advice..." She ignored the contemptuous lift of his eyebrows, "...stop stringing her along. It's not fair. She seems very vulnerable."

David leaned sideways and hooded his eyes. "And if you want some friendly advice, Suze, stick to selling houses, not playing agony aunt. Or you'll find yourself at the job centre."

She pursed her lips and turned back to her desk. She hated these glimpses into David's private life. They always revealed a side of him that she found despicable. Sometime in the future, Iris was going to get very hurt.

¤

The waiting room was packed. In the seat next to Iris, a harassed woman was trying to placate a toddler that was in the middle of a monumental meltdown. Iris wondered how so much noise could emanate from something so little. She had read somewhere that babies' eyes remained the same size into adulthood. Judging by the racket, so did their lungs.

Iris didn't hear her name the first time it was called. She did the second time, when the volume of the Tannoy was turned up. She hurriedly looped the strap of her bag over her shoulder and put the magazine she'd been reading back on the low table at the end of her row. Without attracting attention, she had carefully ripped a page from 'Good Housekeeping' that had a recipe for gingerbread. It was last year's Christmas issue but just as pertinent now, with November approaching. She decided she would buy a gingerbread man cutter and coloured icing to decorate. She would give some to Trish and the rest she and David could have with mulled wine on Christmas Eve, curled up together in front of a roaring fire.

She had given more thought that morning about Suzanna and David and whether there was something between them. Her kindness may have been a smoke screen. And there was no smoke without fire. Working together, she couldn't imagine them not having an affair, but apart from David muttering Suzanna's name once, there was nothing else to suggest it. She imagined a folder in her head with 'Requiring Further Attention' written on it and filed her thoughts away. Quickly, she walked to Dr Whittaker's door, knocked and walked in at his command.

He looked up from his notes and smiled warmly. "Iris, how are you, dear? How are you coping at home?"

Iris sat in the seat he indicated and placed her bag in her lap. "Well, I'm not there any more, George. It's been sold."

"Well, that was fast. Are you still in Didsbury?"

"No. I've got a boyfriend now and I've moved in with him."

"That is good news, Iris." Doctor Whittaker smiled with genuine pleasure. "So, where are you now?"

"Poynton."

He sat back and frowned. "Poynton. Iris, that's miles out of our catchment area. You need to register at a practice there."

"Oh. No. Please, George." Iris's face paled and she clasped her hands to her chest. "You've known me since I was born. I don't want a new doctor who doesn't know me. I couldn't face it just yet."

Dr Whittaker blew his cheeks out as he considered her stricken face. He really was too soft with her but she had suffered terribly losing her parents and grandfather while so young – then, of course, having to care for Dorothea. He leaned forward and rested his arms on the desk. "Iris, don't upset yourself. I'll keep you as my patient for now, even though I shouldn't."

Iris wiped her eyes and gave him a grateful

smile. "Oh thank you so much, George. I'm really, really grateful."

Dr Whittaker waved her thanks away. "Now, why have you come to see me today?"

"Well." She caught hold of the handles of her bag again and pulled her shoulders down. "What it is, George, when I moved in with David, that's my boyfriend, I decided to come off my meds because I didn't need them any more. Gran was dead, I had a new life so, well, like I said, I stopped taking them."

Dr Whittaker raised a hand. "Whoa. You know full well that you shouldn't stop taking antidepressants like that."

"I know and I'm sorry but I've felt no ill effects. Well, not really, except I get a lot of stress headaches these days. Because..." Her face clouded. "...well, I'm going through a sticky patch at the moment so I want to go back on them. Just for a little while."

"Perhaps if you explain what's making you stressed, I can help."

"Please, George, I know I'll be alright if I can take them again."

Dr Whittaker took a deep breath. "Iris, I'm not going to prescribe antidepressants. You're off them now and you can't just start again every time you go through a rough patch. I'll give you a leaflet on coping mechanisms for stress and anxiety."

He opened a drawer and extracted one from a manilla folder. He smiled and held it out.

Iris sat up. Her face became sullen."That's no

good. A bloody leaflet? How's that supposed to help? Am I expected to sit cross legged on the floor, waving bloody joss sticks around and singing Kumbaya my Lord? Well, if you think that, you can bloody think again."

Dr Whittaker sat back in his seat and his eyes widened. Was this Iris speaking? He was speechless for a moment then cleared his throat. "You won't know if you don't try, Iris. I am NOT putting you back on antidepressants. Heaven knows I shouldn't have let you stay on them so long. You'll manage just as well without them, now you have a new and better life with your boyfriend."

"What do you know about what my life's like now? Nothing, that's what. So stop being so bloody patronising. I'm not that stupid little Iris Ferguson any more." She stood and kicked the chair. It teetered on its back legs before falling with a clatter.

Dr Whittaker stood, held the leaflet out again and addressed her calmly. "I suggest you take this, go home and, if it's of no help, come back. With a better attitude."

Iris glared at him, dropped her eyes to his extended hand, grabbed the leaflet off him and stuffed it in her bag. She shot him another seething look. "No. I'm not coming back. I'll go and get another GP. One who's more sympathetic."

"That's a good idea. I've already told you this practice is out of your area, now you've moved. Let reception have your new address for now.

Goodbye Iris." He indicated the door.

When she left, Dr Whittaker walked around his desk and righted the chair. In all the years he'd known her, she had never behaved like this. It was totally out of character. If this is how she had become, now she was removed from Dorothea's crushing influence, he wasn't impressed but he did find it troubling.

CHAPTER 10

Iris was excited about her birthday tomorrow. It was her first away from Gran and Surprise View. That, along with it being her thirtieth, made it doubly special. Instead of having a miserable one with Gran, she was looking forward to David taking her out for a meal. She wondered excitedly what other things he had planned for her.

Things between them were improving. The Porsche had been repaired, they hadn't had a fight since the crash and David was showing more patience.

She'd found a leaflet on coping with stress in her bag when she arrived home on the day she'd been to her doctor and wondered where it had come from. She was happy to give it a go though and was enjoying practising the relaxation techniques. Strangely, she remembered little of the appointment, except that she'd left without a prescription for antidepressants. She mustn't have asked him. She'd replaced them with paracetamol, which was helping and if her relationship with David remained on an even keel, she was convinced that her stress levels would drop and the headaches would stop.

¤

Next morning Iris woke, tingling with excitement. It was her charity shop day and she was going for a birthday lunch with Trish. David had a breakfast meeting in Manchester and had already left. She hurried downstairs to see if he had left a card. He hadn't. She pushed away her disappointment. He was probably saving it for tonight. She was so looking forward to the evening. He said he was booking it for seven thirty. It was their first night out in ages, although to be honest he'd only taken her out once before and that was the day after he valued the house so that hadn't been a date. Well, there was the meal following Gran's funeral but that didn't really count either.

She walked back upstairs with a mug of tea and turned the clock radio up when *Relax* came on. Frankie goes to Hollywood was one of her favourite groups. She danced round the bedroom, pumping her arms when she sang "When you wanna come, come," and thrusting her hips out at every "Uhh! Woo!"

Laughing when the song ended, she washed and changed into her favourite belted jeans. She looked in the mirror and applied a sweep of dark brown mascara and a slick of pink lipstick. That done, she blow waved a flick into her fringe, pulled her hair into a low ponytail, attached her new Fergie bow, tucked in a pink striped shirt and slipped on her new black kitten heels.

She stood back and examined the result. She grinned at her reflection. If the old Iris could see her now, she'd wouldn't recognise herself.

¤

The shop door tinkled as Iris opened it. She took off her jacket and walked to the little tea point behind the counter. Trish was already there and as she heard Iris approaching she turned, threw open her arms and sang *Happy Birthday* at the top of her voice.

Iris laughed in delight and clapped her hands. "Oh, Trish. You daft beggar."

"Happy birthday, my dear Iris!" She reached into her bag and pulled out an envelope and a little package, which she handed to her. "Go on, open them. I'll make us a cuppa."

Iris opened the card first and a tear sprang to her eye. It depicted a circular table covered with a white embroidered cloth on which sat two Delph cups and saucers, a tea pot and a vase of blue irises. Overlaid were the words, in gold embossed letters, *To a Dear Friend*.

Iris hugged her fiercely. "Thank you Trish. It's the most beautiful card I've ever had. You've even got my favourite flower. It was Mum's too. Hence my name."

"...And a very beautiful name it is too." Trish carried their cups through into the shop and perched on the stool to watch Iris open her present. She fiddled with the ribbons and took out a little rectangular box. When she took the lid off, she gasped and looked at Trish with wide eyes.

Trish smiled. "I hope you like it. it's sterling silver."

Iris took out a delicate chain from which was hanging her initial. She held it up and gazed in wonder. "Oh, Trish. It's absolutely beautiful. I love it. Thank you so much." She hugged her friend again and, before she could stop herself, let out a sob.

Trish held her away to look at her. "Oh, dear girl, what's wrong. Here," She took a tissue from her cardigan pocket.

Iris took it gratefully. "Sorry Trish. No-one's ever bought me anything like this before. You're the best friend I've ever had."

"Aw, sweetie, you're my best friend too. Now, dry your eyes, blow your nose and drink your tea, before a customer comes in and thinks I've been shouting at you!"

Iris laughed and handed the necklace to Trish, turned her back and moved her ponytail away from her neck. Once it was on, she moved to the shop mirror to admire it, touching the silver initial with her fingers. "Oh, it's so beautiful. Thank you again, Trish."

Her day was turning into magic already.

¤

Lunch was delicious, the afternoon sped by and soon they were tilling up, locking up and hugging goodbye outside the shop. On the way home, Iris reflected on how special the day had been. It only needed a lovely evening with David to keep the magic going and make it her best birthday ever.

¤

As Trish drove home she was also thinking about David but without charity. He'd not bought Iris so much as a card. Trish had only met him twice, both times when he'd dropped Iris at the shop with donations, and she had taken an instant dislike to him. He was nothing like she'd expected. Iris was warm and funny and kind. Trish had imagined that he would share those attributes, that he'd be her blanket and her wings. Most of all, that he would adore her.

David didn't. He was oily. Smug. Immaculate. Perfect hair, perfect face but a fake smile that turned on and off and never reached his eyes and those eyes were so blue, so intense, cold as an iceberg. There was no chemistry between them either. Trish had noticed that he barely glanced at Iris or acknowledged her when she spoke. What's more. Iris was different around him. Subdued. Her light was dimmed and when she looked at him, it was with awe and fear. All these things greatly disturbed Trish.

It seemed, from things Iris had let slip about her life before and now, that she'd swapped a dungeon for a gilded cage. Trish fervently hoped that one day she would find the strength to leave David. She was a rich woman now. She could buy a lovely little place of her own, where she could blossom and become the beautiful, confident, free spirited Iris Ferguson that Trish could see bubbling under the surface. David was killing her spirit, She feared that he was with Iris purely for her money. Once that was gone, he'd leave her penniless and broken.

¤

The car was caught in traffic. By the time Iris arrived home, it was gone six. The Porsche wasn't there. She let herself in, dropped her keys on the hall table and ran upstairs to shower. She was back downstairs by 6.45. David still hadn't arrived.

She read Trish's card again and put it in a prominent position on the marble mantelpiece. She checked her watch. He hadn't said what time he'd be home but it had to be soon, so he could get ready.

She walked over to the drinks cabinet and inspected the bottles. It wasn't yet seven but it was her birthday so she poured a jigger of Bacardi and added a can of Diet Pepsi from the integral fridge.

Iris walked to the phone to see if he'd rung. The light on the answer machine wasn't blinking. She finished her drink. It was five past seven. She stood, walked back to the cabinet, poured another single Bacardi into the glass and another Diet Pepsi.

By 7.25, Iris was panicking. Had David been in an accident? Was he in hospital? Dead? She took a chance and rang the estate agency. She knew it closed at half seven on Thursdays. Hopefully Suzanna would still be there.

She closed her eyes in relief when the phone was picked up. "David Phillips Estate Agents. Suzanna speaking. Can I help?"

"Suzanna. It's Iris. Is David there?"

"Hi Iris. David? No. He got back from Manchester at six, freshened up and went straight out."

"But he's still not home. I'm worried he's had an accident."

There was a pause. "He wasn't going home, Iris. He went straight to Le Petit Coco in Prestbury."

Iris blinked and held the phone tighter. "But he's not...I thought...I'm waiting for him. It's my birthday." Her face screwed up.

There was that same pause. "Iris, I'm sorry, I don't know about that. He's meeting a business associate there. I booked the table for him this morning." Suzanna's voice tailed off.

Iris didn't answer. She dropped the receiver into the cradle. He had booked a table but not for her. For someone else. Who? Obviously not Suzanna. Was it a really a business associate or another woman?

It was her thirtieth birthday.

It was her first one away from Paraffin Alley. Away from Gran.

It was supposed to be special.

She had wanted with all her heart for it to be special.

Trish had gone all out to make it special.

David hadn't even given her as much as a sodding card.

Iris discarded the jigger, slopped a generous measure of Bacardi into her glass and drained it in one. It was her birthday and he had forgotten. If she couldn't celebrate with him, she'd celebrate on her own. She'd done that for the last sixteen years anyway. She was used to it. Nothing had changed.

Iris choked back a tear and reached for the bottle.

CHAPTER 11

Iris woke abruptly. Her eyelids sprang open and scanned the room before she closed them to shuffle her senses into order.

It was daylight.

She was shivering.

She was dressed.

She was on the sofa.

She was in the lounge.

When her eyes reopened, it was with a sharp intake of breath. The events of last night crowded in. She arranged them chronologically.

Her birthday.

No David.

The missed meal.

Bacardi.

Being sick.

Curling up on the sofa.

Falling asleep.

Iris lifted herself into a seated position, rubbed her arms and shivered. Her gaze fell on the Bacardi bottle. It had been full. Now it was half empty. She moved her eyes to the stain on the carpet in front of her. She would have to clean up her vomit. The next focus was the mantelpiece clock. It was half past ten. She gasped. Was it that late in the morning? Where was David? Had he come home? Why didn't he wake her?

She got to her feet, stumbled out of the room, up the stairs and into the bedroom. On David's side of the bed, the covers were thrown back. She made the bed yesterday morning so that proved he had been back. He would have found her downstairs at some point. Why didn't he wake her so she could come to bed, instead of leaving her there?

Iris ran a hand through her hair and looked around. There was a discarded bath sheet on the floor by the en-suite, so he had showered, dressed and gone to work without even acknowledging her. Couldn't he have at least put a blanket over her to keep her warm?

She slipped out of her dress and hung it up, picked up David's towel and folded it over the radiator. Time for a shower, change, then sort out her day. She didn't have a hangover, which was a relief. She wasn't used to drinking spirits but the vomiting must have cleared it from her system. She would go down and clean it up straight away.

She hadn't eaten since lunch with Trish yesterday. She suddenly fancied smoked salmon and scrambled eggs. Toast. A pot of tea. Then what? She was suddenly hit with a fit of pique. She didn't know. Her days were never about her. They revolved around David, his wants and needs. It felt like he had slotted her into a tiny corner of his life where she sat forgotten amidst dust and cobwebs. As she thought about it, the feeling darkened to anger. Her life with David was no better than it had been with Gran.

Well, today she was going to do what she wanted to do.

¤

Suzanna was already sitting at her desk when David arrived. He raised his eyebrows in mock surprise. "Have you been here all night?"

She curled her hands around her coffee cup and glared up at him.

He indicated her drink. "Do I get one of those?"

"Kettle's back there." She turned away to answer the telephone.

David pulled a face and walked into the kitchen. Back in the shop, he perched on the side of her desk, crossed his legs at the ankle and grinned. "C'mon. What's wrong? You've got a face like a chapped arse."

Suzanna leaned back to look at him and folded her arms. "I had a phone call last night, just before I closed."

"Oh yes? Who from?"

"Iris."

He frowned. "What was she ringing you for?"

"To find out where you were. Apparently you were supposed to be taking her out to dinner last night. For her birthday."

"Ah." David clicked his fingers. "I knew there was something I'd forgotten."

Suzanna's eyes opened wide in amazement. "Something you'd forgotten? We're not talking about putting the bloody bins out. It was Iris's birthday, for God's sake. She sounded really upset."

"So that's why she was flat out on the sofa, dressed to the nines with sick everywhere. She'd obviously got pissed, puked and passed out." He laughed at his alliteration.

"I take it she wasn't speaking to you this morning? Don't blame her."

"She didn't see me. I didn't wake her."

Suzanna pulled her head back in shock. "You didn't wake her. You just left her there?"

"Yes. I don't see the problem. It's only Iris." He stood and walked to his desk. "Now, I bet you're dying to know how I got on with Bill the builder last night? I need to dip into the expense account. That meal cost a bloody fortune. Pass us a claim form."

Suzanna handed one to him.

"Well," He grinned at the downwards curve of her mouth. "I'll tell you, Suzanna. He's already confirmed that I can market and sell the apartments at Surprise View but he's also keeping his eye out for any more coming on that road. So will I. Suze, can you draft up a letter that we can send to the other houses in Paraffin Alley? If anyone is thinking about selling, I want to make sure I get in first. Anyway, Bill's only condition for number 8 is that I open a branch in Didsbury. I've already got enough money for that, so I'll be shop hunting in the near future."

Suzanna looked at him with contempt. "You've got Iris to thank for all this. You should treat her with more respect."

In a flash, David's demeanour changed. He stood and walked to her, spun her chair to face him and rested his hands on the arms. She moved back as he brought his face closer. His eyes had darkened to ink. "If you mention Iris once more today, I'll..."

Suzanna folded her arms again and shoved her face into his. "What, David? You'll do what, exactly? Don't try bullying me or I'll walk. I mean it. I'm not Iris. I bite back."

He broke into a grin and pushed himself up. "You bite back? I like the sound of that, Suze."

She pulled her chair away from him and turned back to her computer. "Piss off, David. You're not funny and you're not God's gift to women, even if you think you are."

David walked back to his desk when his phone rang. He blew Suzanna a kiss and ignored the upwards flick of her middle finger. "David Phillips Estate Agents. David speaking. How can I...Oh, hi Bill. Great night last night. What? Chorlton? I thought you'd already sold them."

Suzanna listened quietly. When he finally replaced the receiver, he turned to her with a triumphant face. "That was Bill."

"You don't say."

He let her remark go. "He's said I can market and sell the current flat build in Chorlton. Not only that, he's bought a house on a large plot of land in Chorlton-cum-Hardy. He's planning to demolish it and build ten luxury apartments. He wants me to market and sell them too. Looks like I've found the location for my next agency. It's like a gift."

Suzanna smiled sweetly. "Well, you'd better do some major grovelling to your little cash cow then, when you get home."

David looked thoughtful. "You're right. Suze. Favour please, sweetie-pie? Will you ring Interflora and sort out a nice bouquet? Then can you ring Le Petit Coco and book a table for two for tonight for 7.30. Then can you nip to the jewellers..."

"David."

"What?"

"What do you think?"

"No?"

"Correct. Do it your bloody self."

David grinned and picked up the phone.

¤

It was cold on the roof terrace of Surprise View. It always was, this time of year.

Back in the day, Grumps had fashioned a firepit from an old galvanised bucket. A simple job – he'd drilled holes in the side and sat it on two bricks. It had still been in use by Iris up to the house being sold. She was delighted to see it still here as well as coals, lighter fuel and a box of household matches in a stay seal box in the coal bunker by the door that led down into the house.

Half an hour after arriving, she was sitting on an old folding chair and sipping a cup of hot tomato soup from a flask. Laid out in front of her on an old picnic table was a plastic container of Brie and cranberry sandwiches, a banana, a tub of grapes, a packet of French Fancies and a smaller flask of coffee.

She tucked her scarf inside her warm coat and pulled her woolly hat over her ears. The old plaid blankets were still there, wrapped in a bin liner and now one was spread over her legs, the other around her shoulders.

Over breakfast, she had planned the picnic, like she and Grumps used to do, but aware that the locks could have been changed. She had handed over what she'd thought were all the keys after completion but found one in an old coat she'd not worn for a long time. David had told her that the house would lie empty until work started next spring. If she hadn't been able to get in, plan B was to go to the beautiful Fletcher Moss gardens on the other side of Didsbury Village.

But she'd been lucky and here she was. Her heart was brimming with wonderful memories. As she settled back in the rusty chair, she relaxed and began to think objectively about her relationship with David. She wasn't happy, the honeymoon period had been brief but she couldn't imagine life without him. Even as she thought this, she knew that a tiny piece of her love had broken away and she knew that even if she found it and fixed it back on, it would never be the same.

So what was she going to do when he got home tonight? Say something and risk him losing his temper or say nothing and risk him losing yet more respect. Her stomach turned over. She didn't want to go home. She didn't want to face him. With a sigh, she picked up the post that she had scooped up from the floor when she'd let herself in. She began leafing through them. As she thought, it was all leaflets and junk mail. She gave up half way through and began to crumple them and feed them, one by one, into the flames.

Once she threw in the last piece, she hunkered back down in her coat, thrust her hands into the deep pockets and stared at the pigeon loft, waiting for inspiration. "Grumps, what should I do?"

She closed her eyes for a moment and listened to the sounds in the street below. A baby crying and the gentle shushing of its mother as she pushed the pram along. A dog barking with excitement as its owner chatted to it on the way to the park, the hollow echo of a child bouncing a football along the narrow street.

She could hear birdsong in the bare branches of the hornbeams that ran along the pavement edge all the way down Paraffin Alley. In Spring, catkins would appear. In summer, the trees would provide nourishment for moth caterpillars. Autumn would bring finches and tits to feed on the berries and at Christmas the residents would string fairy lights across them, all the way to the end of the road and she and Grumps and Mum and Dad would sit up here, so wrapped up that only their faces were visible, gloved hands clutching mugs of creamy hot chocolate, mulled wine and warm mince pies. They would gaze down in wonder at the magical scene as the lights dancing together in the breeze.

Iris lifted her face as a cold wind blew up from the street and curled over the parapet to where she sat. It had a smoky smell and brought a precious gift of more memories. Bonfire night and smoke and laughter and Grumps writing their names with sparklers and Mum and Dad dancing round with her in excitement as each firework transformed the dark skies over their heads into a myriad of noise and colour and brilliance.

She let out a sad breath and freed her hands. She poured coffee from the second flask into a fresh cup, reached for the box of French Fancies and opened it. She ate them, one by one, until the box was empty. Then she drank the rest of her coffee.

Iris came to a decision. She would go home only when she was ready. Whatever time that was and whatever mood David was in when she arrived, she would face the consequences.

CHAPTER 12

Iris arrived home, carried her shopping bag into the kitchen and began emptying the contents, wrappers for the bin, cups and sandwich container for the dishwasher. As she filled the flasks with hot water, David walked in from the lounge.

She glanced at him as she unbuttoned her coat. "Hi."

His brows furrowed as he watched. "Where've you been? I've been worried sick."

"Out."

"Out where? I left you three phone messages here this afternoon. Where were you?"

"Just out." She removed her hat and scarf and folded them carefully on the table.

David felt his temper rising. She was being deliberately obtuse. "Didn't you think to let me know?"

"No."

"What d'you mean 'no'? I get home. No Iris. Don't you realise how thoughtless that was?"

Iris lay her fists on the table and leaned on

97

them heavily. She looked at him. "Thoughtless? Me? After your behaviour yesterday? You promised to take me out for dinner on my birthday. Instead you took someone else. I don't know who it was and I don't care. It was supposed to be me."

David opened his mouth.

"I've not finished."

He clamped his lips together, folded his arms and fixed her with a hard stare.

"I was really upset that I was left to celebrate it on my own, like I've had to do since I was fourteen. So I decided to have a few drinks then I fell asleep. Then, sometime in between last night and this morning, you came home, went to bed, got up and went out and at no point did it occur to you to get me upstairs to bed. Couldn't you have at least woken me up this morning?"

David didn't answer. A warning muscle was twitching in his cheek. Iris ignored it and carried on. "I'll tell you why you ignored me. It's because I mean nothing to you. I'm a fixture, not a feature." She walked around the table and stopped in front of him. "You never give me a second thought. You never treat me with respect and you don't give a toss about me, even though you know how I feel about you. Maybe it's time I moved out."

David sucked in his breath. It was a warning shot across his bows. The thing he had been dreading. He gripped her arms tightly. "Iris, listen to me. You never said yesterday was your birthday. How was I supposed to know? I didn't find out until today, when Suze told me you'd rung her last night..."

Iris drew herself up and clenched her fists. "You did know. The other day, I told you and you said you'd make a reservation at Le Petit Coco."

"Iris, you didn't tell me. When I mentioned Coco's it was to say I was booking it to take Bill Byrne, the chap who bought your house. He's got more conversions planned. I was buttering him up."

"No." Iris's voice sounded unsure. "You definitely said it was for us."

David shook his head and smiled benevolently. "I think you misheard me or mixed it up in your head, Iris. You've seemed a bit absent-minded lately, a bit confused. I've noticed and other people have too."

Iris forehead wrinkled. She didn't know what other people he was talking about. "But why did you leave me downstairs?"

"You looked so peaceful, I didn't have the heart to wake you. I looked in on you this morning before I went off and you were sleeping like a baby."

She gave a deep sigh. "David, I feel like you're putting up with me because you have to. If that's the case, I'll go. I've got the money. I can buy a place of my own."

"No! Listen, Iris, you're not going anywhere. I apologise if I'm making you feel like this. I'm a silly man who can sometimes be insensitive."

He pulled her into his arms and kissed her, taking heart from her lack of resistance. "Hey, I'm not so bad. Today, as soon as I found out it was your birthday, I went all out. I ordered flowers but you weren't in when they arrived so they left them next door. They're in the lounge now, waiting for you, with a bottle of champagne. I rang Le Petit Coco and made a reservation for tonight at half seven but it's too late now so how about I order a Chinese and nip out when it's ready? You can go and get changed, have a shower then let me spoil you for the rest of the evening."

Iris hesitated. He looked down at her, a smile playing on his lips, those ocean eyes searching her face for his redemption. He looked contrite, sincere. She relaxed. "That sounds lovely, David. Thank you."

¤

David reversed the Porsche out of the drive and made his way to the local take-away. As he drove, his hands grasped the wheel tightly, clammy against the leather. That was a close call. She had sounded serious about going. He gritted his teeth. He hadn't liked the way she'd spoken to him though. He'd been that close to slapping her. But for the sake of his plans he really had to learn to control his temper. More than that, he'd have to start making more of an effort with her. Either that, or kiss his ambitions goodbye.

He pulled into the parking bay outside The

Golden Dragon and turned off the engine. Tomorrow was Saturday, his day off. He stared up at the shop frontage thoughtfully. Why not treat her to a weekend away? He could ring Suze and tell her he wouldn't be in on Sunday. She'd probably be pleased that he was making an effort. That would earn him a few brownie points after the earbashing she gave him today.

The last thing he wanted to do was piss her off. Suze was a valuable asset, so much so that he was considering asking her to take over the management of the Bramhall agency while he concentrated on getting the Didsbury shop off the ground. He had already found the perfect premises. Once it was open, the expansion into Chorlton wouldn't be far behind. It was up to him not to fuck up.

His left the car and walked into the take-away, turning a mega-watt smile on the pretty Chinese girl behind the counter. "Hi, Kiki. How's my favourite girl today?"

She blushed, as she always did. "Hi, David. Got your 'phone order here." She read quickly from a pad. "Two portions of Spring rolls. One side order of fried noodles. One 51, vegetable egg foo young and One 69, bean curd with beef and broccoli."

She placed two brown paper bags in front of him. David reached for the handles before she could moved her hands away. He leaned forward, fingers touching hers. "Have you ever had a sixty-nine?"

Kiki blushed again as she shook her head.

David winked. "I'll have to show you one day."

She pulled her hands away and held them to her mouth to mask a giggle. He lifted the bags down and winked again as he left the shop.

Back in the car, he put the bags in the passenger foot well and turned his thoughts back to Iris. Perhaps this weekend would be a good time to approach her about Chorlton before something, he didn't know what, happened.

He had diffused the situation tonight but her sudden changes in personality, the aggression, seemed out of character and he found it disturbing. Recently he had started sensing a darkness lurking inside her. He searched his mind to ratify what it was and why it worried him.

A quote from Macbeth came into his head.

'By the pricking of my thumbs, something wicked this way comes.'

He shivered as he pulled into his driveway. Iris was standing at the lounge window. The lights in the room behind her turned her silhouette black. He couldn't see her features but he could feel her eyes looking into him.

David climbed out of the car, smiled and waved.

The figure stood there for a moment longer then turned and walked from view.

CHAPTER 13

David let Iris sleep in on Saturday morning while he pulled on jeans, tee shirt and a roll neck jumper before creeping downstairs. It was nine am and he wanted to book a hotel before springing the surprise. He wasn't familiar with the Lake District but had once stayed at the Derwent Mount in Borrowdale, a few miles outside Keswick. He found the number, rang them and booked half board for one night in a luxury double room on the first floor with a balcony and views over Derwentwater.

David prepared a breakfast tray for Iris with fresh coffee, orange juice, cereal, toast and her favourite lime marmalade. He plucked a rose and a piece of gypsophila from the bouquet he had bought her and popped it into bud vase. Back upstairs, he put the tray on the upholstered bench at the foot of the bed and tiptoed to where Iris lay.

David bent to kiss her and Iris opened her

eyes. "Happy birthday, babe. It's officially today."

She laughed happily. "How lovely."

"Well, sit up then. Your day starts with breakfast in bed." He collected the tray and placed it on her lap.

Iris clapped her hands in delight. "Oh! What a treat."

He sat on the edge as she ate. "Well, that's just the first. When you've finished, get dressed and pack a weekend case."

Her eyes lit up. "Why?"

"Because we're going to the Lake District for the weekend."

"Oh. Wow! Whereabouts?"

"Keswick."

Iris clapped again. "Oh, you wonderful man. I've not been there since Mum and Dad were alive. I love the Lake District. I love Keswick."

"Well, eat up then. As soon as you're ready, we'll get going." David stood and planted a kiss on her head. "Happy birthday, Iris."

She beamed up at him and it stayed after he left the room. What a super surprise. She hadn't expected anything more after the champagne and flowers last night. That plain talking must have done some good, although she couldn't actually remember much of what she had said, except that she knew it was because she'd lost her temper, which she never did without provocation.

What she did recall though, with a leap of her heart, was him saying that he didn't want her to leave him.

Iris ate the last half slice of toast, pushed her tray away and hugged herself. She was more than happy. She was joyful. Blissful. Ecstatic. She climbed out of bed and skipped around the room, opening drawers and wardrobes, choosing what to wear. She sang to herself as she packed. She couldn't have been more mistaken. David did care.

What a wonderful weekend they were going to have.

¤

Predictably, it was raining. Pouring down. Stair rods. The Porsche's wipers, even at double speed, were ineffectual.

He swore and Iris chuckled. "This is why there are so many lakes in the Lake District."

David forced a smile. This wasn't what he had planned. They had thrown their walking shoes in the boot and his idea had been to book in then go out for the afternoon. At this rate, they'd be stuck in the hotel all day.

Their room restored his mood. The bed was king sized, the views were stunning and on the coffee table by the French doors was a pre-ordered bottle of champagne in an ice bucket, two fluted glasses, a bowl of fresh strawberries and a paring knife.

Iris clapped her hands together as she looked around. "Oh, David, this is perfect."

He wished she would stop clapping like a performing seal. It was immensely irritating. It was three o'clock already and the rain hadn't eased. But at least the forecast for Sunday was dry and bright, a bonus for November. He'd just have to make the best of today. He walked over to the champagne and began to undo the seal.

Iris sighed with pleasure. "Champagne in the afternoon. How decadent!"

David turned to her with a smile. "Well, if you can't have champagne on your birthday, when can you have it?" He deftly extracted the cork with a loud satisfying pop.

With full glasses, the bottle and the punnet of strawberries, they moved to the bed. "I'd better unpack before everything gets creased." She made to stand but David stopped her. "No. Leave it, Iris. Just live in the moment."

She nodded. "Of course, you're right. Perhaps we could..." She gave him a shy smile.

David grinned. "Now there's an idea." He reached for a strawberry, dipped it in his glass and put it to her lips. She opened her mouth, bit into it and drank from her glass, loving the bubbles with their big golden kisses.

When she finished, David took the glass from her. "Stand up and undress for me."

Iris giggled. "Like a stripper?"

He nodded.

"I'll need music."

"I'll improvise."

He started whistling and sat forward as Iris twirled in front of him. Slowly, each item dropped to the floor. Her jeans, her jumper, then she paused as her hands reached behind her bra.

David's breath was coming faster. "Off."

She unfastened it and held the cups to her breasts, hips swaying. He licked his lips, eyes riveted on her. Slowly, she moved them away and the bra fell to the floor. His lips pursed and he nodded at her panties. "Them."

She slid her thumbs under each side and slowly slid them, zigzag fashion, down her body to the floor. After she stepped out of them, she stood upright and opened her arms. "How do you want me?"

David stood and unzipped his jeans. "Kneel down here."

She looked puzzled but obeyed.

He looked down and held her head in both hands. "Now, suck me off."

"What?"

"Come on. Get your gums 'round my plums."

Iris pulled away. "No, I can't. I don't want to."

"What d'you mean, you don't want to?"

She nodded at his member. "That's not coming anywhere near my mouth."

David threw out a laugh. "No. I know. It's going to come in your mouth."

She looked at him aghast.

"Come on, Iris. Be a woman."

"I am a woman and I'm not giving you oral sex."

David grabbed her head again. "Just do it, Iris."

"I said no." She jerked away and stood up. "I mean it, David. Can't we just make love, like we usually do?"

David fell back on the bed. "It gets tedious."

"Tough."

"What did you say?" His voice had gone an octave higher and was delivered through clenched teeth.

"You heard me. I. Am. Not. Giving. You. Oral. Sex. There. Is that any clearer?" Iris pulled on one of the dressing gowns and fastened the cord around her waist as she walked over to the coffee table. She stared out of the window, arms folded tightly across her chest.

David left the bed and moved stealthily until he was behind her. He caught hold of her hair and yanked her backwards. Iris cried out, rammed her elbow into his stomach and spun round, breaking his grip.

His eyes widened. She was holding the paring knife in front of her. He raised his hands and stepped backwards. "Whoa, Iris. Put that down. Don't be stupid."

Her face held the same hard expression that he had seen before. "Don't you ever try and force me to do something I don't want to do. Do you understand?"

"I understand. I'm sorry, Iris. I didn't think you felt so strongly about it."

"I made my feelings very clear."

David smoothed out his voice. "I've said I'm sorry. Please, Iris. I promise I'll never do it again. Just put the knife down. OK? Put it back on the table."

There was a moment. Iris blinked. Frowned. A

perplexed look crossed her features. She looked at David, at the arms held out in front of him, palms facing her. She looked down at her hand and the knife clutched there, the blade pointing towards him.

She raised her eyes, a confused half smile on her face, looking to him for an explanation. He teased the knife from her grasp and placed it at the end of the table away from her reach.

He turned back and took her hands. "Are you alright, Iris?"

She moved her head from side to side and took a hand back to press her forehead. "I don't know. Did I just faint?"

He led her to the bed and she sank onto it. He sat by her. "I think you blacked out. Why don't you lie down and have a nap? I'll wake you before we go down to dinner."

She laid down and let him cover her with a throw. "Could you pass my painkillers? My head's banging."

David passed her two tablets and a glass of water. Iris took them gratefully and within minutes she was asleep. There was an easy chair on each side of the coffee table. He sank into the nearest. His arms hung limply over the sides as he gazed at her. Even in sleep, there were two shallow furrows of tension between her eyebrows, an unnatural set to her jaw.

What the hell had just happened? This was the second – or was it the third – time she had lost her temper with him but this time was different. She had picked up a knife with the intention of using it as a weapon. More worryingly, she couldn't remember doing it. Then there was that weird expression on her face, that thousand yard stare.

It like she had been possessed by something that seemed to leap in and out of her body at will. Her non-recollection of the event seemed genuine. Was this the darkness he had sensed yesterday, that had chilled his bones? Something wicked this way comes?

He quashed that thought. He wasn't given to hysteria.

Did she have a mental disorder then? David rolled forward and gripped the arms of the chair as his face screwed into a deep frown. If she did, that would be disastrous.

He'd better bring forward his plans and get the money he needed from her before she ended up in the nut house.

Or before she became progressively more dangerous.

CHAPTER 14

Breakfast was between 8.00 and 9.30. Iris and David were seated in the dining room at nine. Iris was amusing herself by watching birds flying to and from feeders hanging from shrubs and trees outside the picture windows.

There was an illustrated booklet on garden birds on the window sill by their table and she leafed through it, trying to identify each as it landed.

Tits were in abundance and each time one appeared, Iris announced its arrival to David, with a theatrical snigger behind her hand. "Another tit, David. Look. It's a blue tit. Cold boobies. Oh. Look, David, here's two for you. Great tits."

David glanced at her several times. Iris was her usual childlike self and had been since he woke her last night for dinner. Neither of them had mentioned the incident. It seemed she still had no recollection. When they returned to their room later, they had sex and afterwards she rolled onto her side and slept soundly throughout the night. David, though, was tortured with restlessness and bad dreams. He had hidden the knife in his bedside drawer and each time he woke he quietly checked that it was still there.

This morning, he was tired and irritable but he had to keep it together. Over breakfast, he was going to broach Iris about the money for the Chorlton agency. He wasn't leaving it a moment longer than he had to. From the back pocket of his jeans he took a gift box, inside was an eighteen carat gold necklace with a solitaire diamond pendant. It had cost a fortune but he saw it as an investment. He placed it in front of her, folded his arms and cleared his throat loudly.

Iris transferred her gaze from the window and gave him a quizzical smile.

He nodded at the table.

She glanced down. "What's this? Is it for me?" She pressed her knuckles together excitedly.

"Open it."

She did. Her eyes grew wide as she picked up the chain. "Oh, David. This is beautiful."

"It's your proper birthday present. You like?"

She wrinkled her nose in delight. "Very much, I like."

He pushed his chair away. "I'll put it on for you."

Iris's hand rose to her neck. "Oh. Well, not now, if that's alright? I'm wearing the one that Trish gave me for my birthday. She lowered the neck of her jumper to show him. "Hadn't you

112

noticed it?"

David set his mouth. "No. When did she give you that?"

"On Thursday, at the cat shop. Isn't it pretty? It's got my initial on the chain."

"I can see that."

"D'you like it? It's sterling silver."

"It's cheap. This one's eighteen carat gold." He pointed to it in her hand. "That's a real diamond. I want you to put it on instead."

Iris looked at him beseechingly. "Can I wear it tonight, when we get home."

"I want you to wear it now." His tone was less pleasant and had that familiar barb.

Iris looked at him. She didn't want the day ruined. Not this early. He was being so good to her. She forced a smile. "Of course." She lifted her hair and he left his chair and moved behind her. His hands rested on her shoulders for a moment and she flinched. He undid the silver necklace and dropped it in front of her. She handed him the gold one. He fastened it, moved his fingers over it to the front to arrange the pendant then went back to his seat. "There. It looks lovely."

Iris patted it lightly, gave him a smile and put Trish's chain in the box and the box in her bag. She would change them round on Thursday before she went to the shop. "Thank you again, David. I absolutely love it."

"Good. I like to spoil you, Iris." He reached across the table, picked up her hand and held it lightly, gently rubbing the back with his thumb.

113

"Actually, while I remember, I've got some good news and bad news. Which do you want first?"

Iris answered immediately. "The bad news."

"OK. I'm having to sell the Porsche."

Iris face registered shock. "Why? What's happened?"

"All in good time. Do you want the good news now?"

"I think I need to, after that."

"I've got the money to buy retail premises in Didsbury village for cash and I'm going ahead with the purchase in the coming weeks. My solicitor, is drafting the papers."

Iris beamed proudly. "Oh, you are clever. Two shops. You're building an empire."

"That's the idea. I'm considering making Suzanna manager of the Bramhall shop so I can concentrate on the new one."

Iris was relieved that he wouldn't be working alongside Suzanna any more.

David went on, enthusiasm lighting his face from within. Iris caught her breath at how handsome he was when he was animated. "Bill has asked me to sell the apartments he's building in Chorlton. This is a fantastic opportunity for me to open an agency there, Iris."

"More good news. So why do you have to sell the Porsche?"

David squeezed her hand. "I'm coming to that. Like I said, I've got the money for Didsbury. The premises there include a two bedroom duplex apartment above, which I intend to rent out.

That'll generate a regular income." He turned one of her hands over and, with a finger tip, traced the lines on it with the delicacy of a palm reader. "However, short term, it won't be enough to raise the capital for a Chorlton one. So, there you have the reason for the bad news. I've been investigating retail premises and found one that's bigger than Didsbury for around the same price. It doesn't have the first floor accommodation but it's on the High Street so it's got maximum footfall. I can't miss this business opportunity so I have to sell the Porsche to get the money together. I might be able to get a small mortgage for the balance but the Bank of England base rate is sky high. We're talking fourteen to sixteen percent for loans."

Iris frowned and stared out of the window while she absorbed the information. The sun had broken through heavy clouds and Derwentwater reflected it back in a blinding shimmer. She hooded her eyes against the glare.

David let her hands go, rested his elbows on the table and threaded his fingers under his chin. His foot tapped impatiently on the floor.

She turned back to him. "I don't want you to sell the Porsche. You love that car. It would really upset me. I mean, it was a present."

He shrugged expressively.

Iris blinked into the sunshine before asking, "What if I lent you the money you need to buy it?"

David sat back in surprise. He had expected Iris to give him the money – not offer a loan. He thought quickly. If he was as good as gold with her, he was sure she'd not want it back.

He formed his face around an ingratiating smile. "That would be wonderful, Iris. It's your inheritance so be assured I'll repay every penny."

"Well, as you say, David, it's my inheritance. If the Bank of England base rate is, for argument's sake, fifteen percent, I'll lend you the money at five percent. I know I'll lose interest but I'm not worried, as long as I get the capital back and a bit extra." She stopped and smiled. "Are you happy with that?"

This was getting worse. Her offer came with interest attached but what could he do? She was calling the shots. The waiter arrived with their breakfast. When he had gone, David extended his hand.

She looked at it blankly. "What're you doing?"

David smiled. "Shaking on it."

Iris shook her head. "No, David. We're going to do this properly, draw up a legal contract and loan agreement and everything."

His face fell. "You're joking. Iris, I find it quite insulting that you feel the need to go to these lengths. Don't you trust me?"

"It's not a matter of trust, David. This isn't about us. This is a business arrangement and this way we're both protected."

What could he say? Hers was the only offer on the table. "OK. Tomorrow, first thing, I'll ring Mark, my solicitor and get him to arrange it for us."

"No," Iris refilled their cups and put the cafetière down. "I'll instruct my family solicitor, Derek Collins."

David blinked. "Why can't we use mine?"

"Because he's your solicitor."

"But..."

"I'm using my solicitor, David. I'll ring him tomorrow. By all means, use Mark if you want to, for your side of the agreement."

David had no option but to back down. He didn't recognise this new Iris. It seemed she had more savvy than he gave her credit for. Somewhere along the line, together with the violent episodes, she was growing a backbone and he didn't like it.

Once the Chorlton agency was added to his portfolio, he would have his hands full for a considerable period. At that stage, he thought with intense relief, he could get rid of her. If, in the future, he was successful enough to consider a fourth agency, he was confident he'd be able to find another cash cow.

A woman with the same credentials. Single, rich and gullible.

CHAPTER 15

When Iris walked into Whiskers Galore on Thursday morning, the tinkle of the door chime drew Trish from behind the partition.

She smiled warmly at Iris, "Hello birthday-girl-last-week. How was your meal?"

Iris ran over and hugged Trish tightly. She let go and beamed. "I had the most fabulous weekend, Trish. David took me to the Lake District. To Keswick. We stayed at a fabulous hotel overlooking Derwentwater, in a luxury room and we had champagne and strawberries and he bought me a fabulous gold necklace with a real diamond pendant – not as nice as yours, of course..." She laughed and added breathlessly, "...and it was fabulous."

Trish smiled fondly. She was glad David had made an effort after all. It warmed her to see Iris so animated but it didn't make what she had to tell her easy. "Well, I'll make us a brew then we've got clothes to price and hang and more books to sort."

Iris gathered an armful of jumpers, folded

them over a spare clothes rail and went back to the counter for the tag gun. She had almost finished when Trish came though with two mugs. "Sorry for the delay, Iris. I've finished sorting the books. We can put them on the shelves later. I want a word first."

Iris stopped and looked at her friend. "Why? What's wrong?"

"Well," Trish hesitated, "Nothing, I hope. There's just something I want to tell you and ask you, as I don't want to make assumptions."

"OK." Iris tagged the last garment and returned the gun to the counter. "Right, you have my undivided attention."

They sat together behind the counter and Iris sipped her tea while she waited for Trish to speak.

"What it is Iris, my son Andrew plays golf regularly and he knows a builder called Bill. Andrew was talking to him at the weekend and Bill told him about a house he'd just bought on Paraffin Alley. Number eight. That was yours, wasn't it?"

Iris nodded, wondering where this was leading. The house was sold. It was nothing to do with her any more.

"Andrew's an architect and Bill was telling him about the conversion. Now, he told Andrew that he bought the house for a hundred and ten thousand. But I thought you said David sold it for one hundred thousand, before deduction of fees."

Iris tilted her head. "I did."

"So..." Trish didn't want to spell it out but Iris was staring blankly at her. "...what happened to the ten thousand?"

Iris shrugged. "More fees?"

Trish answered carefully. "No, Iris. You pay the sale fees from the sale price. The purchaser doesn't pay them."

"I don't know, Trish. I just left it to David."

"But didn't you read over the contract and see the amounts?"

Iris squirmed in her seat. Her headache was returning, despite the tablets she'd taken before she left home. "No. David did all that. He just told me to sign and date where the crosses were."

"Oh, Iris. You're too trusting. You've only known David for a couple of months. That's not long enough to give him carte blanche over your financial affairs."

"You don't like him, do you?"

Trish sat back in surprise. "That's nothing to do with it. My only concern is with you."

"But you don't like him."

Trish sighed. "I don't know him. I've only met him twice but both times I didn't get a good impression. So to be honest, Iris, no. I don't like him."

Iris said nothing. She spread her hands out on her lap and looked at them thoughtfully, then used the thumb nail on her left hand to push back the cuticles on her right. She repeated it with the other hand.

Eventually, she looked up and met Trish's

worried gaze. "Trish, I'm going to be honest now. My instinct is to be angry with you and defend David."

Trish took hold of her hands. "I'm only looking out for you, Iris. You're a wonderful person but naive in so many ways. If I've got it wrong, I will apologise and beg your forgiveness. But I don't think Andrew, and certainly not Bill, got the numbers wrong."

Iris gave Trish a conciliatory smile. "Trish. Shh. You don't ever have to apologise to me. I said my instinct was to be angry but I can't. Not with you. I love you to bits. To be truthful, I'm beginning to have a few doubts about David myself, so if you think he might be swindling money from me, I'm prepared to keep an open mind until I know the facts."

Trish leaned forward and hugged her. "All I'm asking you to do is follow this up. Have you got your copy of the contract?"

"No."

"Oh, Iris, for goodness sake. It was your house. David was only acting as your estate agent. All the legal documents should be in your possession. The fact that you live together has no bearing."

Iris's face folded. She didn't want proof. She wasn't prepared for that. Trish put her arms around her and shook her head sadly. Was Iris getting conned left right and centre by that creep? If what Andrew had told her was true, what else was David doing behind her back?

She looked kindly at Iris's teary face and

handed her a tissue. "Now, don't get upset, love. We can sort this out. You've got me to help you and I won't put up with any of his shit."

Iris hiccuped a laugh. "Trish, you swore!"

Trish laughed with her. "Well, he'd make a saint swear. That's better. Now, blow your nose and wipe your eyes. Preferably not in that order..."

Iris laughed again.

"...and we'll decide how to sort this out. OK?"

Iris nodded. She wouldn't tell Trish that she was going to lend David a large proportion of her money at a ridiculously low rate of interest. It was already in the pipeline. She had rung her solicitor on Monday and his PA had told her that as soon as he had returned from a skiing holiday in France he would ring her for her instructions.

¤

David bounced into the house, called Iris's name and dropped his briefcase and keys on the hall table. He switched on the lamp and walked through to the kitchen, guided by a delicious smell. Iris was by the stove, stirring something in a pan. He shimmied up behind her and put his hands on her waist. She turned into his embrace with a smile.

"What's for dinner? Smells wonderful."

"Coq au vin."

"Oh. It smells like chicken." He laughed at his own joke, placed a kiss on her lips and moved his hands to her breasts. "What're we having with it?"

She moved away and opened the oven to check inside. "Roast vegetables." She moved a finger round to point to each in turn. "Carrots, onions, potatoes, sliced garlic and broccoli."

"Roast broccoli? Never heard that one before."

Iris closed the oven door. "I found it in a recipe earlier this week. I think you'll like it."

He moved behind her again and began to lift the back of her skirt. "Any chance of a quickie before I go for a shower?"

Iris was tempted to push him away but she was going to bring the matter into the open tonight and didn't want to antagonise him. She laid her hands on the counter top and braced herself. "It'll have to be. Dinner won't be long."

He bent her forward, a hand pressing down hard between her shoulder blades. In one quick movement, he opened his zip, pulled aside her panties and laughed. "Neither will this."

¤

David opened a bottle of Chablis while Iris filled their plates. He poured a generous measure into crystal wine goblets and smiled at Iris. "A toast."

"What to?"

"The contracts are underway for the Didsbury shop and as soon as your solicitor gets back, I'll be negotiating a deal on the Chorlton premises. My man's waiting for the agreement from your man. So, a toast."

Iris raised her glass. This was moving nicely into the right arena. She asked a few relevant questions and sat back as he enthused. David hadn't been in such a good mood for a long time. He complimented her on the meal and on her appearance. She'd visited the hairdresser that week and had her hair cut and coloured. It was now light honey blonde, and styled in a soft perm that suited her heart shaped face.

When they had eaten and Iris had stacked the dishes, she looked at him as he refilled their glasses. "David, can I ask you something?"

"Anything. Go on."

"Do you know when you sold my house?"

"Yes."

"Well, how much did I get for it again?"

David's hand paused on its way to his glass. "One hundred thousand. Why are you asking?"

"Just something Trish said today." She placed a napkin down nervously. Should she have mentioned her? But how else would she explain her question.

"Go on."

Iris gathered her courage and told him. About Andrew. About Bill. About the one hundred and ten thousand pounds.

David picked up the glass and examined the colour in the light of the drop pendant above the table. Iris pressed her hands together in her lap. "So I'm wondering where the other ten thousand went?"

David continued to stare at his glass before dropping his eyes to her. "Land Development Tax."

Iris frowned. "What?"

He put the glass down and rested his fingertips on the base. "The ten grand was to pay Land Development Tax."

"Was it?" She sounded unsure.

"Let me explain." He sat forward. "Bill's converting the house into flats, so he has to pay tax for each one because the land is being developed for multiple occupancy. Now do you understand?"

"Not really." She wrinkled her nose and propped her cheek on her fist. "Why would that put an extra ten thousand on the price on the house?"

David blinked. He took a sip of wine and smiled patronisingly as he placed it down. "OK, Iris. Let me try and explain another way so your pretty little head can get round it."

"Please."

He paused and thought for a moment. "Now, listen this time because if you still don't understand, I'm not going to keep trying. I've had a long day and I'm tired. I want to put my feet up, watch 'Dallas' then go to bed."

He finished his wine and poured more.

Iris gave him a nod of encouragement. "Go on then."

He emitted an impatient sigh and paused for a moment longer. "OK. It's quite simple. Bill paid one hundred grand for the house. Then he paid ten grand to the Inland Revenue. So, when he told that chap he paid one hundred and ten, he meant that's what he'd paid in total. For the house and the tax. One hundred thousand plus ten thousand is...?"

"One hundred and ten thousand," Iris answered obediently.

David raised his eyes to the ceiling. "Hallelujah!" He dropped them and grinned at her. "I'm glad that's sorted. Right, I'm going to watch my programme while you clear up. Can you pour me a double scotch when you've finished?"

The theme tune drifted into the kitchen, where Iris was loading the dishwasher. She straightened and smiled as she wiped the counter tops.

She was hoping David would have a simple explanation and he had. She was feeling more than a little guilty that she had doubted him and she was looking forward to telling Trish that she'd been wrong after all.

CHAPTER 16

On Tuesday, Iris and Trish went for a walk. Trish picked her up from David's and drove them to Lyme Park in Disley. They changed into walking shoes and trekked for miles around the historic parkland, then turned back to stroll round the formal gardens and admire the beautiful Edwardian Hall. It was an icy cold, dull November day and most of the other visitors were dog walkers.

As they walked, Iris went through her conversation with David.

Trish nodded. "So the ten grand was what the builder had to pay the Revenue."

"That's right."

"For Land Development Tax."

"Yes."

"Do you believe him?"

"Why wouldn't I?"

Trish frowned. "I've never heard of Land Development Tax."

"Is there any reason why you should have?"

"No, but it just doesn't ring true. Listen Iris, I'm not saying David's lying. I don't know anything about the property business. But

127

please will you do something for me? Do you have a solicitor?"

"Yes. The family one."

"Well, will you call him and ask him about it? You could ring the Inland Revenue but you'd probably be passed from pillar to post and kept hanging on for hours."

"But he's away for two weeks."

"Is he? Oh. Have you already tried to contact him then?"

Iris kicked a stone from under her shoe and shoved her hands deeper into her pockets. She couldn't lie to Trish. She told her everything. About the property in Chorlton, the loan she had agreed to pay David and the call to her solicitor to handle the paperwork.

Trish listened in silence. Once Iris had finished, she nodded slowly. "At least you're proceeding with the loan through your solicitor. That's a safeguard. Well done, Iris."

"So, you're not mad at me?"

"Why should I be mad at you?"

"Because I'm lending him my money."

"Iris, it's your money and you're doing the right thing by going through a solicitor but if things go wrong, I hope you've left yourself enough to buy a place of your own."

Iris shrugged and gave Trish a smile. "I've got enough put aside for a nice little house. Don't worry, Trish."

Trish relaxed. "Good. But if, for whatever reason, you have to move out, please, please tell me. You can stay with me as long as you need to."

"That's so kind of you, Trish but it won't come to that. I think David and I could have a future together. I just need to try harder."

Trish pressed her lips together. That was the saddest and most worrying thing that had ever come out of her friend's mouth.

¤

Iris was ironing in the kitchen when David arrived home from work. It was four o'clock.

She answered when he called her name and smiled a greeting as he walked in. "You're early?"

"Yes. I had a valuation in Higher Poynton so I didn't bother going back." He picked an apple from the ornate bowl on the breakfast bar and gave her a perfunctory kiss on the lips. "Been quite busy today though. What did you get up to?"

Iris finished a pillowcase and set the iron on its side. "It's been lovely. I met Trish and we went to Lyme Park for a walk. It's beautiful there. Then we had coffee and cake in the cafe before she dropped me home."

David frowned. He threw the apple in the air a few times then looked at her. "I thought you only saw that woman on Thursdays at the shop?"

Iris reached for another pillowcase and smoothed it out on the ironing board. "Well, I do usually but we decided we needed more exercise so we're going to go for a walk every

Tuesday, if the weather's dry."

David bit into the apple and crunched it loudly, nodding slowly.

Iris ironed the pillowcase. "Next week, we're going to Tatton Park."

"I don't think so."

She had folded it and placed it on top of the first before she realised what he'd said. She rested her hands on the ironing board and laughed. "Sorry? What did you say?"

"I don't want you socialising with that woman."

"You don't want me...Why ever not?"

"Because she's trying to turn you against me."

Iris laughed again. "Don't be ridiculous. Trish is my best friend. How can you say that?"

"What about the matter of the ten grand she told you about?"

"She was just asking for clarification, that's all. I'd told her I'd got a hundred thousand."

"It's no business of hers."

"David." Iris leaned hard on her hands and frowned. "It was an innocent question. I'd have asked the same, if the situation had been reversed. There was no malice or anything intended."

David threw his apple in the bin, walked over and stood at the other side of the ironing board. "That woman's toxic. She's an interfering old bitch. I don't want you seeing her. In fact, you can stop working at that stupid shop."

"What? No chance. I love working there and I love Trish. She's a wonderful friend."

"Oh. I see what's going on."

"What?"

You two are dykes, aren't you? I bet that's it."

Iris's mouth dropped open. She looked at David in amazement. "You think I'm a lesbian?"

"Either that or you swing both ways."

Her expression altered. It made her look different. Harder. There was a set to her mouth and her eyes were darkening to green-black serpentine.

She looked at him with contempt. "Oh, grow up, David. You're like a spoilt child, d'you know that? Don't you like me having a friend? Does it upset you when I'm happy? Do you think you're the only one I need in my life? God help me if that was true."

His face didn't change. He stared hard at Iris, as if pondering her words. Then, without speaking, he put his hands under the ironing board, lifted it and threw it across the room. The iron tipped and fell to the floor with a loud clatter.

There was nothing separating them now. Iris stepped back but not quickly enough. She hunched her shoulders instinctively when David grabbed the back of her neck. He pulled her close and snarled, "You're lucky you've got anyone in your life. You're fat, ugly and useless. You should be grateful I put up with you."

He slapped her hard across the face and threw her against the wall.

Iris slithered down and came to rest on the floor. She stared up at him, tears splashing over her reddening cheek. David stood looking down at her. He was breathing heavily and his hands had balled into fists by his side.

One unfurled and he jabbed a finger at her. "I told you before. Don't wind me up. Now get up, lard arse."

Iris curled her legs under her and pushed herself up on her hands. Her ears were buzzing. It felt like acid was dissolving her brain. She lifted her head as David turned his back, then looked to the side, where the iron lay, still attached to the socket. She leaned over, pulled out the plug, picked it up and got to her feet. The buzz became a million bees as she watched David walk towards the hall without a backward glance.

She lifted the iron and followed him. As she came up behind, she let out an animalistic scream. David turned in time to see the iron coming towards him. He raised his hands and it glanced off the side of his palm. David screamed in pain and pressed his hand to his chest. Iris grabbed his collar and held the underside of the iron close to his face. The heat was intense. He jerked the top half of his body away, fear draining his colour.

Iris spoke in the same fluid, controlled voice that she'd used at the hotel, when she'd been holding the knife. "I've warned you about ordering me to do things I don't want to do. I will see my friend as and when I want. Is that clear?"

David 's head spasmed but he managed a nod.

"And I am neither fat, ugly, useless or a lesbian. OK?"

A second nod.

"And if you ever lay a hand on me again, you'll regret it. Do you understand?"

A third, more pronounced.

At that moment, the telephone rang. David escaped into the lounge to answer it.

Iris put the iron on the counter to cool, retrieved the ironing board, placed it back in the cupboard and stacked the clothes and bedding, ready to take upstairs.

Suddenly her breath fractured and she leaned her arms on the counter for support. She blinked away a mist, pushed herself upright and held on to the top as she looked around. Had she finished the ironing? There was still laundry in the basket. She remembered David coming home early. Where was he?

She rubbed her forehead and touched her cheek delicately with her fingertips, wondering why it was smarting. As she walked to the lounge, she heard him coming off the phone.

"Who was that?"

David jumped and wheeled round. "What?"

Iris was standing in the doorway, a smile on her face. "On the phone. Who was it?"

He kept his eyes on her and pointed to it with one hand, the other held defensively in front of him. "It was just a friend of mine."

She danced over and wrapped herself around him. He looked down at her in trepidation. She didn't seem to be armed. He folded his arms gingerly around her and she settled against his chest with a contented sigh. "What did he want?"

"He's invited us to an evening reception at the Midland Hotel in Manchester. He's getting married a week on Saturday."

Iris lifted her face and smiled up at him. "Oh, how lovely. I've never been to a wedding."

"It's only the evening do."

"It'll still be lovely. I've never met any of your friends."

"No. Yes. It'll be nice." There was a tremor in his voice.

"I'll buy a new dress for it. Now, go and have a shower and I'll start dinner. OK?"

David nodded and waited until she moved away before releasing his breath properly. Upstairs, in the en-suite, he examined his hand while he ran cold water over it. It didn't look bad but it hurt like hell.

What was happening to Iris? These episodes were escalating. He reminded himself that as soon as her solicitor was back, he would push Mark to get the loan agreement set up urgently.

In the meantime he would tread very carefully.

PART TWO
SOUTH DAKOTA, USA

CHAPTER 17

A patrol car turned into the driveway and pulled up outside the wooden veranda that ran the width of a neat two-storey clapboard farmhouse. The engine stilled and a young man climbed out. He was good looking and smartly attired in the uniform of the Pennington County Sheriff's Office.

He looked around while he hitched up the waistband of his trousers then looped his thumbs inside the belt and made his way over a patch of lawn to a partly built cabin in the corner of the front yard.

He stopped and called to the two men working on the roof. "Hi folks. It's coming on real well."

The younger of the two, well built and in his late thirties with dark blond hair and a trim beard, straightened and looked down. "Morning, Warren. She's in the kitchen. Ask her to put the kettle on, will you?"

"Sure thing." He strolled off and walked round to the back of the house. A border collie rose from a blanket by the porch and met him, barking as her tail wagged furiously. A miniature version detached itself from behind her, shot up the steps and bounded into the house.

In the kitchen the door slammed followed by claws scrabbling on stone flags. The woman washing plates in the sink took the impact of twenty pounds of muscle and fur on the back of her knees.

She grabbed hold of the edge of the sink then turned to the excited pup bouncing behind her. "Bunty, will you stop doing that."

She knelt and grabbed the pup in a hug. "You're very naughty but you're still gorgeous."

"Sorry, Bunty. That description belongs to my lady here."

She looked up and smiled. "Morning, Deputy Fisher. How are you today?"

"Better for seeing you." He danced across the kitchen, reached her and broke into into song as he waltzed her around the table in the centre. "Joanna, I love you. You're the one, the one for me. Ooh, yeah..."

Joanna laughed and pushed him away. "Behave!"

He chuckled. "Eddie says put the kettle on."

"Right. Do you want tea or coffee?"

"Tea for a change, thank you ma'am. Have you got that posh one with the fancy title? You know, tastes like cat pee."

"Earl Grey?"

"That's the one."

"Of course." Joanna filled the kettle and

clicked it on. "How's things?"

"Fine." Warren took a seat, rested his chin on the palm of his hand and fell quiet as he watched her. She had a great ass.

"Warren, are you looking at my bottom?"

"Yup."

"Well don't."

Warren grinned. He'd had a crush on Joanna since their first meeting back in the Spring. She was blonde, grey eyed, had a smile that lit up the room and a sexy English accent. It made no odds that she was in her thirties, at least ten years his senior.

The screen door opened.

Joanna turned. "Hi, Eddie. What d'you and John want to drink?"

"Coffee would be great, sweetheart. Same for Dad. We've nearly finished the roof. Want to come see?"

Outside, the three stood with Eddie's father, leaning into their cups for warmth. Above them, in the chill of the October morning, a weak sun sat low, its colour bleaching into a watery sky.

Warren broke the silence first. "What did you say it's going to be?"

"A tea room." Joanna turned to him. "A posh cafe, if you like. The speciality will be afternoon tea, which people will book in advance. It'll have a selection of food presented on a three tiered stand."

She flattened her hand and raised it in front of her to illustrate each layer. "The bottom will have finger sandwiches with a selection of fillings. The middle will have an assortment of cakes and fancies and the top will have two types of scone with jam, butter and, if it's available, clotted cream, but there's a problem in the States with unpasteurised milk so it might have to be pasteurised, which isn't as nice, unfortunately."

She warmed to her subject. "There'll be a choice of leaf teas as well as coffee and the optional extra of a glass of sparkling wine. We'll have six tables, each seating up to four. They'll be outside in good weather, inside in bad. Each one will have a different coloured tablecloth and a posy of fresh flowers in the centre. The crockery will be mismatched china." She looked up at Eddie. "Have I left anything out?"

Eddie looked down at her proudly. "No, sweetheart. Just the name."

Joanna leaned against him and his arm slipped around her waist. "Of course. I'm calling it The Willow Tea Room. It's a nod to my favourite designer, Charles Rennie Mackintosh."

Warren looked at her blankly, moved his gaze to the cabin then back at her. "Are you doing proper food as well?"

John and Eddie exchanged glances.

Joanna turned to face him, her voice steady. "It is proper food."

Warren grinned at Eddie and John, winked at Joanna and handed her his empty cup. "I'm sure you'll do very well. Well, better be off. See you again, folks. Thanks for the tea."

Eddie shook his head as Warren drove away.

"How the hell did he ever make uniform."

John laughed. "Nepotism. His dad was in the force and he and Sheriff Brody go way back."

Eddie shook his head. "I swear, if his brain exploded, it wouldn't part his hair."

"Don't be rotten." Joanna tutted. "Warren's a nice lad. He's just happy-go-lucky. A bit immature. Plays the fool. You should try and look below the surface."

"I'll take your word for it." He said dryly. "But I remain unconvinced."

¤

The telephone rang through the house. Eddie picked up from the kitchen extension. A familiar voice was speaking before the receiver reached his ear.

"Ed? Is that you? It's me, Bronsky."

He leaned his shoulder against the wall and smiled. "Art? Well, long time no see. How are you?"

Lieutenant Bronsky snorted. "Oh, same old, same old, you know. Right. Listen up..."

Eddie found himself straightening his spine.

"What it is, Ed, I've had a call from our friends at Greater Manchester Police. They're holding a training course. A pilot scheme, apparently."

There was only a few hours of workable daylight left. They needed to complete the roof before dark. Eddie interrupted. "Art, what's this got to do with me?"

"Give me a chance, will you. Jesus wept."

Eddie could visualise his former boss, fifteen

139

hundred miles away in New York, perched behind his desk at Precinct 13, chewing a cigar stump, flicking ash at an overflowing ashtray and barely visible behind a mountain of paperwork.

"How's the lovely Joanna, by the way?"

"She's great. She's out with my mom, buying tubs and flowers."

"Interesting." His voice suggested otherwise. "You know, I always knew you two would get together in the end. The way you used to eyeball each other, I could've sold tickets." He roared with laughter. "Anyway. They want me to put forward two officers. One from here and one from another state. Now, I've figured South Dakota, 'cause of you."

"Art, didn't you notice I handed in my badge six months back?"

"Very funny. Will you listen? Right. You know when you took Joanna to your place, after Vermont? You called Sheriff..."

Eddie filled in the gap. "Brody."

"That's the guy. Well, as you know, I spoke to him a couple of times and he was real obliging. I was thinking maybe he could spare someone for a couple of weeks. Have you still got his number? I can't find it."

"Hang on." Eddie reached for the directory and read out the number scribbled on the cover.

"That's great. Thanks Ed."

"So when's all this happening?"

"Starts on..." A pause as papers shuffled, "...Monday November twenty-five through

Friday December six."

"Short notice, pulling two officers that time of year."

"Well, not great timing but everyone will be back before it kicks off for the holidays. Right. That's it. Sorry to have interrupted your day. You can go back to whatever you were doing."

"We're in the middle of building a cabin for..."

"Whatever. Go on. Fuck off, Ed. Take care though. OK?"

There was a click and the line went dead. Eddie grinned as he replaced the receiver. He walked to the back door and his hand was just reaching for the handle when the phone rang again. He swore and walked back.

"Hello? Is Joanna there please? It's Samantha, from England."

"Hi Samantha. How are you?"

"Is that Eddie? Oh, how lovely to speak to you. We're all fine here. How're you two?"

"We're great, thanks Samantha. Joanna's out with my mother. Can I get her to call you when she's back?"

"Well, it's eleven at night here. We're off to bed shortly. I was just finishing off some bits. Can you give her a message?"

"Of course."

"It involves you as well. I'm getting married on Saturday, November the thirtieth. The invitations have gone out but I thought I'd ring, you know, belt and braces, in case yours arrives late, or gets lost. You're invited to the whole shebang. I'll give Joanna chapter and verse tomorrow. I'll ring her at ten am, your time."

He smiled, "I'll be sure and tell her."

"Thanks, Eddie. I hope you can come. Dying to meet you at last."

"You too. Thanks, Samantha. Take care now."

Eddie replaced the receiver thoughtfully. Joanna had been away from England for over six months. A trip back might do her good. Sometimes he worried that she'd get homesick. She loved South Dakota, loved the farm and he knew how much she loved him but it was still early days for their relationship and everything was so different here.

He liked the idea of them going back to where they first met, before everything went crazy. Before they nearly lost each other. Before they found each other.

CHAPTER 18

Eddie's mother and Joanna were kneeling in front of a pair of garden planters. Between them were bags of compost, potted conifers and trays of winter flowering pansies and cyclamen.

Laura sat back on her heels to admire two that they had finished. "These look beautiful. They'll look fabulous by the tea room door. Are we agreed that the other two will flank the veranda steps?"

"Yes." Joanna arched her back and settled forward again. "We've done well..." She stopped when Eddie emerged from the house.

"Joanna, it's Samantha."

She stood and brushed the soil from her apron, "Sorry Laura, it's the call I've been waiting for."

"No hurry, honey. Go have a good catch up with your friend."

¤

"The wedding's at the end of November." Joanna looked at Eddie's parents across the kitchen table. "Now, Eddie and I had a chat when I came off the phone and he suggested we stay for a couple of weeks. We thought we'd fly

143

out on Wednesday the twenty seventh and come back on Wednesday the eleventh."

John held his hand up. "Joanna, we're more than happy to stay on until you two get back."

"But won't you want to get back to California?"

Laura laughed. "We're in no rush. My sister can keep an eye on the house while we're away. Anyway, we love being here with you and the work on the tea room is so exciting, I'd hate to leave without helping it through to completion. You don't want to be asking the neighbours to come over when you've got us."

John folded his arms on the table. "Eddie and I should have all the exterior work done before you leave. While you're away, I'll arrange for the electrician to come and do the first fix but I need you and Laura to complete the plans for the interior."

"That's no problem." Laura patted his arm. "We can thrash it out in a day. Joanna knows exactly what she wants so it's simply a case of putting pen to paper."

Eddie looked at Joanna. "That sound OK to you?"

"Brilliant. Thank you both so much. Now," She paused and exchanged a glance with Eddie. "There's another reason why we're going for so long. As you know, I rent out my flat in Manchester. Well, the agents contacted me recently to remind me that the lease is up shortly. The couple who are renting aren't asking for an extension – they've bought their own place, which is great and it'll be vacant by the time we arrive. I spoke to Eddie about a plan I've had for a while. He thinks it's a great idea." She caught Eddie's hand and squeezed it. "I've told the agents not to re-let it. When we get to England, I'm going to put it on the market. When it's sold, I'd like to use the money to built an extension here."

Laura and John looked surprised.

Joanna went on quickly, "That's only if you don't mind."

John leaned forward and rested a hand on Laura's arm. "Joanna, It's Eddie's place now. And yours. You can do what you want with it."

"Let Joanna finish." Eddie smiled. "I think you're going to like this."

"The extension's for you. We want you to visit as often as you like and hopefully spend summers with us. So, it's going to be single storey, on the left hand side of the house and accessed from the hall. It's a bedroom and en-suite, for you. To stay in. When you come..." She tailed off with a smile.

John's face lit up. Laura looked at Joanna in delight. "That's wonderful, Joanna. I don't know what to say. Thank you. Thank you. Thank you. Ooh, I love you, my darling girl." She jumped up, ran round the table and enveloped Joanna in a hug.

¤

"You know, It's a big leap of faith, using your apartment money for the extension." Eddie climbed into bed and ruffled her hair as he settled against the pillows.

"We've already been there, Eddie." Joanna curled up against him. "I've a pretty good idea that you and me are for keeps."

"That's true. I just want you to be absolutely sure." He began to plant small kisses on her neck.

"I am. Otherwise I wouldn't have told them today. That feels nice."

"Good." His lips moved to her shoulders.

She freed her arms, wrapped them around his neck and kissed him.

¤

Joanna curled up in the afterglow, Eddie's arms reassuringly strong around her. She had so much to do once they got to Manchester. She would sell the flat fully furnished. Maybe she'd scour the charity shops for the china tea sets while they were there. A frisson of excitement made her shiver and, in sleep, Eddie held her closer.

She moved her head slightly to look at him then turned back with a smile and fell asleep, warm and safe in his arms.

CHAPTER 19

The familiar sound of steel toe capped boots on the porch decking drew Eddie's gaze from the agricultural accounts he was checking at the breakfast table to the glass panel in the back door. He glanced over at Joanna as she loaded the washing machine. "Your boyfriend's here."

Deputy Fisher knocked, opened the door and shoved his face inside. "Only me. Hope I've not caught you two at it." He ignored the look Eddie gave him. "Just kidding, folks."

Joanna straightened up. "Come in, Warren. Want a cuppa?"

"Ooh. Love one. Coffee please, anyway it comes." The young man walked to the table, sat down and set a bundle of papers in front of him. "I've come to ask a favour."

Eddie put his pen down. "What?"

Warren pushed the papers over to him. He squared his shoulders and folded his arms over his chest. "I've been selected to attend a seminar and..." A vague hand wave, "...other stuff, in Manchester, England on..." He reached over and grabbed the top page from Eddie's hand, "...November twenty-five. It finishes on..." He

147

scoured the page, "...December six. Can you look it over and tell me what it's about?"

Eddie looked at him in surprise. "Sheriff Brody put you forward?"

Warren nodded proudly. "Yup."

Eddie took the page back and scanned it before turning to the rest. He was silent for a few minutes while he read. "OK. It's pretty straightforward. There's going to be a series of lectures and workshops looking at IT programming and information sharing between national and international police forces."

Warren's face was blank.

Eddie glanced up briefly. "Technology's becoming more sophisticated, Warren, and this means that computer systems will become compatible. This'll enable inter-regional, national and eventually international databases to improve co-operation in detecting and arresting criminals." He sifted through the last few pages and looked up. "Clear so far?"

Warren pinched his chin between finger and thumb and looked up at the ceiling as he considered Eddie's question.

Joanna brought their coffees over with a plate of biscuits and sat down.

"Warren?" Eddie asked patiently.

"Just one thing really." He propped his elbows on the table. "What's 'it'?"

Eddie threw out a breath and shook his head at Joanna.

She kept her face straight as she answered. "It's not a word Warren. It stands for

148

Information Technology."

"Oh. Right."

Eddie took over. "Anything else before we move on?"

"Err, no. I don't think so."

"OK. The second week focuses on grass roots policing. You'll go out with different units, on foot, in cars, motorway policing, crowd control. You know, at soccer stadiums and the like. It shouldn't stretch you too much." His eyes drifted to Joanna and back. She pressed her lips together and looked down at her cup. "Looks like you may be spending some time with CID. That's the Criminal Investigation Department. Sounds interesting. You can play detective."

Warren brightened. "Oh. I like the sound of that. Thanks, Ed." He helped himself to a biscuit and looked at Joanna. "I think this'll be good for me. Actually, I'm already preparing research into different policing methods. You know? So I can hit the ground running. I've made a list of TV programmes to watch. Here." He handed Joanna a sheet of paper covered in an untidy scrawl.

Joanna looked then made a shield of her hand to hide her face. Her shoulders began to shake. She kept her head down as she handed it to Eddie.

He ran his eyes down the page, then looked over at Warren. "Seriously?" His eyes dropped to the sheet again. "Cagney and Lacey. Hill Street Blues. Kojak. Miami Vice." He looked up. "The A Team?"

"Ah." Warren held up a finger. "You noticed that last one. I put them in alphabetical order but couldn't make my mind up whether to put it under 'T' for The A team or 'A' for The A team."

"I think you were right with the first one." Joanna offered kindly.

"That was my choice too. Ed?"

"What?"

"What do you think? Go on. Best of three?"

"Warren. You've already got the best of three."

"Have I? Oh. Right. Well, can you cast your vote anyway? I value your opinion."

Eddie dropped his arm with a thump and glared at him. "Warren. I haven't got time for this. Have we finished now?"

Warren dissolved into laughter and pointed at him. "Got you!"

Joanna smiled at him indulgently. "Very funny. So, what are the logistics?"

"The what?"

"Your flights, accommodation. That sort of thing."

"Ah, now. Sheriff Brody said Manchester police haven't arranged anything. I've to sort my own and they'll refund the costs. The Sheriff's giving me an advance."

"Right. But you've not looked into it yet."

"No. I thought you'd help me. I'm not so good at organising stuff."

Joanna felt a pang of pity. She sat forward. "Look, I'll tell you what. Eddie and I are going to the travel agents in town tomorrow. Why don't you come with us? You can get everything sorted there."

Warren flopped back in his seat with a grateful smile. "That would be great. I've got some leave so I thought I'd tag another week onto the end and make it into a vacation. See some sights. So, where're you two going?"

She ignored a miniscule but desperate shake of Eddie's head.

"Well, actually, we're going to Manchester too."

Warren sat up. "That's spooky. Can we go together?"

Eddie broke in quickly. "No. We leave after your Seminar starts. I suggest you fly out on Thursday the twenty first. That'll give you a few days, depending on the connecting flights, to get over jet lag."

"OK. Sounds good. Where are you staying?"

Joanna answered. "At my flat in Manchester. We're going over for a wedding but staying for two weeks to put it on the market."

"Oh." Warren's eyebrows lifted hopefully. "Is it big enough for..."

"No." Eddie stood and handed the papers back to Warren. "Tiny. Just one bedroom and a bed that barely sleeps two."

Warren winked at Joanna. "Not a problem, Ed. You can take the sofa."

Joanna ignored him. "I presume this event is based in and around Manchester? If it is, you could book into the hotel I stayed at before I came to the States. The Grosvenor. It's near the city centre, just off the main road. Very central.

Eddie's stayed there too. In fact, that's where we met."

She and Eddie shared a smile.

Warren dropped his gaze to a small knot in the honey pine surface and scratched it with a fingernail. "I'm really grateful, 'cos, thing is, I've never booked a flight before. I've never even flown before."

Eddie rolled his eyes.

Joanna patted Warren's arm. "Don't worry. The travel agent will do all the work and we'll be there in case you're not sure of any of the details. OK?"

He nodded. "That's great. Right." He stood, "About time I was off. What time tomorrow?"

"Get here about ten." Eddie sat back in his seat, "And don't forget to tell Sheriff Brody what you're doing."

Warren nodded, turned to Joanna with a smile of thanks, then lunged and caught her in a bear hug. She grunted and rested her palms lightly on his shoulders.

Eddie shook his head as the young Deputy strolled out.

Once the screen door closed, Joanna started laughing.

"What?"

"The 'A' team. You must admit, it was funny. He had you fooled."

Eddie grinned. "It just confirmed my low opinion of him." He became serious. "Are you looking forward to going home?"

She looked around expressively. "I am home."

"You know what I mean."

"Yes, I am. Especially now so much has changed. Now we're us and not you and me, if that makes sense. It'll be lovely." Joanna walked round the table and straddled him. She brought her hands to his chest and kissed him, her lips moving gently over his.

Eddie loved it when she did that. Grateful that his folks were out for the day, his hands began to explore under her tee shirt.

"Hi! Just me again. Whoops! Looks like I have caught you at it, this time."

Joanna sprang off Eddie's lap and arranged her top before turning.

Eddie's voice was like thunder. "Warren! What do you want now?"

"Just checking on the time again. Am I getting here for ten tomorrow or...?"

"Yes. Here. At ten. In the morning. Tomorrow. Got it now?"

"Yup. That's great. Well, I can see I'm stopping you good people getting on with your day." He smirked. "I'll see you tomorrow then. At ten. In the morning. Here."

Eddie called to him as he reached the door. "Warren, in future, whenever you come here, please go to the front door, ring the bell and wait to be invited in, like a normal person. Never, and I mean NEVER, just wander in through the back door again. Is that clear?"

Warren winked. "OK, Ed. See you."

As soon as the screen door shut, Joanna shook her head. "You know, I think we'd better keep

153

an eye on him while we're over there."

Eddie's face dropped. "You're not serious."

She chuckled. "I'm not suggesting a short term foster. Just make sure he's OK. Maybe take him out with us a couple of times. I'm sure he'd appreciate it. He'll be a fish out of water. Sheriff Brody shouldn't have put him forward."

"I think his decision was based solely on whose absence would have the least negative impact on his team." Eddie shrugged. "Anyway. OK, sweetheart. We'll keep an eye on him. Now...before we were so rudely interrupted..."

With a happy sigh, Joanna caught hold of his hand, followed him upstairs and pushed the bedroom door closed behind them.

PART THREE
NORTH WEST ENGLAND

CHAPTER 20

"David and I have been invited to a wedding. Well, the evening do. I need something spectacular to wear." Iris looked at Trish with a worried expression. It meant so much to make a good impression on his friends.

Trish gave her a hug. "You'll look like a princess when I've finished with you. Now. Do you want a dress? Or trousers and top, or skirt and top?"

"Oh. I don't know, Trish. I'll leave it to you. Whatever you think suits me. Well, it all depends what we've got in the shop, doesn't it?"

Trish's eyebrows raised. "Excuse me but I don't think so. This is a special occasion. It calls for a special shop. We'll close up at one and go out. Right?"

¤

The door of Crowthers boutique tinkled musically when Trish entered, a reluctant Iris trailing behind her. She'd passed this trendy boutique many times but had never had the nerve to go in.

Trish ushered her in front as a tall, slender assistant floated over to them. She glanced at the name badge on her blouse. "Hello, Francesca. We need your help for a special outfit for my friend here."

To Iris's surprise, Francesca's beautiful, perfectly made up face softened into a warm smile. "Call me Frankie." She tilted her head to one side and tapped a long pink fingernail against full pink lips.

"And the occasion is?"

"An evening reception with her boyfriend, this coming Saturday. She wants to dress to impress."

Frankie nodded thoughtfully. She took one of Iris's hands and turned her round slowly. "What a beautiful figure. How tall are you?"

Iris spoke for the first time. "Five foot two."

Frankie wrinkled her perfect nose. "You petite ladies are so feminine and cute. I wish I was a few inches shorter."

Iris's eyes widened. "But I've always wanted to be tall, like you."

Frankie laughed. Of course, Iris thought, it had to be silvery and mercurial. "We all want to be someone else. Now, I think I have the perfect thing for you. Just one moment." She walked off and ran her fingers delicately along a rail of dresses before nodding in satisfaction and extracting one.

She moved elegantly to the far end of the

boutique and called behind her, "Shoe size?"

"Four," Iris called back.

Frankie selected a pair and was off again, this time to the lingerie section. "Bra size?"

"Thirty-six B."

"OK. Now we're getting somewhere." They could see her searching through tiny hangers draped with what looked to Iris like gossamer. She walked back to them quickly, her face animated with pleasure, "I think I have the absolutely perfect ensemble for you." She caught Iris's arm and gently let her to the changing rooms. "Take these and come out when you're ready."

Frankie draped the garments reverently over Iris's arm. After an encouraging nod from Trish, Iris vanished behind the curtain.

Five minutes later, she emerged. Collectively, Frankie and Trish drew in their breath.

"What?" Iris looked uncertainly between them. "Do I look OK?"

Frankie shook her head in wonder. "You look stunning."

"She's right." Trish clapped her hands together. "Iris, you do."

Iris turned and walked back into the changing room and stared with more confidence into the full length mirror. They weren't exaggerating. She did look stunning. She turned this way and that, admiring herself, then looked out at Frankie. "I'll take everything."

Frankie smiled in delight. "I'm so glad. Now get changed and come to the till. You need a nice little clutch bag to complete the outfit. I'll pick one out and have it waiting."

Iris took another long look at herself. She couldn't believe how different she looked, even better than her earlier makeovers at Trisha's hands.

David was going to love it and he was going to be so proud of her when she walked into the reception on his arm. All she wanted in the world was for him to love her and respect her. If he wouldn't, or couldn't, she would just have to keep trying. There was nothing else for her to do.

CHAPTER 21

Warren took his seat in the lecture room with the other delegates. Today's speaker was a woman in her fifties with steely grey hair and a blue suit with her name, Brenda, typed on a badge pinned to the lapel. On the screen behind and to her left was an enlarged photograph of a man's face and shoulders. He had black frizzy hair that sharpened into a widow's peak, a beard and an enigmatic smile. Brenda paused, while the delegates looked at the image, then smiled. "Good morning everyone. I think most of you will recognize this man?"

There were murmurs of assent. The British bobbies muttered, "Too bloody right."

Warren didn't have a clue. The guy looked like a vampire.

Brenda continued more seriously. "On this, the fourth day of our seminar, you may still be wondering why we need cutting edge technology. In real terms, how can it help police catch criminals? Well, I have a case study which illustrates its importance." She glanced behind her and said, "This is Peter Sutcliffe, commonly known as the Yorkshire Ripper. Sutcliffe murdered thirteen women across Yorkshire and North West England between 1975 and 1980. His crimes led to the development of a computer system for dealing with major enquiries. This is the HOLMES system. Anyone know what it is?"

Warren put his hand up.

Her eyes flicked to his badge, "Yes, Warren?"

"Is it to do with Sherlock Holmes, the way he solved crimes?"

Brenda chuckled. "Very good!"

There was laughter. Warren looked around. He was being serious. He joined in anyway.

"HOLMES stands for Home Office Large Major Enquiry System. Bit of a mouthful, I know. But let me rewind so you can understand how the necessity for this came about."

Warren settled back and folded his arms.

"The five-year investigation into Sutcliffe's crimes became one of the biggest in British criminal history. It cost four million pounds. Two hundred and fifty thousand people were interviewed, thirty-two thousand statements were taken and over five million car registrations were checked.

"But a manual card index system was used and a bottle-neck happened at the main incident room at Millgarth police station in Leeds. The inquiry was so intensive that new cards were arriving before existing ones could be processed and cross-referenced." She paused for a moment to look at each delegate before continuing. "Eventually there were so many cards that the floor of the incident room had to be reinforced to support the weight."

This drew gasps.

She folded her arms and perched on the edge of the projector table. "Eventually the manual system was overwhelmed and this resulted in evidence against Sutcliffe being lost. He was actually interviewed nine times but each time he was released.

"Two Home Office inquiries were set up to review the lessons from the investigations. The outcome was the development of HOLMES. The scheme made it mandatory for all police forces to share intelligence, which some constabularies had previously resisted or even refused to do."

¤

When the day drew to a close, Brenda explained the format for Friday's class, but Warren was looking ahead to next week's programme with the police. He'd made up a great strap line: on the beat with the feet on the street. He'd let them have that one. Eddie and Joanna should be in Manchester by now. He was hoping he'd see them while they were here. He was homesick, his first time so far away from South Dakota. The Grosvenor was fine, the food was good and his room comfortable but he got bored at night. He supposed many of the delegates felt the same, scattered as they were around the area.

He was glad to get back to the warmth of the Grosvenor that evening. It was cold in

Manchester and Warren was glad he'd packed some warm clothing. The snow was already falling in South Dakota but there the air was cold and crisp. The weather was warmer than back home but here it was chilly and damp. It stuck to his skin and seeped into his bones.

When he collected his key, the receptionist handed him a telephone number. "You had a call from a Miss Joanna Brooks, Mr Fisher. You can ring her back on the phone in your room. Dial nine for an outside line. We'll charge the call to your account."

"Thanks." Warren pushed the paper into his back pocket and took the stairs two at a time. In his room, he threw his anorak on the bed, clicked on the kettle, emptied a sachet of coffee into a cup and unwrapped the complimentary biscuits. After turning up the heating, he rang Joanna.

She answered on the third ring.

"Hi Joanna, it's Warren." He held the phone to his ear as he poured boiling water into the cup. "Did you have good flights?"

"Hi, Warren. Yes, thanks. No delays and we slept most of the way, mercifully. We got here late last night. So how are you? Enjoying the course?"

Warren wrinkled his face. "It's OK. Today's was good but some of it goes over my head. At least it's nearly weekend."

"Actually Warren, we were wondering. Are you doing anything on Saturday evening?"

"Hanging round here, I guess. Why?"

"Well, we're at the wedding that day. I was on the phone with my friend this afternoon. She's invited you to the evening reception. Fancy it?"

Warren's face lit up. "Oh, Joanna, I do. That's if you don't mind me playing gooseberry."

"Don't be daft. Have you got something suitable to wear? A clean shirt? Smart trousers?"

Warren walked over to the wardrobe and peered inside. "Black trousers and a blue shirt. Will that do?"

"That sounds fine. It starts at seven at the Midland. We're nipping back to the flat to get changed then getting a taxi back, so we'll pick you up about ten past. Can you wait in reception?"

"Yup. Thanks Joanna. You're an angel."

Warren put the receiver back in the cradle and grinned. It would be great seeing them and getting out. Who knows. He might even meet someone like Joanna and have some fun while he was here.

CHAPTER 22

Eddie and Joanna arrived back at the Midland with Warren in the wake of the evening guests. Warren was impressed at the Christmas tree in the main hall, twenty feet high, decked in champagne baubles and festooned with soft tone lights. They were directed to the function room by uniformed staff and left their coats at the cloakroom by the entrance.

Eddie bent to Joanna's ear. "You look gorgeous, sweetheart."

"Thank you." Joanna smiled. She was wearing a forest green voile knee length dress with a dark green lining, sequinned bodice and cut out back.

Eddie looked over at Warren. "Close your mouth."

Warren snapped it shut. She looked...wow. He was about to say so when a voice detached itself from the noise.

"Joanna! Oooh, here you are. Ravishing as always." Samantha hurried over and enveloped her in a hug.

Joanna laughed in delight. "Hi, Samantha. Today was wonderful. I'm so happy for you and

Richard."

Samantha let her go and fell on Eddie. "Ooh, you hunk, It was lovely meeting you at long last. You're gorgeous. Love your accent. Very sexy. I must say, Joanna's never looked happier. You're obviously good for her."

Eddie smiled. "I think it's the other way round. Congratulations again, Samantha."

Samantha beamed up at him then turned to Warren. "Oh...hello! You must be Warren. You're rather gorgeous too."

He grinned and shook her hand. "Hi Samantha. Congratulations on your wedding."

She kept hold of it, pulled him to her and kissed him hard on the lips. "I've decided to start being a proper married woman tomorrow, so I'm making the most of tonight. Now, go off and get a drink. It's a free bar, so fill your boots."

She spotted more guests arriving behind them and rushed to meet them. "Oooh! Lorraine, you look stunning and William, how fabulous to see you!"

¤

Iris followed David though the crowds to the bar and stood by his side as he waited to be served. She turned to him with a chuckle. "The bride, Samantha? She didn't look very pleased to see you. Didn't she know you were coming?"

"Apparently not. What d'you want to drink?"

"White wine please."

He shouted his order and looked around. The

dance area covered a third of the floor space and beyond it was a stage where the DJ stood behind a bank of equipment and speakers. The rest of the room was taken over with tables and chairs. A few people were dancing to a Temptations hit. He spotted the buffet bar, nudged Iris and nodded over. "Can you go and get us some food? I skipped lunch for this."

"OK." She kissed his cheek and walked off, singing along with the song. He noticed a group of young lads, standing against the wall clutching their beer glasses, watching her as she passed. She did look eye catching. Her dress was blue satin, the top close fitting with a plunging neckline. The ra ra skirt was short and flared. It was perfect for her. She looked cute and incredibly sexy. So sexy in fact that, before they left, David had pushed her into the kitchen and had her against the fridge.

He finished his whisky and signalled for a double. Iris arrived back with two laden plates and hoisted herself onto a bar stool. She sipped her wine and began eating. As she wiped her fingers on her serviette, she glanced at David. His eyes were following someone behind her. She turned and saw an attractive blonde in a green dress walking between the tables.

Iris looked back at him. His gaze followed the woman as she passed the buffet table and into the corridor beyond. Iris's brows furrowed. He seemed transfixed.

She tapped his arm. His head turned. She nodded towards the woman. "Who's she?"

David ignored her. He sat for a few moments more then pushed away from the bar. "I'm going to the loo."

Iris climbed down from her stool and followed him discreetly. She paused at the buffet table to watch his progress. He followed the woman through patio doors at the end of the corridor. Iris drew a sharp breath. He obviously knew her.

Her insides tumbled with jealousy but she held back from jumping to conclusions. She would return to her seat, have another drink and when David returned, casually ask once more who the woman was.

Iris turned and bumped into a man, who uttered an apology and strode off in David's direction. As she walked back to her stool the groom rushed past and disappeared down the corridor as well. What on earth was going on? It felt like there was a drama being played out that she had no part in. She pushed her plate away, drained her glass and asked the bartender for a refill.

He leaned forward, breath hot against her ear. "If your boyfriend doesn't come back, gorgeous, fancy coming home with me tonight?"

Iris wished she could. She gave him a slow smile and raised her glass into the space between them. "Same again, barman. Right to the top."

He grinned and refilled it.

¤

The function room was getting hot with so many bodies milling around. Joanna, needing fresh air, opened the patio doors and stepped down into a square courtyard. An early frost had dusted the ground and the evening had a crispness that quickly cooled her. She hugged herself. She wouldn't be staying out here long, that was for sure. She heard steps behind her and turned, expecting Eddie.

A weight dropped into the pit of her stomach. "David."

"Well, hello there, Joanna. Nice to see you. I'd wondered where you'd been all these months."

She tried to go back inside but he blocked the entrance. As she faced him, he leaned in to her, whisky heavy on his breath. He was still heartbreakingly handsome but, up close, she could see strands of silver running through his dark hair and delicate lines fanning out from the corners of his eyes. There were the beginnings of thread veins on his nose, due, she guessed, to his predilection for scotch whisky.

"I heard you got yourself a new man."

She held his gaze. "Is that any of your business?"

"Don't get cocky with me, darling. You might have moved on. I haven't. I never got a good reason why you walked out on me."

Joanna answered calmly. "I think it was quite obvious."

He moved nearer. It was purposely intimidating. "Come on, I hardly ever touched you. Believe me, if I'd really meant to hurt you,

you'd have known about it."

Her heart was beating faster. With a rush of relief, she saw Eddie walking swiftly towards them.

David tipped his head. "So, where's this new man then?"

"I'm here."

David turned. His jaw dropped. "You. It's you...when she came for her things. You're the bastard that decked me..."

Eddie pushed past him and moved Joanna close to his side. "I'll do it again if I have to."

He gave Eddie a dismissive look and turned back to Joanna. "Now, where were we, before Guy the Gorilla rocked up?"

Eddie answered, his voice calm. "You were just about to turn round and walk away."

"David." Richard was puffing as he ran through the doors. "There you are. I've been looking for you everywhere."

"Well, you've found me."

"Yes. Look, I don't want any trouble tonight. Samantha didn't know I'd invited you. I've just had a right earbashing. So be on your best, please? Don't do anything to spoil her day. If you kick off, she'll call the police. She means it, so I'm warning you."

David took a step back and patted Richard on the shoulder. "Don't worry, mate. I was just saying hello to my old girlfriend. I'm not going to cause trouble. I didn't know she was going to be here. You never told me."

Richard grimaced. "Sorry. I know, I never paid

much attention to the guest list. I left it to Sam. Look, you'd better go in. I think your girlfriend's looking for you."

David turned and walked inside.

Richard extended a hand to Eddie. "Hi Eddie. Sorry about this. He can be a bit...awkward."

Eddie shook it and smiled, "It's OK. We'll keep out of his way."

Richard nodded and followed David. Eddie kept his arm around Joanna. "You OK, sweetheart? We don't have to stay, if you don't want."

Joanna shook her head. "Thank you but I don't want to go, Eddie. I'll be damned if he's going to scare me. Anyway, it'd be a shame to drag Warren away."

Eddie wrapped his arms around her and rested his cheek on her head. "It's up to you. I know to my cost that you're not for running away. As I recall, you weren't the easiest person to serve and protect."

He felt a warm breath of laughter on his neck.

"Anyway, he's with his girlfriend and he's been threatened with the police so I doubt he'll make a scene." He dropped his head to kiss her. "Come on. It's freezing out here. We'd better get back to Warren before he starts fretting."

Joanna laughed again but seeing David had stirred a pool of dark memories. The first time he had lost his temper, only a few months into their relationship and over something inconsequential, he had hit her. The writing was on the wall. She left him and booked into the

170

Grosvenor. "Well, one thing we have to thank him for, it's down to him that we met."

"True...but I'd love another swing at him."

Joanna raised her head. "I hope you never have to. I want David Phillips firmly relegated to the past, where he belongs."

"Don't worry, sweetheart. You won't see him again after tonight."

She nodded with a shiver. She had been standing too long in the freezing courtyard. As they stepped back inside, she hoped that was all it was.

¤

Iris sat back in her chair and stroked the stem of her glass with her finger and thumb. They had moved to a table on the edge of the dance floor. David was sprawled in his seat, nursing another drink. She'd lost count of how many they'd had but their glasses never stayed empty for long.

It was half past nine. The dance floor had cleared for the moment. She'd decided not to ask David what had happened. She didn't want to hear a lie and she was frightened of the truth. Miss Green Dress and her boyfriend were at a table further back from theirs. It was hard to see them through the other occupied tables and the traffic of people.

She wished she had the nerve to go to the woman and ask her who she was. She'd seen a dishy young man with them and had noticed his appearances on the dance floor with different girls. He was obviously unattached.

There was plenty of time for observation. David hadn't said two words since returning. He was sitting now, an impenetrable look on his face. She had given up trying to engage him in conversation.

The DJ's voice sounded over the speakers. "Right, people, it's time for luuurve. Here's Hall and Oates with their 1982 hit single, 'One on One'. Come on, Samantha and Richard get up here now. And everyone else!"

Iris sat back and folded her arms miserably then craned her neck to see Miss Green Dress again. She was standing up and pulling at the hands of her boyfriend. He was resistant at first, then laughed as he got to his feet. Now they were weaving between the tables towards her. She looked away as they passed and glanced at David. His eyes were riveted on them.

She turned in her chair to watch. They were dancing together now. Her arm was around his neck and his hand was open against the small of her back. His other hand was holding hers to his chest. They were looking into each other's eyes. It was obvious that they were in love. The floor was filling up but for them, in that dance, for that song, no-one else existed. They could have been alone on the dance floor, so completely wrapped up in each other as they were. Iris studied her. The woman's hips were moving in time to the music, pushing into his. He had a smile on his face, gently drawing her even closer.

Suddenly Iris felt tears prick her eyes. They

had what she wanted. What she craved. Real love. True love. Love that David would never give her.

"C'mon. Let's dance." David stood. She looked at him. His face was pulled down in a scowl, his cheeks flushed. She didn't want to dance with him like this. He walked round the table. "I said let's dance."

She shook her head and winced as he took hold of her upper arm, his fingers digging into the soft flesh. He marched her to the middle of the floor and put his hands on her waist. She rested hers lightly on his chest. As the record drew to a close, another started on the second turntable. The DJ's voice broke in. "No sitting down yet, you lovely lot. Here's another smooth smooch. It's The Four Seasons and guess what? They've got you under their skin."

David and Iris were only a foot away from them now. When the announcement was made, she was close enough to hear Miss Green Dress say, "Eddie. It's our song!"

She heard them laugh and saw the kiss he placed gently on her lips. David saw it too. He pushed Iris and they both staggered slightly. She was beginning to realise how much they'd had to drink.

David knocked Eddie's shoulder and shoved his face into the narrow space between the couple. "Having a good time then?"

Joanna dropped her smile. Eddie shot him an angry look and moved Joanna to another part of the dance floor.

Iris tried to pull away. "I want to sit down David. I don't feel well."

He hissed in her ear, sending spittle into her hair. "You'll sit down when I tell you." He followed them, pulling her along in his arms. Iris stumbled against the woman, who looked at her sharply.

David spun Iris round so he was shoulder to shoulder with Joanna. He gave her a look filled with loathing, then danced Iris away to their table. She fell clumsily into her chair.

"I need another drink." He walked off to the bar.

Her gaze returned to the dance floor. The song had finished and they were walking off, coming towards her again. She cowered in her seat, trying to make herself invisible, keeping her face half hidden behind her glass. When they levelled with her, Miss Green Dress paused momentarily to look down at her. To Iris's complete surprise, she gave her the warmest, kindest smile before moving on. Iris's eyes followed her back to her seat. Eddie's hand was placed protectively on her back.

Her gaze moved to David. He was at the bar, leaning heavily on the counter, holding another glass of scotch. His face was turned to the side and she could see his profile. He was watching them too.

Her throat was tightening. How pathetic she must look, sitting alone, her boyfriend somewhere in mind and body. Hot tears began to spill onto her cheeks. She wiped them away with her fingers, drained her wine and closed her eyes. When they opened, David had gone. There was only his empty glass on the bar. She sat up straight and looked around the room. There was no sign of him. He must have gone to the toilet.

Fifteen minutes passed. She began to fret. It was nearly half ten. A few people had already left and others were starting to make a move. The DJ was playing a song she didn't know, the volume turned lower. She stood and walked to the bar, stumbling past chairs on the way.

She smiled at the bartender and asked politely if he would check the Gents for her. She could hear the slur in her voice. It sounded quite pronounced. He shook his head. He had just been in. It was empty. Iris thanked him and walked off. Another thought struck her. She hoped she was wrong.

She made her way to the cloakroom and waited impatiently in the queue until she reached the front. "Excuse me, has a tall dark haired man been here to collect his coat, a navy blue Crombie?"

The girl behind the desk nodded. "Oh yes. I remember him. He collected it about twenty minutes ago. Was he with you?"

Iris's face reddened. She couldn't face more humiliation. She forced a smile. "He's in our group. I volunteered to look for him." She stopped, tapped the counter lightly a couple of times and backed away.

Holding her tears, she pushed through the

queue behind her and stumbled back into the party, keeping her eyes down. She traversed the obstacle course of tables and chairs, praying she wouldn't pinball between them, or vomit, or do anything to draw attention to herself. Her pace quickened once she passed the buffet table.

When she entered the corridor, she broke into a run and fell through the door into the ladies toilets, mercifully empty. She shuddered to a halt, crying uncontrollably. David had gone home without her and left behind the devastating truth that she had been avoiding all evening. He didn't love her. He didn't even like her. In fact he held her in utter contempt.

She rushed into a toilet cubicle, fell to her knees in front of the bowl, clung onto the sides and emptied her stomach noisily.

When she crawled out, she curled up on the tiled floor beneath the sink and passed out.

¤

Joanna scraped her chair back. "I've just seen David's girlfriend going past. She looks upset. I'd better go and see if she's OK. I can't see him anywhere."

Warren interrupted. "Is he the jerk-off who was hassling you on the dance floor?"

She nodded.

"I was watching. Saw him going for his coat a while back."

"He's gone home without her?" Joanna fumed. "The bastard. Right, that's it."

Before Eddie could say anything, she walked

off. The corridor was empty. Joanna guessed she'd made for the Ladies. When she walked in, she saw Iris curled up under one of the sinks.

Joanna ran over and sank down by her side. She rubbed Iris's arms gently. "Hey, come on love, wake up."

Iris didn't respond. There was vomit around her mouth and chin and in her hair. Joanna stood, pulled a handful of paper towels from the dispenser, ran them under the hot tap and wiped Iris's face, threw them in the bin and reached for more. This time she soaked them in cold water and pressed them to the unconscious girl's forehead.

Slowly, Iris began to move, groaning quietly. She lifted a limp hand to her face.

Joanna took her other and squeezed it gently. "Hello? Can you hear me? I think you fainted. You're safe. You're in the ladies toilets. I've just found you."

Iris felt a rushing in her ears that rose to a crescendo. There was a sudden 'zoop' and it stopped. Her eyes half opened and she squinted in the glare of the fluorescent light overhead. A concerned face floated into focus above her. She recognised it straight away and sat up, sucking in pain as her skull connected with the U-bend under the sink.

Joanna put an arm around her. "Careful. Come on, I'll help you up. Lift your head and shoulders last and do it slowly, so you don't go dizzy."

Iris was too weak to protest. She rose gingerly

to her feet. When she was upright, she pushed Joanna's hand away and steadied herself against the rim of the sink. She stared into the mirror and groaned. She was a mess. Her face was streaked with mascara and there was vomit in her hair. She started to sob.

Joanna ran the taps and filled the basin. With soap and hot water, she helped Iris wash her face properly and clean her hair. While she dried herself on more paper towels, Joanna retrieved Iris's clutch bag from the floor and found lipstick and mascara inside.

She clicked on the hand dryer and Iris fluffed her damp hair under it. Once it was dry, Joanna handed her the make up and waited while she fixed her face. With a final blink at her appearance, Iris turned to Joanna. "Thank you. You didn't have to do all this. Especially after David was so rude to you and your boyfriend. I'm sorry."

"That wasn't your fault. Has he gone home without you?"

Iris dropped her head in embarrassment and nodded at her feet.

Joanna pulled her into a hug, "Oh, love, I'm sorry. Look," She held her away, "You can't stay in here. Come and sit with us. We'll look after you and get you home. OK? What's your name?"

Iris's twisted her mouth into a wan smile. "It's Iris. Iris Ferguson."

Joanna passed her bag to her and linked her. "Come on, Iris. It's quieter out there now."

Back at their table, Joanna went through the

introductions. Eddie reached for a spare chair and they shuffled round to accommodate her.

Once they were all seated, Iris looked at her. "I'm sorry. I don't know your name."

"Oh, sorry, it's Joanna."

Iris stared hard at her for a moment before a memory hit her with the force of an express train. David, half asleep. Quick fumbled sex, the words she'd strained to catch. Three syllables. The first: incomprehensible, the second and third: 'anna'. He hadn't said Suzanna.

He'd said Joanna.

Warren was smitten. His eyes roamed over Iris, absorbing her face, the bodice that coddled two plump breasts and the shapely crossed legs visible up to her thighs in a cute little frilly skirt. He thought she was gorgeous.

Eddie and Joanna were speaking to her in gentle tones. She was clearly very upset. Warren sat forward and cradled his beer while he listened.

Eddie spoke. "When we leave, we'll drop you home."

"No!" Iris's face wrinkled with panic. "I don't want to go home tonight."

Eddie frowned. "Why not?"

Iris took a couple of deep breaths and a sip from the schooner of water she'd been given. She kept her eyes low. "I don't want to see David."

"I don't understand."

Joanna squeezed Eddie's arm and shook her head. She turned back to Iris. "You can come back with us then, if you like? We're in Didsbury."

Iris looked at Joanna without expression. She didn't want to go anywhere with this woman. Not now she knew who she was. She didn't want any more of her kindness or her pity. Somewhere in their past, this woman and David had meant something to each other. Maybe he still cared. His behaviour tonight suggested that. Jealousy and hatred rose like bile in Iris's throat.

Warren saw his chance. He sat up straight and looked at Joanna. "She can come back with me. I'm sure there'll be a room at the Grosvenor. Iris, would you rather do that?"

She'd felt Warren appraising her since she'd joined them. Perhaps he liked her. He was very good looking. He had David's colouring but he was much younger and his face was boyish, open and kind. She turned to him with a grateful smile and let her hand rest on his thigh. "Oh, Warren, I would."

He gave her a joke salute and a cheeky grin. "Deputy Warren Fisher at your service, ma'am."

¤

It was eleven o'clock. The DJ was packing up. The bartender was cleaning the counter. The pot collector was clearing the tables. Only a handful of guests remained. Before long the overhead lights would come on.

They collected their coats and located their hosts by the Christmas tree to say goodbye.

Samantha's whispered apologies to Joanna for David's attendance didn't go unnoticed by Iris. She felt piqued. He wasn't a gatecrasher. He'd had as much right to be there as Joanna, with her smokey eyes and her smile and her body and Eddie. Iris thought it monumentally unfair. All she'd ever wanted was David but then Joanna turns up and in a split second, he'd forgotten all about Iris. She may as well have not been there.

As she waited outside with the others for a taxi, she felt her anger resurging. Everything she had given him, not only the Porsche and the promised loan for the Chorlton agency but the things she did every single day to make his life comfortable and happy. It was all futile. But at the beginning, when she'd had nothing, she'd given him the most precious gift of all. Something she could only give once. Her virginity. She had offered it willingly and trustingly but he had taken it carelessly and greedily.

Iris had often wondered what had attracted him to her. Now she knew. Her inheritance. That was the reason he'd moved her in. It wasn't kindness and compassion. Nor any growth of feelings. David didn't possess any of those traits. Just greed and self service. Even now, he was waiting on the loan. God only knew how he planned to part her from the rest of her money but she knew now that he intended to wring her dry then he would discard her empty husk.

How could she have been so stupid, so naive,

not to have realised this from the beginning? Had she been so blinded by desire?

Things had to change. She wouldn't lend him the money now, but she wouldn't tell him yet. He would have to screw someone else for it. Iris mouth twisted. He'd happily screw Joanna for nothing. That would be something to see, the destruction of that woman's nauseatingly perfect relationship. Maybe she should try to seduce Eddie, let his guilt destroy what he had with Joanna.

Iris picked up that thought and inspected it for a moment but laid it down again gently. No. He seemed like a good man and so in love with Joanna, she doubted he would betray her. She wanted to punish David though for his callous betrayal. Because Joanna had caused it, she had to suffer too. There had to be a way. Iris's fingertips pressed against a growing headache.

Warren chanced slipping an arm around her waist. "Iris, the cab's here."

She looked up and leaned into him with a sweet smile.

CHAPTER 23

"Hi. Can I book a room for this lady, please?" Warren pointed to Iris, "She's unable to get home tonight."

Iris smiled brightly at the receptionist.

"Certainly Mr Fisher. Would you like the room to be," His eyes settled at a spot somewhere between them, "Close to yours?"

Warren looked down at Iris.

She nodded. "Yes. If that's possible?"

"Let me see. Ah. You're in luck. The adjacent room is vacant. Will that be bed and breakfast or room only?"

"Bed and breakfast please." She glanced at Warren. "May as well make the most of it."

Warren kept his eyes fixed on the receptionist. He'd been getting vibes from Iris since they'd climbed in the taxi together. Sitting that bit too close, touching him each time she spoke. It had been only a short journey from the Midland but packed with promise.

"Oh," Iris stopped as they moved away. "Is it possible to get a toothbrush?"

"Certainly Madam." He handed her one from a drawer under the counter. "I'll add it to your bill. Do you want toothpaste too?"

Warren jumped in, "No. Iris. You can borrow mine."

"Thank you Warren, you're very thoughtful." Iris hid her pleasure. He'd just handed her opening gambit.

They took their keys, Iris signed the register and they climbed the stairs silently. Outside their respective doors, Warren turned, "When do you want the toothpaste?"

She shrugged, "Maybe in about half an hour? I'm going to have a shower first. Shall I come to you or..."

Warren nodded. "I'll be ready. With the toothpaste, that is."

Iris wrinkled her nose prettily and vanished inside.

¤

Warren ran to the door as soon as he heard a gentle tap. He opened it and inhaled quickly. Iris was standing there wrapped in a small bath towel, with a big smile. "I'm ready."

"What?" His eyes widened.

Iris held her toothbrush up in front of her face.

"Oh. Of course." He opened the door wide. "Come in, quick."

As he ushered her past him, she noticed that he'd changed into grey jogging pants and a black tee shirt, which moulded around his toned arms and torso. He closed the door and hurried into the en-suite. When he came out, she was sitting on the bed, holding the towel to her chest. He handed her the toothpaste.

"Thanks Warren. This is good of you. Can I use your bathroom?" Without waiting for an answer, she disappeared into the en-suite, to emerge a few minutes later. He had taken her spot on the bed so she padded over and sat next to him. "I feel much better now."

He nodded. "I'm glad. You know, your guy was a bastard to leave you like that. You didn't deserve it and you looked so gorgeous." he paused, then blurted, "I wish you'd been with me."

Iris turned her eyes upwards and tilted her head. "So do I, Warren."

They gazed at each other for a few moments. Then Iris leaned sideways and kissed him.

She let her towel drop away and when he lifted from the kiss, he was presented with two naked breasts. He dragged his breath in.

Iris snaked her arms around his neck. "Warren, would you like to make love to me?"

Warren bent to kiss her again then paused. He couldn't do this. Iris was still drunk. He gently pushed her away and folded her towel back over her breasts, sighing inwardly. They were magnificent.

Iris sat up. "What's the matter? I thought you liked me."

"I do, Iris." He gave a shrug, "I just think it's better if you go to bed and sleep it off."

Her face fell. "No. you don't. You think I'm fat and ugly. That's why you don't want sex with me." She clutched her towel. "I'll go back to my room. Don't worry. You won't see me again."

She stood, ignoring his helping hand and began to walk to the door.

Warren rose and followed her. "Iris, it's not that at all."

Iris turned, looked up at him and vomited.

¤

Warren woke. He yawned, shifted carefully on the chair and sat up. Over in the bed, Iris lay on her back snoring loudly. Warren stood, groaning as his back uncurled, folded the bedspread he had covered himself with the night before and walked into the en-suite. When he came out, showered and dressed, Iris was sitting up and rubbing her eyes. She gave him a startled look.

"Morning, Iris. How you feeling?"

She looked around the room and back at him. "What did I do last night? Did we...?"

He grinned, shook his head and nodded towards the chair. "No. I slept over there. Don't worry."

Iris blinked. She remembered making a pass at him but nothing else. She was glad he hadn't take advantage but now, sober and rested, she still wanted this gorgeous sexy man. She smiled back coyly and hugged her knees. "You're a gentleman. Thank you."

"Thank you! Now, how're you feeling?"

"I feel OK. I think I sicked up most of it last night." She had a memory. "Ugh! Was I sick here as well?"

"Yup. I cleaned it up, don't worry. I'm not squeamish. Now, I put you to bed with your towel on but if it's not around you now, that's not down to me." He grinned again.

Iris peeked under the sheets. "I'm naked, actually."

Warren felt himself grow hot. He turned away to the kettle. "You want a cup of tea?"

"Yes please."

"Milk?"

"Yes please."

Sugar?"

"No, thank you."

Iris watched him in amusement, His movements were clumsy, his hands shaking as he lifted the kettle to the cups.

When he walked over with them, Iris took a breath. "Warren?"

He set them down and looked at her.

She tipped her head to one side. "I thought. Well, I wondered. If you feel like it...would you like to make love?"

"Would I?" Warren hadn't been with a woman in a long while. Especially one like Iris. He needed no second bidding. He smiled, shed his clothes and jumped in next to her.

Iris sighed in pleasure. Even after only a few minutes, she could tell the difference between him and David. Warren's touch was tentative and gentle. There was no hint of dominance or control. He asked how he could please her. She led, he followed. As she approached orgasm, she knew this was how she had always thought it would be.

¤

Warren buttered a slice of toast and looked at Iris across the breakfast table. "Eddie and Joanna are picking me up at ten. They're taking me to the Peak District for the day."

She cut into a hash brown. "Oh, it's beautiful there. You'll love it."

"Why don't you come with us? I'm sure they wouldn't mind," He asked suddenly.

She shook her head, "I can't Warren. I have to go home. David will be frantic by now."

Warren's face clouded, "Then he shouldn't have walked out on you last night. I don't know why you're bothered."

"I don't know either." She took two painkillers from her bag, popped them in her mouth and took a drink from her cup.

"Do you love him?"

Twenty-four hours ago Iris might have answered after only the slightest pause but now she looked away, lips pressed together, a frown wrinkling her forehead.

"That's a no then."

"It's complicated, Warren."

"Why?"

"Please, Warren, don't ask any more questions."

Warren gave her an apologetic look. "I'm sorry. It's your life and your business, Iris. I respect that. Could I ask you something else, though? Not related."

"Of course you can."

"The seminar ends this coming Friday but I'm staying for another week on vacation." He paused for a moment then ploughed on. "Could I see you again?"

He usually made it a rule to only date single girls but he was prepared to make an exception for Iris, seeing as her relationship with that creep clearly wasn't rock solid. More like on the rocks. Besides which, he really liked her.

Iris set her cup gently on the saucer and examined the pattern of black dots on the white china surface while she considered the question. He moved in his seat, waiting for her reply. After a moment, she smiled up at him. "I'd love to, Warren. Thank you."

¤

Warren waved to the hire car as it pulled up outside the Grosvenor. Joanna climbed out and gave Iris a hug. "Hi, Iris. I hope Warren took good care of you?"

Iris looked at Warren. "Yes, thank you."

Joanna saw them exchange smiles. Looks like they'd slept together. That worried her. She didn't want Warren to be drawn into a conflict between Iris and David. It would only end in tears. She continued breezily, "Well, can we give you a lift home now? Does David still live in Poynton?"

Iris turned to her with cold green eyes. "Yes. He does. I expect you know the address. Don't you."

189

It was a statement, not a question and delivered with accusation and heavy sarcasm.

Joanna blinked. There was an uncomfortable silence. Eddie broke it. "Is anyone getting in any time soon?"

Warren put his arm around Iris as they climbed into the back seat. Joanna returned to her seat next to Eddie, her face troubled. The journey was quiet, broken only by pockets of conversation behind them. Iris had obviously guessed that she and David shared a past and it had clearly upset her.

Joanna whispered to Eddie, "Can you not drop Iris right outside, in case he sees us?"

He glanced at her and nodded. He had no desire to cross horns again.

¤

Warren gave Iris one final wave and turned back in his seat.

"Was she alright last night?" Joanna glanced behind at him. "She was in a dreadful state."

She had voiced her anxieties to Eddie that David would do something to hurt Iris when she got home. Eddie hadn't shown the same concern. To him, the solution was simple. Iris should do what Joanna did. Leave him.

"She was OK. Bit drunk. Spewed. But she was fine this morning. I really really like her, you know and she's agreed to see me again."

Joanna's face clouded. "Warren, no. You mustn't. She's in a relationship with David. He'll kill her if he finds out."

Warren's chin jutted out defiantly. "He's not likely to, is he?"

"That's not the point. She's not available."

"We're not planning to elope, Joanna. There's no strings attached. We like each other and she's obviously having problems with him. Anyway, what was going on last night with you and him?"

Eddie broke in. "That's none of your business."

"No, it's alright Eddie." Joanna glanced at him then turned back to Warren. "We were in a relationship once. He hit me. I left him. He's a bastard. I expect Iris has found that out for herself."

Warren transferred his gaze to the window. He knew about domestic violence. He'd had enough call-outs to incidents and he could never understood why women – and men – put up with abuse from their partners.

He replied, almost to himself. "While I'm here, I'll be good to her. Give her a nice time and show her how a woman should be treated. Who knows, it might be a wake up call."

Joanna's face softened. He was a good man. She turned to face the front. "OK Warren. But I don't want to see you get hurt, emotionally I mean."

Eddie rolled his eyes.

"No. She's a sweet kid but I'm not about to fall in love." He opened his arms and looked down at himself, "I mean, it would be cruel to keep this from all those women out there."

Eddie stopped the car at a red light. They

turned to stare at him.

Warren looked from one to the other and grinned. "What?"

CHAPTER 24

There wasn't a sound when Iris walked into the house. She paused in the hall, unsure whether or not to announce her arrival, then shrugged off her coat and draped it over the bannister. She brushed down her skirt, ran her fingers through her hair and walked into the kitchen.

She froze. David was standing against the sink, legs crossed at the ankles, a mug of coffee cradled against his chest. They stared at each other for a few moments until he sniffed up loudly, cleared his throat and picked up another mug. "Coffee?"

"Um. Yes, please."

He turned his back to pour from a freshly brewed cafetière.

"Milk?"

"Please."

He walked to the fridge, took out a jug, walked back to the counter and poured some into her mug. He dropped a spoon into it and stirred it round and round, each clink against the side making her flinch. She glanced at the wall clock to her left. It was quarter to eleven.

David turned again, the mug in his hand. He

held it out. Iris walked slowly through the room and stopped in front of him. She reached for it.

David smiled. "Here it is."

He threw the contents at her.

Iris screamed in shock and pain. The hot liquid covered her neck and chest, soaked her dress and dripped to the floor.

David tutted. "All over your lovely outfit. What a pity. You'd better take everything off."

She rubbed at herself and began to walk backwards. "I'll get undressed upstairs and have a shower."

"No. Take them off here."

Iris was by the table now, her hand feeling for the edge. "No. I'll do it upstairs."

"You'll do it here. Get them off!" He shot forward and gripped the top of her bodice. Iris curled up to protect herself but he was too strong. His hands ripped the garment away, propelling her towards him. With two more violent tugs, the dress lay ruined at her feet. She began sobbing, hugging herself, vulnerable in her underwear.

David hadn't finished. "Where were you last night? I waited for you to follow me but you didn't."

Iris felt the buzzing in her ears. She straightened and met his gaze. "You don't get to ask me questions. You left me on my own. You walked out without a word. I didn't even know you'd gone. How do you think that made me feel?"

"I don't give a fuck how it made you feel."

"You made that blindingly obvious." Iris moved closer, anger shunting away her fear. "And who is this Joanna? What is she to you? I want to know what was going on last night."

David laughed. "If you could only see yourself. You look ridiculous, standing there half naked, trying to act tough. You're just a silly little girl who's way out of her depth. Go on then, get upstairs and put something on. Then come back down with some answers. I want to know where you spent last night."

The buzzing was getting louder. It was coming from everywhere. Iris looked down at her tattered dress. She thought about Warren this morning, how considerate and gentle he had been when they'd made love. How lovely he said she was. How respectfully he treated her, like she was his equal. Like she mattered.

She blinked, aware that her head was throbbing in tandem with the buzzing. "No. Not until you tell me who Joanna is."

David rolled his eyes before fixing them on her. They narrowed as his hands gripped her arms. "OK. If you must know. Joanna used to be my girlfriend. She walked out on me in April. Just upped and left."

Iris tried to pull away, her face ashen, body shaking uncontrollably but he drew her closer and looked into her face. "And d'you know what? I'd have her back like a shot."

"You bastard. What about me?"

"Well, You know the old saying, a bird in the hand? I can't have her but I can have you. Any

195

time I want." Without warning, he moved his hands to her bra and pulled the straps down. She struggled as he forced his mouth on hers while one hand pulled at the back of her panties and ripped the delicate lace away.

Iris tried to break free but his grip was too strong. He pushed her down on the table and began to unbuckle his trouser belt. Iris's back was bent painfully over the edge. He moved from her mouth and pressed his cheek against hers as he unzipped his jeans and freed himself from his underpants. His knees forced her legs apart.

Iris flipped her eyes desperately to each side. On her left was an empty fruit bowl. She reached out her hand, caught it by the rim, lifted it and brought it down on his skull. David yelled in pain and pulled away, clutching the side of his head.

This was her chance. She darted to the counter, picked a carving knife from the rack, spun round and ran at him with such speed, it knocked him off his feet. Iris fell on top, straddled his chest, pinned his arms to the floor with her knees and held the knife to his throat. He tried to dislodge her but she was too high up his body.

Iris bent over him, her face inches from his, the length of the blade pressing on his Adam's apple. He roared at her, his voice distorted, "Get off me before I kill you."

Iris shook her head. "No. You're literally not in a position to do that, David."

He flopped down. "OK. So why don't you just get off me and we'll forgive and forget."

"So you can try and rape me again?" She shook her head.

"Iris, don't be so stupid. I only having a bit of fun. Couples do you know. Just get off me. Please." A note of pleading was pushing through the anger.

"You threw hot coffee over me. It's lucky there was milk in it or I'd have been seriously burnt. You ripped my dress off me and tried to rape me. That isn't my idea of a bit of fun." She sat up and pressed the point of the knife against the top of his rib cage, just to the left. "Your heart is here, in between these two ribs." She wrinkled her brow, "Oh, but you don't have a heart, do you, David?"

"Iris, please, I'm sorry, really, really sorry for trying to force you to have sex. I honestly thought you'd enjoy a bit of rough."

Her voice was scornful, a laugh bubbling between the words. "When have I ever given you the impression I like a bit of rough?"

David's rolled his eyes expressively. "I don't know. Look, I was out of order leaving you on your own last night and even more for asking where you spent it. I promise I won't mention it again. I promise I'll never touch you again, unless I get a specific invite. How's that?"

She ignored his attempt at sarcasm. "What about Joanna? Are you going to try and see her? Get back with her?" Her voice changed and took on a mocking tone to equal his. "You'd be wasting your time, you said so yourself. I've seen her with Eddie. You've seen them. They've got something really special. It's obvious they're in love."

David refused to be riled. "I only said those things to hurt you. I didn't mean it."

"But you dream of it though. You said her name one night when you woke and had sex with me. Don't try and deny it. I heard you."

He ignored her and pressed on with his platitudes. "Iris, we make a good team, don't we? We're great together. I don't want her, I only want you."

Iris blinked several times and screwed her face up. The wrinkles in her forehead deepened. The buzzing became a chainsaw carving up her brain and clearing a path for firecrackers that were beginning to follow.

She looked at the knife in her hand, looked at David, pushed herself back and up. She dropped it, pressed her fists to her temples, walked out of the room, up the stairs and into the bedroom.

She climbed onto the bed, laid down and passed out.

CHAPTER 25

The bedroom was dark. In the middle of the king size bed, Iris stirred, uncurled, rubbed her face into the pillow and rolled onto her side. Her eyes opened. The first thing they registered was the digital clock. It was five pm. She propped herself up on her elbows. That couldn't be right. She looked around. How did she end up here? She sat upright and dropped her head in her hands.

She remembered arriving back that morning, taking her coat off, going into the kitchen. David was in there drinking coffee. After that, nothing. She turned on the bedside lamp, pushed the covers away, and looked down. She was naked. There were pressure marks on her upper arms and shoulders, bruises between her thighs. There were dried coffee stains on her skin and in the bed.

She turned her legs and placed both feet on the carpet, rubbing her soles into the soft pile to ground herself.

The house was cold. She showered quickly and hugged her dressing gown around her as she descended the stairs and looked into the empty lounge. She continued on to the kitchen. There was a note on the table in David's handwriting. She picked it up and walked to the kettle, shook it to make sure there was enough water then clicked it on. While she waited for it to boil, she leaned against the counter top and read the note.

Dear Iris,

Sorry about yesterday. I felt ill, so I went home. I did tell you but you were in a mood and didn't say anything. I was upset that you stayed out all night but at least you got home safely.

You weren't feeling well when you got back and went straight to bed. When I went up to check on you, you were fast asleep. Must have been the booze last night. You ripped your lovely dress and underwear taking them off!

I'm away until Wednesday at the estate agents' convention in London I told you about. Should make it back by noon. Getting the train to Euston this afternoon from Piccadilly. I'll call you while I'm away to make sure you're OK.

David x

Iris read it twice then went straight back up to the bedroom. On the cocktail chair by the window was her dress. She picked it up and shook it. Her panties and bra fell out. Everything was torn and coffee stained. She frowned in puzzlement.

She took them downstairs and threw them into the flip top bin, brewed her tea and carried the mug through to the lounge. She lit the fire, turned on the television and sank into the chair nearest the warmth. There was a war programme on TV. She fixed her eyes on the screen while she thought about the content of David's note. She didn't remember him saying he felt ill before he left. Today was almost a total blank too. She brought her cup to her lips. So what did she remember about last night? Joanna and her boyfriend Eddie. The friction between them and David. Fainting in the toilet. Joanna finding her, cleaning her up, taking her to sit with Eddie and Warren. Going to the Grosvenor with Warren. Booking a room. Making love with him in the morning.

Her insides somersaulted with pleasure before it hit her that she'd been unfaithful to David. Why didn't she feel guilty? Why wasn't she mortified? Why did her infidelity bring only a smile to her face and a feeling of warmth and happiness?

She felt unable to dissect her emotions right then. She rested her cup on her chest and her head against the back of the armchair. On the screen, there was a sudden explosion. Iris jumped and spilled her tea. With a feeling of deja vu, She stared down as it soaked into her dressing gown. The feeling that sprang from this was infused with fear. No. More than that. Sheer physical terror.

Her face caved. David had thrown coffee at her. She put her cup on the floor and pressed her fingers to her forehead. Her dress. David had done that. He was angry and ripped it off her. Bra and panties too. Iris inhaled loudly and a sob escaped her outward breath.

She remembered being held down on the kitchen table, bent backwards, the edge cutting into her coccyx.

Legs forced apart.

She cried out, exploded into noisy tears and wrapped her arms over her eyes for protection against the images.

David had raped her.

No. No, he hadn't. The images still poured in. He'd tried to but she'd stopped him.

She hit him with something.

There was a knife.

She was holding it.

Sitting on him.

Blade across his neck, above his heart.

Running upstairs.

Then waking.

Iris dropped her arms and found a handkerchief in her pocket. She wiped her eyes and dabbed at her gown. The note he had left her had been a complete fabrication. This thing she did, blacking out, had happened to her before but she'd assumed she'd simply fainted. But this time she'd recalled both cause and reaction. The other times? Had they been triggered too?

This was nothing to do with stress. This was something else. Something she didn't understand. This was dangerous. What if her behaviour spiralled out of control? She could actually kill him.

Maybe she really was ill. Maybe she was going insane. The thought induced more tears.

Then another memory surfaced. Before his attack, she had asked him again who Joanna was. Now she knew. Iris's face wrinkled with the sting of his words.

He walked out last night. Because he couldn't bear to see Joanna with another man. If it hadn't been for that woman, Miss Green Dress, none of this would have happened. Iris felt her desire for revenge becoming insatiable.

¤

Warren got out of the shower in time to answer the phone.

"Mr Warren? I have a call for you."

"Thanks." He rubbed a towel over his wet hair and waited for the connection. "Hello?"

He heard a little voice at the other end and recognised it straight away. "Hi, Iris! Well how weird is that? I was just thinking about you. How are you?"

"I'm OK, Warren. Just thought I'd say hello

203

and wish you good luck for your course this week."

"Aw thanks, babe. How did you get on when you got back today?"

A pause. A shuffle through the line, like she was changing ears. "Um. OK. He's away on business now until Wednesday."

"Oh. Right. What plans have you got then?" He held his breath in hope.

"Well, I was wondering if you'd like to meet..."

He jumped in. "I'd love to."

"How about tomorrow night?"

"Tomorrow's good. I should be finished by four and back around half five. Wanna grab something to eat?"

He heard her shuffle the phone back again, "I thought perhaps you could come to me? I mean where I used to live. It's empty. I've got a key. I'll bring food and wine. We can have a picnic."

Warren's grin split his face. "That sounds great. What time?"

"Is seven OK?"

"Yeah. Can I bring anything?"

"Just yourself. Tell the taxi to drop you at Paraffin Alley, Didsbury. I'll be waiting outside the house."

"Will do."

"OK. See you then. Bye."

The line went dead. He dropped the receiver into the cradle and punched the air.

¤

Iris took her last painkillers of the day and snuggled under fresh bedding. She had turned the electric blanket on and now she was wrapped in a warm cocoon.

David had phoned her earlier. The journey had been good, he was in the hotel and was just going down to the bar for a few drinks with the other delegates before he turned in. The seminar was in the same hotel and was she alright now? Iris had played up to him but by the end of the call, which had been mercifully short, she was clenching her fist, pressing her nails into her palm. How could she go on living with this man with all the things he was doing to her? She was tougher than she thought but she didn't want to be. She shouldn't have to be.

These and other dark thoughts crowded in, demanding to be heard. Iris was still in shock and too tired to be receptive.

Tomorrow morning she would go to Surprise View and take everything for her evening with Warren. She'd be able to spend some time alone and let happy memories blanket her.

She didn't know herself any more. She pined for the girl she had been before she met David. She grieved for the loss of her innocence. She even missed the tedium of life with Gran. Living here with David was a relentless battle, walking on eggshells, fearing his temper, evoking his violence. This wasn't the life she'd envisaged and it wasn't the life she deserved.

In Paraffin Alley, up on the roof, she could breathe and think. She could let her thoughts bubble up to the surface. Then Grumps would help her sort through them and guide her back to herself, where ever she was and whatever she was becoming.

CHAPTER 26

It was cold on the roof terrace but the sky was a delicate china blue and the winter sun pierced through the chill to sneak pockets of warmth to the small figure sitting on the fold-up chair.

Iris had been at Surprise View for an hour. She arrived at 11am with clean blankets, pillows, plates, cutlery and wine glasses, Back at the house there was white wine chilling in the fridge and a selection of cheese and a packet of cream crackers wrapped up on the counter.

She settled back with her flask and lunch box. She was warm and cosy in a thick winter coat and her old woollen hat, scarf and mittens. She had taken one of Gran's Zopiclone tablets last night and slept really well. She'd handed back all Gran's other medicines to the chemist except these and was glad she'd kept them.

The fire in Grumps' bucket was burning low. Iris hoisted herself out of the chair to collect more coal. There wasn't much left in the store but it didn't matter. In Spring, the builder would started the renovations and she would never be able to return. This made her feel incredibly sad. She was beginning to wish she hadn't sold Surprise View. It wasn't the house she'd miss, it was here, on the roof terrace, where she had been at her happiest. It was the only place she felt happy now.

She opened the front of the store and glanced back for a moment to the pigeon loft. She remembered one traumatic day soon after Grumps' death. It was the day that Gran decided to get rid of the pigeons by poisoning them. Iris had panicked. She couldn't let her murder these innocent creatures. In desperation, she rang Grump's pigeon fanciers club. Her pleas galvanised his army of friends and they descended on the house a few hours later armed with carriers. Before she knew it, every feathered soul was on its way to a new home. From that time the big loft had remained empty and hauntingly silent.

Iris took a deep breath and looked back at the coal store. She couldn't wait to show Warren her little sanctuary tonight. Hopefully they could make love under the stars.

She pushed the shovel to the back to reach the remaining coals. It clanged against an object jammed against the wall. She worked the shovel under it and pulled out a metal box. Her face lit up in recognition.

She hurried back to her chair, placed the box on her knee, wiped the coal dust off the lid and opened it. She lifted out an Enfield No 2 mark 1 gun. It was Grumps' service revolver. He had brought it home when he was demobbed in 1945. On occasions, he would take it out and lovingly clean it when Iris was with him, even letting her do it under careful supervision.

Iris opened the chamber and examined inside. It was in great condition, considering that it been tucked away and forgotten for the last sixteen years.

She looked back in the box. There was still ammunition in there. She hugged herself in delight to have rediscovered this piece of Grumps' life.

¤

Warren arrived at Surprise View at half seven. Iris heard the diesel engine turn into the street and ran excitedly downstairs. She ushered him inside, took his hand and led him up the three flights of stairs to the attic, then on up to the terrace. As he walked onto it, he stopped in his tracks. In the light from a bulkhead by the entrance, the terrace was bright and welcoming. A fire was burning in the bucket, flames licking the air. Arranged around it were two chairs with a blanket over the back of each one. In the middle, a folding table held the cheese, biscuits, wine and glasses.

"This is really cool." Warren took the seat she indicated and thanked her when she handed him a glass. She sat beside him and they held hands for a while and looked up at a cloudless night sky, the velvety blackness studded with pinpricks of light.

Iris eventually cut a piece of Edam and motioned him to help himself. "So, tell me about

Warren."

Warren grinned. "Jeez. OK. I'm twenty-five, born and bred in Custer, South Dakota, I live with my folks but I'm saving up for my own place. My dad was Pennington County Sheriff until he took early retirement and now I'm a Deputy at the same office." He shrugged, grinned and his voice morphed into Looney Tunes' Porky Pig. "Th-The, Th-Th-The, Th-Th...That's all, folks!"

Iris clapped her hands together delightedly. "Gosh! I'd swear Porky was here just then!" Warren laughed along with her. She refilled their glasses and asked. "So, is there a girl back home pining for her handsome deputy?"

"Nah. I'm young, free and single."

A sigh escaped. "You're lucky. I wanted so much to have a boyfriend. Then I met David. They say be careful what you wish for."

Warren pressed his lips together for a moment then leaned forward, "Why don't you leave him Iris? I still don't understand why you don't. You can tell me to butt out."

Iris smiled and rubbed his shoulder. "I'm sorry, I was a bit precious the other day. I was still hurting. The thing is, I fell hard for David the moment I saw him. I still have feelings for him, even when he's being horrible. Don't ask me to explain. I can't." She tried anyway. "It sounds crazy but when he hits me...don't get me wrong, he's not done it much...but afterwards, he's so loving, I forgive him straight away and put it behind me. I've been living in hope that he'll grow to love me and things will be better."

Warren gave a small sad shake of his head. "Even once is too much, Iris and you must know he'll never change. It'll only get worse. I've seen enough domestic violence in my job to know that."

Iris rested her elbows on the arms of the chair and looked up at the dark sky. "I'm beginning to realise that. Believe me, Warren, the scales are falling from my eyes. One day, I'll have had enough but I don't know when that will be, but when I do, then I will go." She lifted her shoulders and dropped them expressively.

Warren waited but she offered nothing more.

¤

Over the next hour, the temperature dropped rapidly and they could see their breath freezing. Even the thick blankets and the heat from the fire wasn't enough to stave off the ice that was splitting the air into shards that sliced their throats when they inhaled.

Eventually Warren looked apologetically at Iris, "Sorry, babe, I'm freezing."

"Me too. Do you want to go?"

"We can go back to the hotel, if you fancy it?"

Iris gave a happy sigh. "I'd love that, Warren. We can get a taxi in the village."

They extinguished the fire, packed the food and stored the pillows and blankets inside the pigeon loft.

An hour later, they were at the Grosvenor. Warren went into the en-suite and as Iris waited she spotted a courtesy note pad on the dressing table. In idle curiosity, she looked at the top sheet. On it was written a telephone number and above was Joanna's name.

She blinked at a suggestion that inexplicably nudged its way into her head. She obeyed it without question, picked up the pencil next to it, copied the number onto another sheet and pushed it to the bottom of her bag before Warren walked back in.

"Wouldn't go in there for a while, if I were you." He grinned and pointed at her. "Only kidding."

Iris laughed as they fell on the bed. Warren leaned on his elbow and let his hand rest on Iris's stomach. His face lowered until it was a few inches from hers. He pursed his lips and watched his hand as it glided over her trousers and under her blouse. Iris felt that familiar sweet sensation down below but when he reached her breast, she froze.

Warren didn't notice. His fingers began tease their way under her bra.

Iris slapped his hand away. "No. Stop."

"What? What did I do?" His face was puzzled, confused.

She wriggled away and stood with her back to him. She looked to the side. "This was a mistake. I can't do this. I'm sorry."

Warren climbed off the bed and walked around her. He put his arms on her shoulders and bent to look into her stricken face. "What have I done? Tell me, Iris, so I don't do it again."

His gentleness touched her heart. She dropped her head into her hands and burst into tears.

Warren was lost. He wrapped his arms around her as she cried. He didn't know what else to do. He waited until her tears subsided. "What is it, Iris?"

She pushed him away with a loud sniff. She took a tissue from the dressing table and blew her nose, then reached for another and wiped her eyes. When she turned back, he was shocked at how pale she was.

She started talking in a small voice. She told him about her headaches, the blackouts that David's temper triggered. She told him about yesterday, David's rage. Her voice became lower. Then she sank to her knees and folded her arms over her head. Warren had to crouch to hear the rest of the story. In a voice breaking with emotion, she told him how David had thrown coffee over her, ripped her clothes off. How he had tried to rape her. At this, she dissolved into more tears.

Warren was horrified but he had to do something. She was breaking her heart and his. He gathered her up and lifted her back on the bed. When he set her down, he lay behind, his arms around her. Iris's sobs became quieter, softer, then only detectable by the slightest movement of her shoulders. She pulled his arms tighter and her breathing began to slow. There were a few more sniffs, some sighs, then her breath evened out and she fell into an exhausted sleep.

He stayed awake as long as he could to make sure she stayed asleep. That bastard had hurt one of the sweetest, nicest, most loveable girls he had ever met.

One day, he was going to get what he deserved.

CHAPTER 27

Warren was awake by six am. Iris was still asleep and judging by her position on the bed, hadn't moved an inch during the night. He extracted his arms carefully, slipped out of bed and into the en-suite where he quickly showered, shaved and dressed.

Back in the room, he put the kettle on. Iris began to stir.

He walked over and perched on the side of the bed. "Morning, sleepyhead. How you feeling?"

Iris opened her eyes and blinked then gave him a wide smile and held her arms out. "Wonderful. Gosh, I slept like a baby."

He leaned over to hug her. "Good."

She sat up and rubbed her eyes as he returned to the dressing table to make their drinks. "Warren?"

"Yup?" He filled the cups and fiddled with the little plastic pots of milk.

"About last night. I'm sorry I reacted the way I did and I'm sorry for unloading all my troubles on you."

"Hey, less of that." He looked sternly at her as he brought over their cups.

215

Iris took the one he held out. "No, it wasn't fair. You're not here to play Agony Aunt."

Warren reached for her free hand and squeezed it gently. "Iris, whatever else I am, I'm your friend and friends are there for each other."

"But you've only known me for two days."

"It doesn't matter. I think you're a lovely girl and I enjoy your company."

"Thank you. I feel the same about you." She paused then looked at him shyly. "Warren, I know I was distraught last night and freaked out when you touched me but..."

He smiled. "But?"

"That was last night and you're you, not him. So, that's if you'd like to, could we?" She traced his jawline with her fingers.

Warren tilted his head, "Are you sure?"

She put her cup on the bedside table and raised herself up. "Yes. I want you to chase away my demons. I want you to..."

Warren stopped her with a kiss. He lay next to her, wrapped his arms around her and planted delicate kisses on her face and neck. Iris pressed into him, her breath coming in deep sighs.

Then, when they could wait no longer, when she whispered how much she wanted him, they made love.

¤

On the stroke of seven, they were having breakfast. The receptionist had booked a taxi for Warren for eight to get him to Wythenshawe

216

police station, where he would be out with uniformed officers for the day. Iris would share the taxi and travel on to Poynton.

As they talked, David's name came up again. Warren was curious about how she had met him. Iris told him the story and found herself confiding in him about David's attempt to end her friendship with Trish because of an issue with the money from the sale of the house.

Warren was confused. "What's she got to do with it?"

Iris explained.

"And you believe him over her? Look, Iris, I think he's got more to gain by lying than your friend has. Did you look into it?"

"Yes. I asked David about it and he had a plausible explanation."

"Did he take anything else, during the house sale?"

"No. Well, he organised the house clearance and the auction but he paid me for that."

"Did you get proof? I don't know anything about auctions but surely they give invoices? When was this?"

Iris's face dropped. "About two months ago and no, he just told me how much and had the money paid into my bank."

"Do you know who the auctioneers were?"

She shook her head.

Warren pressed on. "Would anyone else you know have the information?"

Iris lifted her tea cup and frowned over the rim. "Not that I know of. Do you really think he'd keep back some of my money?"

"What do you think?"

Her brows knitted. "Oh dear. Oh no. I don't think...I mean, it would be theft."

He closed his mouth. Iris was too trusting. That crock of shit must have seen her coming a mile off. Warren didn't want to upset her again or pile more worry on her. "I'm probably wrong. Sorry, babe. Ignore me."

He turned back to his plate and lifted his fork. He was with Manchester CID at the end of the week. It wouldn't hurt to mention it to them.

¤

It was pouring down when Iris arrived home. She ran inside, shivering as she took off her coat and shoes. She hurried into the kitchen to make a hot drink. Her mood had vastly improved from the day before. Warren had been so good, bless him and he'd made her promise to ring him if she needed to talk or wanted to go out again. He was a caring friend, a considerate lover and made her feel good about herself. She needed that.

She wandered into the hall with her mug and glanced at the phone. The light was flashing. It was probably David. His was the last voice she wanted to hear. She pressed the play button anyway. It was Trish.

"Hi Iris! Only me. Hope everything's OK with you? It's supposed to be our walk today but it's throwing it down, so I think we'd better cancel. Give me a call when you get this. Oh, and let me know how your wedding reception went on Saturday. Did David like your gorgeous outfit? Bye, pet."

Iris's hand flew to her mouth. She had completely forgotten. She picked up the receiver to call her back.

Trish answered on the first ring. "Hi sweetie. How's everything?"

"Hi, Trish. I've only just got home. Sorry. I forgot it was today. I was out last night."

"Whoa. Rewind please. You were out last night and only just got in? Where have you been?"

Iris found herself smiling. "I was with someone."

"Someone? I take it not David?"

"No. Someone I met on Saturday night. At the do."

"But I thought you went with David?"

"I did but he went home without me. I met a lovely chap called Warren. I stayed the night at his hotel. With him..."

The gasp from Trish was audible. "He went home...You stayed with...? Well, you have surprised me."

"It kind of just happened. I'd had a few and Warren's so lovely."

"Warren? Well, good for you, Iris. About time you had some fun."

Iris began laughing. "I did."

"Are you seeing him again?"

"Probably. He's over from America on a police funded seminar. He goes back a week on Friday."

"That's a shame. I bet you'll miss him."

Iris's voice sounded cheerful. "Yes, but not in that way."

"You go girl! Anyway. I've got to dash. I'll see you on Thursday."

Trish hung up and sighed. For a moment there she'd dared to hope that Iris's anecdote about Warren would have had a different conclusion, like she was going to leave David for him. Sadly not.

Still, she had a few things to tell Iris tomorrow that might just give her a push in the right direction.

¤

Iris rose early on Wednesday and cleaned the house from top to bottom. Back in the kitchen, she put diced chicken and a jar of mushroom sauce in the slow cooker for dinner that evening. There was a Riesling chilling in the fridge, carrots and broccoli prepared and potatoes washed and ready to be pricked with a fork for baking in the oven.

The table in the dining room was set and she was making soup and sandwiches for lunch so there wasn't much else to do before David got back. He'd rung earlier to let her know that he was on the train and due to arrive at Manchester Piccadilly at noon. He'd jump a taxi and be home soon after one.

At first, Iris couldn't understand how he could phone her from the train. Then he explained in a loud voice, which she assumed was for the benefit of the other occupants of the carriage, that he had spent nearly two thousand pounds in London on a Motorola 8000X mobile phone.

Iris wasn't impressed but made encouraging noises.

"You see, Iris, when my Didsbury agency opens, I'll be out and about a lot, so this means I can always be contacted. And once my Chorlton agency's in the bag, it'll be even more indispensable. Have you heard from your solicitor yet?"

Iris rolled her eyes. Something couldn't be more indispensable just like something couldn't be more unique. She decided not to correct him. "Not yet, no."

"Well, chase him up then. See you later."

The phone went dead. She dropped the receiver back in the cradle. It had been hard to be civil with him. She'd had such a lovely time with Warren and these last few days had enabled her to compare David with someone else. Someone who was a better person in every way. But there was more. Warren's opinion of David matched Trish's. It was making Iris sit up and take note. They couldn't both be wrong.

The more she considered it, the more her anger grew. It had two focuses. One on the growing belief that David was stealing from her and that their relationship had been built on a foundation of lies and deception. The second was how he had taken her and shaken her until the best parts of her had been scattered to the winds. She only found remnants of herself when she was with Trish or Warren, good people who respected her and liked her for who she was.

She was lucky to have them as friends. When she was with David, he filled her spaces with anger and suspicion, fear and resentment.

Another thing was the attempted rape. To him, it wasn't. In his mind, she realised, he genuinely believed he was just taking what was his right to take. That included not taking "No" for an answer.

This train of thought took root as she went upstairs to change their bedding and she found herself despising David even more. Yet you could discover the absolute worst about someone, realise how miserable they made you, how badly they treated you, and still have feelings, still be unable to let them go.

She had tried to explain it to Warren but it was unfathomable. What Warren didn't see, what she couldn't tell him about, was the evil inside her, the dark, violent side. The side she had no control over. The side that had yet to reveal how destructive it could be. That frightened her more than anything.

Iris couldn't cope with these thoughts any more. She left the fresh bedding on the armchair, lay on the bed and pulled the silk counterpane over her. It was soft as gossamer, soothing as a mother's touch.

She was always so tired these days.

¤

"Iris, wake up, you lazy mare."

Someone was shaking her. David was leaning over her, his grip tight on her shoulder.

She jolted upright. "Oh! You're home."

"Well, give the girl first prize for stating the bleeding obvious."

Iris pulled her head over to the clock on the bedside table. "Oh, goodness. It's quarter past two. When did you get back?"

"At one."

"She looked back at him with a frown. "Why didn't you wake me?"

"I was waiting for you to wake yourself. Obviously wasn't going to happen. I've already showered and changed. Thanks Iris. Nice welcome back. Not."

His sarcasm pricked like hot needles. "Sorry. What else can I say? I fell asleep. I worked hard all morning cleaning and getting lunch and dinner sorted. I only came up to change the bed. I just wanted to lie down for a moment. It's not a crime."

"My heart bleeds for your life of servitude." He softened his jibe with a smile. He couldn't afford to piss her off. "Only kidding. Thanks, Iris. I can tell you've worked hard. It looks like I've just walked into a show home."

She felt placated. She slid out of bed and retrieved the clean bedding. "I've done soup and sandwiches for lunch."

He stood back and watched. "Not got time now. I'm off to the shop to touch base with Suzanna."

"OK. Would you like me to unpack for you?"

"Yes. Thanks. What time's dinner?"

"Half six. Or is that too late?

"No, that sounds fine. Should be back in good time."

Iris nodded and welcomed a few extra hours of peace.

¤

The suitcase was open on the bed. Iris started emptying it, sorting out what to wash and what to hang back in the wardrobe. The last item was a pair of red satin French knickers. She held them up and tilted her head. They still had the label attached and the hygiene strip on the gusset. David had bought her a present. There was a note attached with a safety pin. She began to read it. Her face fell.

David,

Tuesday night was a blast. Here's a souvenir.

Look me up next time you're in the area. Or any time!

Hayley x

Iris sat on the bed and scrutinised each word, looking for answers. So David had had sex with someone called Hayley who, presumably was another estate agent at the seminar. She stood, pushed the knickers and the note in her bedside cabinet and carried the laundry basket downstairs.

His infidelity didn't upset her. After all, she was guilty of it herself. She knew it wouldn't mean anything to him. She thought back to the wedding. It hurt her every time she recalled David's expression when he first saw Joanna and his behaviour that followed. They had been the actions of a jealous man. She knew it was Joanna's name he'd mumbled that night but now she had to face the fact that every time she had sex with David, in his head and his heart, he was making love to Joanna.

That was worse. Much, much worse. That was infidelity of the heart.

CHAPTER 28

Iris was quiet on the journey into Bramhall on Thursday morning. Her VW Golf was in for servicing so David gave her a lift.

She kept reminding herself that the only power she had over their relationship, the only weapon in her arsenal, was the loan for the Chorlton shop. She wanted to wield that power and see him crawl to her when he discovered it wasn't forthcoming. She was looking forward to that day. That was the only thing of hers he wanted.

When Iris walked in the shop, Trish was organising dresses into size order on one of the rails and didn't look up when the bell tinkled.

"Morning Trish."

Trish acknowledged her and continued her task.

"What's the matter?"

Trish paused for a moment, fiddled with a tag on one of the dresses, then turned to her. "If you must know, Iris, I'm getting really worried about you and it's really upsetting me. David's playing you like a fiddle and I honestly don't think you know just what you are dealing with. I love you to bits, Iris, but you're so naive. David is a chancer and he seems to spend most of his time working up shady deals. He's hard faced and I don't think he'd think twice about hurting you if you got in his way. Seriously. He's a nasty piece of work."

"I know," Iris's reply was simple.

Trish looked surprised but continued. "Listen Iris, please don't get cross with me for bringing it up again but I spoke to my son about this Land Development Tax. He's never heard of it, so he made a few enquiries. Iris, it doesn't exist. He's also heard rumours that David's been scamming home owners into accepting offers below the market price then selling on above it. I think he did that with your house."

"Wouldn't surprise me." Iris's voice was resigned.

Trish caught hold of her hands. "But that's not all that's bothering me. The few times I've seen him with you, his attitude leaves a lot to be desired. You're different too. Subdued, on edge. I care about you, Iris. I can't stand by and see what he's doing. He's not only stealing your money. He's destroying your soul. You must leave him and go to the police."

"I daren't report him."

"What do you mean? Has he ever hurt you?"

Iris didn't answer.

"He has, hasn't he? Oh, Iris, you must get away from him. He's evil. Can't you see?"

"Yes, I know. And when I feel I can, I will. But not now. Not yet. Do you understand?"

It was Trish's turn to stay silent.

"Trish?"

"I understand." Her friend sounded sad, "But he'll take everything from you."

Iris's voice was firm. "No, he won't."

Her tone resonated with Trish. She recognised her own determination and strength, traits that she hadn't seen in Iris before. She knew it was time to pull back but she would maintain a careful watch over her. "OK. Sorry. I'm interfering."

Iris tried to smile. "No, you're not. You're my best friend and you're looking out for me, like best friends do. Like I would for you." Then, suddenly and unexpectedly, she burst into tears.

"Oh, Iris, don't." Trish walked her quickly to the back of the shop. She sat her down, put the kettle on and found her a tissue. Iris sobbed loudly into it as Trish sank onto the chair next to her and put an arm around her shoulders.

Iris calmed, wiped her eyes and twisted the tissue in her fingers. Then everything poured out. Why David left the evening reception without her. Why she stayed with Warren rather than go home that night. The showdown with David on Sunday morning. The rape attempt. The discovery of Hayley's knickers when he returned from London. When all that was said, Iris went on to describe the physical and mental abuse she had suffered at David's hands since she had moved in with him.

Trish listened in silence. When Iris finished speaking, Trish stood, made coffee, resumed her seat and set her features to disguise how close to tears she found herself. "Iris, this has got to be it. I don't care what you said before. You have to leave him. Right now. I'll drive you home, we'll pack your things, bring them back here then you're coming home with me tonight and staying for as long as you want. This man's a monster. You can't stay with him a second longer."

Iris looked up, her face grey. "I'm not ready yet."

"Why ever not? For god's sake, Iris, you're not married to him. You don't have kids. You've no reason in the world to stay. I know what he's done. He's made you think you're worthless, that you can't survive without him, that no-one else will want you. That he's your whole world. He's destroyed all your self confidence. He's controlling you. He'll never treat you well. Once he has no more use for you, he'll cast you out."

"I know." Iris knitted her brows.

"So why wait for him to do it?"

Iris pressed her mug to her chest and breathed in the aroma. Trish was right. She was her own jailer. Why was it so important to put herself in the firing line with David by reneging on the Chorlton loan? It would be a victory but a short lived one. It wasn't revenge.

She opened her eyes. Trish was looking at her with the same love that she used to see in the faces of her mum, her dad, Grumps.

It gave Iris courage. She sat up and squeezed Trish's hands. "OK. I'll do it. I'll leave him. I'll do it today. Now."

229

Trish grabbed her shoulders. "What, now? Do you really mean it?"

Iris gave her a firm nod. "Yes."

"Come on then."

Iris held up her hands. "No. You're not taking me and I'm not staying at your house. I don't want you involved. Believe me, he's got it in for you already. I'll leave him but without your help."

Trish looked disappointed. "What are you going to do then?"

"I'll book into the Grosvenor, where Warren's staying."

"Right. Good. So, I'll take you home, help you pack and take you to the hotel."

Iris shook her head firmly. "No. I told you. You're not to get involved."

Trish felt tears welling. "Can't I even do that for you?"

"No. Once he sees my stuff gone he might ask the neighbours. If they tell him they saw you... you see? I'm not being awkward, Trish. I'm trying to keep you safe. I'll get a taxi home, pack, then get a taxi to the hotel. I know they've got vacancies."

They finished their drinks in silence before Trish walked her to the door. "Be careful, Iris, please. Ring me as soon as you're at the hotel so I know you're safe. You're doing the right thing."

Iris nodded, her throat constricting. "I know I am. I'll leave him a note saying it's over and I don't want to see him again." Iris pressed her lips together to stop her chin wobbling. "Right. I'm going. I'll get a taxi at the station."

Trish hugged her. "Take care, love. I'll meet up with you as soon as you feel ready."

Iris flung her arms around her friend's neck. "Oh, dearest Trish, I don't know what I did to deserve a wonderful friend like you..."

"You didn't have to do anything. It's enough just being you. Remember that."

Trish watched from the door as Iris walked away. Then she dropped her head, walked back inside and burst into tears.

¤

It was one o'clock by the time Iris arrived home. The driver dropped her outside and gave her the number to call for a pick up.

She wasted no time once she was inside. She ran upstairs, collected her suitcase from the guest room and began to gather her clothes and possessions together. It was surprising how little there was. Iris packed as if her life depended on it, which in a way, she thought sadly, it did.

She left the case by the front door, hurried into the kitchen and took the magnetic notepad and pen from the fridge. Leaning against the breakfast bar with the nib hovering over the paper, she bit her lip. How much should she tell him? Should she explain why she was leaving? Her laugh was brittle. She'd be there all day if she tried and there wasn't enough paper in the world. He wouldn't give a damn anyway. She would keep it simple.

She thought for a moment more, then bent her head and began to write.

David,

I'm leaving you.

I've taken only what belongs to me.

I won't be coming back.

Iris.

She read it out loud. It was fine. Short and to the point. It told him all he needed to know. She tore out the page and put the pad back on the fridge. She would leave it on the hall table and ring for the taxi. It would be all over then. That thought sent a curl of happiness through her. This was so easy. She had Trish to thank. Her wise words had been the catalyst Iris had been waiting for. She folded the paper in half as she walked into the hall and only looked up when she reached the phone.

Her breath caught in her throat. She stopped dead.

"Going somewhere, Iris?"

David was standing by the front door, his arms folded, his feet planted on either side of her case.

CHAPTER 29

David stood between Iris and freedom. Yet her new life was beckoning, beyond him and beyond the carved oak door behind him.

"I'm leaving you, David. I've written you a note." She hid the tremor in her voice.

"What does it say?"

She held it out with a shaky hand.

He walked over and reached for it. Iris flinched involuntarily.

David opened the single fold and read it silently. When he finished, he refolded it and placed it gently on the console. Iris waited in trepidation. What was he going to do? Could she run past him and get out before he could stop her? Impossible. Could she escape though the patio doors at the back then? She could leave her case behind. She didn't need anything. She just had to escape.

David stepped forward. Iris stepped back. Sadness bloomed on his face.

He shook his head slowly and followed through with a heartfelt sigh. "Oh, my sweet Iris, what can I say? I'm so, so sorry. I never knew you were so unhappy that you'd want to leave me. I thought you loved me. I've given you everything, haven't I? A beautiful home, an enviable lifestyle. Wasn't that enough for you? Isn't it what you always wanted?"

Iris stared at him in confusion.

"Look, darling. Please stay – I'd be lost without you."

Iris couldn't speak. What was he saying? This wasn't what she'd expected.

David took her silence as a good sign. "Maybe you've needed more assurances about my feelings. Was I too focussed on the business? Working too hard to expand it, to make a future for us? I had hoped you'd understand and support me. Iris, If you still care for me as much as I care for you, we can learn from this. We can make it work but you need to understand that relationships are full of complexities. You've never been in one before so you won't know. You have a lot to learn about them."

To her astonishment, David dropped down on one knee, caught hold of her hands and smiled up at her. "Iris Ferguson, I love you. Will you marry me?"

Iris's brain was swirling. Was it her fault? Had she concentrated too much on her own feelings and not considered his? Had she not fully appreciated how hard he worked for her, for their future?

David's hands clutched hers tightly. "Iris?"

She had to say something. "David, this is all so sudden..."

He stood and pulled her into his arms. "I'm

sorry. Iris. Of course it is. Look, take as long as you want to think about it."

Marriage? To David? He'd actually told her he loved her. Could they make it work? Wasn't it worth a try? She nodded wordlessly.

David's face lit up and he kissed her. "Why don't we go upstairs?"

She let him lead her to the bedroom. Inside, he began to undress her but she stopped him. Her head was pounding. She needed her painkillers.

He went into the en-suite for water and she opened her bedside drawer. Her eyes alighted on Hayley's knickers. How could she have forgotten? His words blew away like dust. When he came back, she swallowed her tablets and drained her glass. Then she lifted out the knickers, turned to him and shook them out by the waistband.

His face fell. Iris tilted her head as she gazed at them. "I found these in your suitcase when I unpacked it. I take it they're yours?"

He tried to laugh. "Nah. Not my style."

"So, whose style are they, David?"

He spotted the price tag on the hem. "Yours, I hope. I got them for you in London. I thought you'd like them."

"Oh. Did you?" She laid them out on the bed. "Was the note for me too?"

David shifted uncomfortably, his eyes darting between Iris and the knickers. "The note?"

She undid the safety pin, picked it up and began reading in a falsetto voice. "'David, Tuesday night was a blast. Here's a souvenir.'"

Iris stared pointedly at the knickers. "'Look me up next time you're in the area. Or any time.' Exclamation mark. She signs off, 'Hayley' and closes with a kiss." She looked up at David again. "So?"

David arranged his face. "Can I see that note?"

She handed it to him.

He read it and burst out laughing.

"You find it funny?"

David screwed it up and threw it on the bed. "For God's sake, Iris. It was a joke. One of the women at the seminar kept coming on to me and the lads found it hilarious. They must have bought them and stuck them in my case for a joke. I didn't sleep with anyone. I wouldn't do that to you. You should know that."

"So why did you say you bought them for me?"

David squirmed under her gaze. "I thought it was more believable than the truth."

Iris deflated. Was it the truth? It could be a lie. There was no way of knowing. David shook his head and smiled. "Come here, silly. I'm like that song by Dean Friedman, you know? Lucky Stars?"

She shrugged sulkily.

He walked around the bed, wrapped her in his arms and sang. "I may not be all that bright but I know how to hold you tight and you can thank your lucky stars that we're not as smart as we like to think we are."

Despite herself Iris began smiling. He was being so sweet. She looked up at him. "Do you really love me?"

"Let me show you just how much." He eased her back gently onto the bed, undid her bra and pulled down her panties.

His lovemaking was more gentle than usual and his kisses chased away the last of her reservations. She would give him one more chance, just one, to prove he cared and to prove that they could be a real couple.

¤

David left for a viewing soon after. It was too late to go back to the cat shop. Anyway, Iris couldn't face Trish after everything she had promised her friend that morning.

In the afternoon, while she was in the kitchen, the phone rang. She walked quickly into the hall to answer it.

There was silence, then a hesitant voice. A female one. "Oh. Hi. Is David there please?"

Iris cocked her head. "No, he's not. Can I take a message?"

"Would you? That'd be great. I've tried his mobile but it's switched off. I rang his agency and his assistant gave me this number."

Iris frowned. "I'm sorry? Who is this?"

"My name's Hayley. David and I were at the convention in London. I'm coming into Manchester next week and thought we could meet up."

Iris jerked her head back in shock. Her mouth opened and closed but nothing came out.

"Hello? Are you still there?"

Iris felt it. The roaring. The pressure. She held

the phone away. No. Not yet. She took some deep breaths, looked at herself in the mirror above the console and returned the phone to her mouth. "Yes. By the way, I'm Iris, David's fiancée."

There was silence again.

Iris kept her eyes on her reflection and gripped the phone tighter.

"Yes. Iris. Hello. Right. Could you tell him I called. Sorry. I'm late for a meeting. Got to dash."

The line went dead. Iris gently put the receiver back in the cradle. So that was Hayley.

She walked into the kitchen, sat heavily on a bar stool, and dropped her head on her arms. If only she'd left sooner, she would have been spared all this.

Now she was as confused as ever, just when she thought she'd worked it all out.

CHAPTER 30

A sharp wind was blowing over the parapet, whipping Iris's hair around her face. It was four thirty and already dark. The bulkhead light would have been too bright for her mood, so she had packed a torch along with a flask.

She settled in the old chair and laid back against the plastic weave. "Oh Grumps. What should I do? If David's been unfaithful, I will leave him. But what if he hasn't? The thing is, he's asked me to marry him. I still can't believe it."

Iris poured herself a hot chocolate and sipped it thoughtfully. She was giving him one last chance because Hayley's phone call didn't really count against it. David had said she'd been chasing him at the seminar. Maybe that's what this call was.

"Well, Grumps, I've made a decision. I'll go home, tell him about the call but I won't make it a big deal. I'll just have to trust him. Right. I'm going now Grumps. Love you. Miss you."

Iris stood, threw everything back into her bag and left. She caught a cab in Didsbury Village and arrived back in Poynton at six o'clock. The

Porsche was in the driveway. Iris paid the driver and quickly let herself in the house. She heard David's voice in the kitchen and smiled. She would sneak up and surprise him.

When she entered, he was standing at the breakfast bar, his back to her, talking into his mobile phone. She tiptoed up behind him.

"I know. It was great. No, she didn't suspect anything. Not really."

Iris's arms dropped to her sides. She was incapable of doing anything but listening.

He started laughing. "You mean we used a full pack? Christ. You came prepared, you dirty bitch. No. I'm not complaining. Yes. I can get away next week. I'll make some excuse to her. Let me know where and when. OK. See you. Bye."

Iris didn't move.

David turned and jumped when he saw her. "Iris. Hi. How long have you been standing there?"

She was breathing heavily, her face white, lips pressed tightly together, eyes emerald with animosity. The answer came through gritted teeth. "Long enough."

"You heard then?"

She didn't reply.

"It's not like it sounds, Iris." He tried a casual laugh, a hand outstretched in appeasement.

She knocked it away.

"Look, darling..."

"So you did have sex with her."

His mouth opened and shut.

"Quite a lot too, although I don't know how many condoms come in a packet. No pun intended."

"It meant nothing..."

"Nothing means anything to you, David. Actually, That's not strictly true, is it, David?" She nodded sagely. "There's Joanna."

His expression changed. Just a tiny inflection but enough to show that the name resonated.

"As much as you are capable of loving anyone, you love her. Don't you?" Her voice became more strident. "Don't you, David?"

He didn't answer.

Iris stepped back a pace and took a deep breath. "Well, as it's confession time, I may as well come clean too. Last Saturday night? When you walked out of the wedding reception and left me all on my own?"

A tic was visible in his jaw.

"Well, I spent the night with a man I met there after you'd gone and d'you know what, David? We saw each other again on Tuesday night. The sex was fantastic. He knocks spots off you. So, I can't really criticise you for being unfaithful but like you said, it meant nothing."

David stepped closer. "You let some random guy shag you and you're bragging to me about it? ME?"

"I'm not bragging. I'm just being open and honest, something you're incapable of."

"You've turned into a slag, Iris."

Her shoulders lifted. "No difference to what you did."

"Yes there is. I'm a man, I'm allowed to."

"Oh, please. What century are you living in?"

They were inches apart, facing each other off.

David stared down at her. Her infidelity didn't hurt but his pride had taken a tumble. No-one did that to him. He wanted to punish her but he wasn't sure how far he could go before she disappeared inside one of her violent rages.

When she folded her arms and tilted her head, his anger grew. Iris being brave and divisive was even more irritating than Iris being sweet and compliant.

He couldn't resist saying the thing that he knew would hurt her most. "OK. I admit it. I love Joanna. Always have and always will."

Iris set her jaw but it couldn't stop the tell tale wobble of her chin.

David smiled. Bullseye. "And do you know what else? I spoke to Joanna after the wedding. She wanted to meet up. Said she needed closure after our breakup. Wanted to talk. So I left on Tuesday, straight after the seminar finished.

She met me at the station. We booked into a hotel. Let's just say it was incredible. Do I need to elaborate? I was still with her when I rang you yesterday. I wasn't on the train. And, you know what, while I was talking to you, she was sucking my dick. Now there's a woman who knows how to satisfy a man."

Iris's eyes widened. Tears pricked the corners. She didn't want to hear any more.

The roaring that had started in her ears wasn't enough to blot out his words. She brought her hand back to slap his face.

He caught it. "That's the last time you touch me, you mad cow."

Iris snarled, wrestling him, "And this is the last time you touch me. I'm leaving and you know what? I'm not instructing my solicitor about the loan. You're not getting a penny more off me. You've stolen enough already."

"What? That's rich, coming from you. Your feet were under my table like a shot when you got the chance. It was only ever a temporary arrangement but you had some ridiculous notion about me and you. Now look at you, still here, in my house, in my face. Stuff your money. I'll get it elsewhere. Just get out. I'm sick of you. Go on, fuck off." He sent her flying against the breakfast table.

She levered herself upright, her face brimming with emotion. "You've really shown your true colours. I deserve better than this. Better than you."

Iris stumbled out of the kitchen. The roaring was still there but she was holding it in, keeping it under control. She could do that now. It was getting easier.

Hayley, she didn't give a fig about. But Joanna? Now that cut her to the core. For all her kindness, Joanna was no better than David. They deserved each other.

David was still in the kitchen. She heard a glass tumbler being brought down from the cupboard, the sound of a bottle being placed on the breakfast bar, the scrape of a metal top as it was unscrewed. The glug of liquid in the glass.

He was starting on the whisky. She needed to leave now.

Iris ran upstairs and used the phone in the bedroom to order a taxi, then grabbed her suitcase from the spare room, still packed from before. Twenty minutes later she was on her way to the Grosvenor.

That was it. She'd done it. She'd left him, but she wasn't about to let him or Joanna get away with what they had done, what they were doing.

She would see David Phillips again very soon.

In fact, she would see them both.

CHAPTER 31

Iris took two painkillers before returning to Warren's bed.

He smiled with pleasure as he pulled her against him. "I'm so glad you've left that creep."

She closed her eyes, her cheek resting against his chest. She didn't want to talk or even think about David.

Warren went on happily. "I couldn't believe it when Reception rang last night to say you were here. How long did you say you're staying?"

A gentle shrug. "I don't know Warren. I have things to sort out."

She had called Trish as soon as she'd arrived yesterday and confirmed that she'd left David but omitted her stupid, but thankfully short, about-face. She was too ashamed to say that she had fallen for his lies yet again.

Warren was looking forward to his last day of the seminar and spending it with CID. He glanced at his watch and kissed the top of Iris's head. "Got to get up, babe. Are you coming for breakfast?"

"Ooh, yes. I'm starving." Iris smiled up at him. Their night together had been a delicious blend of passion and cuddles. When he went back to America, she would always remember him as the man who shone a light into her darkness. She hoped he would remember her as fondly.

He left after they ate and Iris made her way back upstairs. She was in the room next to Warren again and it was obvious that she hadn't slept there so she jumped on the bed and rolled around, squashing the pillows and laughing at her silliness.

¤

David woke with a grimace. A pneumatic drill was going off in his head and minutes elapsed before he was able to peel one eye, then the other, open. Christ. How much had he drunk last night? He laboured his body into a sitting position against the headboard. At least he'd woken up in bed and not downstairs on the sofa, surrounded by bottles, like he had when Joanna left him.

The irony of the situation hit him. First Jo, now Iris. He turned his head to look at the empty side of the bed. What the hell had possessed him to throw away his third agency and what the hell was he going to do now? He slid back down and covered his face with his hands.

The solution came to him half an hour later in the shower. He would prostrate himself in front of Iris and beg her to forgive him and come back.

Downstairs, making coffee and toast, he was

convinced that Iris wouldn't turn him down. After all, she was in love with him. It was a fait accompli.

At 9.30 he picked up his keys, pulled on his coat and scarf and let himself out. It was a bitterly cold December morning. The Porsche was covered in a layer of ice and his breath was clouding in front of him. He unlocked the car, climbed in and turned the heaters to full blast.

While he waited for the windows to clear, he finished outlining his plans. With Christmas coming up, he would whisk her away to a five star hotel for a few days. She'd love that. While they were there, he would propose to her again and take her for an engagement ring. She would give him the loan for Chorlton and everyone would be happy. Well, for the moment.

He threw the Porsche into gear and pulled out of the driveway. The council would have to grit the roads if this weather continued. The car was warm now and he loosened his scarf. He wondered where Iris had gone. The only one who might know was that interfering friend of hers at the charity shop. He would pay her a visit later.

¤

Whiskers Galore was having a quiet morning. The cold snap was keeping everyone away. So far Trish had only taken a couple of pounds. The shop was cold and the two small electric radiators made little improvement. She sighed and retreated behind the counter to make another hot drink. It was nearly noon.

As she stirred her coffee, she heard the shop door tinkle. She called out in her best customer voice, "Won't be a minute!"

A man replied. "No hurry."

Trish peeped out and her heart jumped. David Phillips was standing in the middle of the shop. Slowly she emerged and stood behind the counter, hands resting on the glass top.

"Hi, Trish." He gave her a film star smile.

She nodded. "David."

"Do you know where Iris is? We had a misunderstanding yesterday afternoon but she wouldn't see reason and went off in a huff."

Trish was caught off guard. Iris hadn't mentioned that when she rang last night. She lifted her shoulders and looked vague, "I'm sorry, I have no idea."

The smile was still on his face but it had turned cold. His frown challenged her words. She found his expression unnerving. She felt the need to puncture the silence. "The last time I saw her was here, yesterday."

"Has she been in touch?"

Trish ignored the question. She busied herself tidying a box of greetings cards on the counter.

David kept his eyes on her, the air heavy between them. Eventually, he spoke again. "You don't seem worried that your best friend has gone missing."

Trish looked him squarely in the eye. "I'm sure she'll turn up, David."

"I think you know where she is and I think you should tell me."

"If she contacts me, I'll tell her you're looking for her. That's all I can do."

He stared at her for a moment more then came to life. "If she does get in touch, tell her to ring me. Tell her it's urgent. Will you do that?" His tone had altered completely. Now it was soft, concerned, emotional. Trish blinked. The difference was sudden and unnerving.

David walked over and leaned on the counter. "Will you, Trish?"

She kept her voice level. "If she contacts me, I'll tell her."

"Thank you." He pushed himself away and smoothed his hair. "I know we've both got her best interests at heart. She has mental problems and needs to be seen by a doctor. I'll get her the help she needs before she becomes even more dangerous."

Trish grabbed at his words. "What mental problems? Dangerous? What're you talking about?"

David rolled his eyes expressively, "Where to start? Well, she's attacked me on several occasions, completely unprovoked, I might add. Twice with a knife and once with a hot iron. But she never remembers after. I'm deadly serious, Trish. She needs help. She seems to be plagued with headaches and virtually lives on painkillers." He shook his head sadly. "The poor darling. She needs to be seen by a professional. She might even need to be sectioned, for her

249

own safety, as well as mine. I'm in BUPA. I can get her help virtually straight away. She will have the best care and the best treatment possible. All she has to do is to take that first step by coming home."

Trish was stunned. "David, if she contacts me, I swear I'll tell her to ring you straight away."

He nodded. "Thank you. I hope you will."

She watched him walk out of the shop. Was he telling the truth or was he lying? She wasn't prepared to gamble when Iris's health was at stake. She walked to the window to check David had gone then hurried back to the counter and picked up the telephone.

With shaking fingers she began to dial.

CHAPTER 32

On Friday morning, Iris left the Grosvenor for some fresh air. Her head was pounding. Paracetamol had long since stopped having any real effect. She bought a coffee from a street vendor and made her way past Manchester University and Whitworth Art Gallery towards Whitworth gardens. She entered and took a seat on one of the benches to enjoy what warmth the sun could offer against the chill of the day.

She had discarded the memory of Joanna dancing with Eddie. The love they shared, that she had coveted so desperately, had been a misconception. It existed only in Eddie's heart. It shone through his eyes, it was in his smile, the way he held her.

As she sipped her coffee, she became aware of a thought trying to push through. A way to punish Joanna and David. She tried to concentrate, to bring it forward so she could hear it but the noise in her head drowned it out.

Iris closed her eyes and offered her face to the sun. The brightness turned the inside of her lids translucent pink.

It would come to her. All she had to do was

wait.

¤

"Miss Ferguson?" The receptionist at the Grosvenor smiled as she walked though.

Iris stopped.

"I have a message from you. From a lady called Trish. She rang while you were out, said to ring her back urgently. Here's her number."

She looked at the note he passed her.

"Dial nine for an outside line. We'll charge the call to your account."

"Thank you." Iris hurried upstairs and struggled to turn the key in the lock. The fact that it was urgent scared her. She fell into the room, ran to the telephone and dialled, her fingers trembling.

Within seconds of the connection, Trish answered. "Iris. Hope I didn't frighten you but I need to speak to you. David came into the shop earlier."

Iris's stomach turned over. "Are you alright? What did he say? Did he hurt you?"

"No, of course he didn't. Listen, Iris." Trish breathed deeply. "He told me about your headaches, about all the painkillers you're taking. About your blackouts. That you've been violent towards him."

Iris hung her head. There was no way she could brazen this out. "Yes. It's true."

"Oh, dear Lord. I'd hoped he was lying. Well, have you been to see a doctor? You've never mentioned anything to me."

252

"I was going to go to my GP but I can't remember if I did. I forget a lot these days."

Trish's voice became strident. It made Iris sit up. "You silly girl, Iris. you could be really ill."

Iris sat on the bed and pressed a hand against her forehead.

Trish sighed loudly. "Listen, Iris, David seems genuinely concerned. I'm not convinced of his motives but he's insisting that he wants to help you. He said he's in BUPA and can arrange for you to be seen straight away."

Iris was quiet. Trish paused and waited for her to speak. Finally, she did, abruptly. "I'll ring him, Trish. OK? Thank you for calling."

Iris put the receiver down and clasped her hands between her knees. She was already frightened of this demon inside her but she knew David didn't care about her. His only reason to want her back was financial. More than ever, she need retribution. It was chomping at the bit, waiting impatiently for her to run with it.

Then it happened. The lightbulb moment. The idea that had stayed tantalisingly out of her grasp had now stepped forward and was coming through loud and clear.

She smiled, recovered the piece of paper that had lain in the bottom of her bag all week and picked up the phone.

CHAPTER 33

On Monday, after the wedding, Joanna began to look for estate agents to value the flat. Her trawl through Yellow Pages had produced more than she'd anticipated. She turned to Eddie. "How many d'you think I should ask?"

"Where are we exactly?"

"Didsbury Village. Well, the outskirts."

"And the estate agents you bought this through?"

"Mortimer Briggs. They're in the village."

"That's a good start. Let's concentrate on this area. Put them on your list and add the other local ones. We can find out their record for selling properties like yours and the prices they achieved, what their fees are. How does that sound?"

Joanna nodded. "I'm impressed. Brains as well as brawn. I like that in a man."

"Ah, you see? You wouldn't get such good advice from Warren."

She sighed deeply. "I won't get anything from Warren now. My heart is broken. He's discarded me for a younger model."

"Good thing for you then that I like my women

like I like my cheese. Mature and blue veined."

"Ha ha. Very funny."

¤

In the village, they worked through the list. It began to rain as they reached the junction of Wilmslow Road and School Lane. They stopped at the traffic lights. Joanna had just pressed the button to cross when a shop on the opposite side of the road caught her eye. Above the whitewashed windows was a commercial sale board, a sold sign nailed diagonally across it. Inside the window, in a clear section of glass, was the following notice:

DAVID PHILLIPS ASSOCIATES
OPENING SOON
A NEW AND EXCITING ESTATE
AGENCY

Joanna stared in disbelief. "Look at that shop. That can't be right. How can he afford to buy premises for a new agency already? He's only had the Bramhall one for a year."

Eddie shrugged. "Maybe he sold the last one."

"No. The Bramhall premises were rented. I wonder who he's ripped off this time?"

His voice was impatient. "I don't care, Joanna and neither should you. The rain's getting heavy and I'd quite like to go somewhere for lunch and dry off. Can we?"

She pulled her eyes away from the shop and felt that resurgence of relief that she'd never see him again. Judging from his behaviour towards Iris at the evening reception, he hadn't changed for the better.

The green man flashed. Eddie grabbed her hand and they ran across the road.

¤

Next day Joanna rang the four agents they had shortlisted. Two were able to fix a date to visit then and there. One returned their call a short time later.

On Friday, while they were preparing lunch, the phone rang.

"That'll be the last agent. He took his time." Joanna reached over the breakfast bar and picked it up from the wall. "Hello? Joanna Brooks speaking."

She wasn't expecting a quiet little voice with a local accent. "Hi. Joanna."

"Hello, who is it please?"

"It's Iris. David's girlfriend. From the reception on Saturday.

Joanna's eyes flashed to Eddie. He mouthed, "Who?"

She mouthed back, "Iris."

He rolled his eyes.

Joanna turned in her seat. "Iris. How are you?"

"I'm fine, thank you. I won't keep you. Why I'm ringing, I wanted to thank you again for helping me on Saturday night and for the lift home on Sunday. It was so kind of you."

"It was the least I could do, Iris." She hesitated then continued, picking her words carefully.

"Was everything alright when you got in?"

A pause from the other end. "Yes. Everything was fine. It was just a misunderstanding."

Joanna shouldn't have asked. She should have known Iris would lie. In a relationship like that, pride in how others perceived you was all you had and it was something you would protect. The line went quiet. Joanna filled an awkward gap. "So. Anyway. You don't have to thank me."

"Well, I want to, so I thought it would be nice if I took you out for a drink. I was thinking maybe tomorrow night?"

This time the pause was Joanna's.

Iris's voice sounded in her ear. "Joanna, I thought about the Cellar Vie in Albert Square. My treat."

"Well, we're pretty busy with my flat. We're putting it on the market, you see."

Iris put a smile in her voice. "I'm only talking an hour or so. That's if Eddie will let you out without him?"

"Of course he will." Joanna realised she'd boxed herself into a corner. "OK then. Yes. Just for an hour or so."

"Sorted then. I'll meet you outside at seven-thirty?"

"Yes. That's fine."

"Lovely. See you then. Bye."

The line clicked.

Joanna hung up. Eddie nodded. "Well go on then. You're going out with Iris. I gathered that much. Where and when?"

"Cellar Vie in town. Tomorrow evening. She's

257

meeting me there at half seven." She gave him a deadpan look and circled her face with a hand. "Notice how I can hardly contain my excitement?"

He chuckled. "You're too soft, sweetheart. You could have just said no."

"Bit rude."

"You could have said no because you used to be in a relationship with him and wouldn't feel comfortable."

"Oh, I couldn't have said that."

He shrugged. "More fool you then."

She glared at him.

He reached for her hand. "Look, you can't go back on it now. Like you said, it's not for long."

"I know and I do feel sorry for her. Maybe she needs a night out, a break from him. Actually, I've got an idea. Why don't you come in with me and have a few pints with Warren at the Grosvenor?"

"You're joking."

"No, I'm not. We can share a taxi. It can drop me off at the Cellar Vie, then drop you back at the Grosvenor. I'm sure Warren would appreciate the company." She batted her eyelashes and pressed her hands to her heart. "And you can tell him all about how you met the love of your life standing at that very same bar. Then, at nine at the very latest, Iris and I can get a taxi back to the Grosvenor, pick you up, we'll get out in Didsbury and she can continue on to Poynton. What d'you think?"

Eddie studied her without expression.

258

"You're clearly impressed."

He blew his cheeks out loudly. "Oh, all right then. At least I won't be far away. I don't like the thought of you being on your own in the centre of Manchester at night anyway."

"I won't be on my own. I'll be with Iris."

"I'll repeat my last sentence."

"You know something? I'm beginning to think she's right. That you might actually not want me to go anywhere without you."

"Iris said that?"

"As good as." She kept her face straight. "Well? Is she right? Are you turning into a control freak? You won't let me out of your sight?"

"Hey, no need for that."

"Well, sometimes I feel you can't."

Eddie stared in astonishment. "Like when? Go on, give me an example."

"OK. Like when I'm in bed." She lifted her shoulders and opened her palms.

"What d'you mean, when you're in bed?"

"Well, you're always there."

"Isn't that connected to the fact that we sleep together?"

"Ah! Yes, but I bet if I went to the bedroom now, took all my clothes off and turned round, you'd be there."

Eddie narrowed his eyes. "Want to try it?"

Joanna held his gaze. "I think we should. Just to prove my point."

"Go on then."

¤

"You see? I was right."

"I'll give you that."

"Well, while we're here, we may as well..."

The telephone rang.

"Should I get that? It could be the Estate Agent."

Eddie moved her gently under him. "Nah. Too busy proving a point."

CHAPTER 34

David was on his way to a viewing in Hazel Grove when his mobile phone rang. He reached for it on the passenger seat. He knew Iris's voice straight away.

"I believe you want to speak to me."

"Iris!" David's voice filled her ear. "Thank God. Where are you? I've been worried sick."

"I'm fine. I'm quite safe."

"Iris, please come home. I'm worried that you're ill and need medical help. Tell me where you are and I'll come for you straight away."

"No." Her voice was clear, abrupt. "I'm not coming home. If we're going to talk, it's got to be somewhere neutral."

"OK. I can understand that." David pulled over and put on the handbrake. "How about I pick you up tonight and take you out for a meal? We can talk then."

"No. I want somewhere private, where we won't be overheard."

He stared out of the windscreen, fingers tapping lightly on the curve of the wheel. "Have you anywhere in mind?"

"Yes. Surprise View."

"What? We can't go there. Iris, it's not your house any more."

"I've got a key."

David frowned. "You can't have. I gave them all to the purchaser."

"I found it in an old coat."

"Have you been there since the sale then?"

"Yes. A few times. The first was on an off chance. The locks haven't been changed."

"Shit. I forgot. Bill asked me to sort it. I'd better put it on my list."

He was going off subject. Iris broke in. "It's the only place I'm prepared to talk to you, David. Are you going to meet me there or not?"

He was taken aback by her directness. "Yes, of course. Let's get everything out in the open and sorted. You need to see someone about your health, Iris. I'm in BUPA. I can get you the best care possible with the best doctors."

"But I'm not, so how can they treat me?"

David clenched his teeth. She wasn't as stupid as he'd thought. He replied smoothly, "I added you to my policy, as my partner, when you moved in."

On the other end of the line, Iris rolled her eyes. Yet another lie. He had made it abundantly clear before she walked out that it had been a temporary arrangement.

"Iris? Still there?"

"Yes. Can we meet tomorrow, your day off? Half past two?"

"Of course. I'm overseeing some work at the Didsbury shop so that'll be ideal."

"OK. I'll meet you at the house." She put the phone down before he could reply.

¤

Iris turned up the heating in her room, stripped off and walked into the en-suite to shower. When she came out, she wrapped herself in the bath sheet and switched on the kettle. With tea brewed and the complimentary biscuits placed by her mug on the bedside table, she lay on the bed with a smile. The second part of her plan had been as easy as the first.

Now it was time to pull the threads together.

CHAPTER 35

David stood outside the entrance of the Didsbury shop and surveyed the streets around it. He gave himself a pat on the back. This was a prime spot, visible from all four corners of the busy junction. The shop fitters were steaming ahead and he hoped to be up and running by the middle of January.

Suzanna had devised the marketing strategy and had been instrumental in rolling it out. David was confident that she would have a few houses ready to fill some of the space in one of the double fronted windows, which would quickly garner interest. She was currently in negotiations with a letting agent to let him rent the other window space on a short term basis, giving David some additional income at the outset.

David knew that Suzanna's dedication was partly because he had suggested he might let her manage the Bramhall agency. He knew she already had ideas to improve the business, which suggested that she didn't think it was achieving its potential under his management. Cheeky cow. He glanced at his watch. It was time to meet Iris. He collected the Porsche and was outside Surprise View at two-thirty.

Since Iris woke that morning, she had been running on a high octane mixture of hate and adrenaline. It was the fuel she needed to do what she had to do. It had killed off her headache and she had never felt more lucid, more sure of herself.

When David pulled up, she was waiting by the gate, hands casually hitched inside the sloping pockets of a short denim jacket. Her hair was newly highlighted and tousled and she was wearing a denim mini skirt. He liked her in short skirts. She looked cute as a button and he felt the urge just looking at her.

"Iris. How are you feeling?" He locked the car door and stepped up to her.

She nodded a greeting but didn't speak.

He looked past her to the house. "So, you really want to talk in there?"

"Yes."

Inside, once she had closed the door, David pressed her against the wall, his breath hot on her neck. His hand pushed under her ribbed jumper.

She shoved him backwards. "Not here. Up there."

He glanced up towards the first floor and back at her. "Where?"

"Upstairs. I've got something for you."

David licked his lips and followed her. At the top, she walked along the landing to the next flight.

"Iris, where are you taking me?" He reached for her and swung her round, hands under her skirt, cupping her bottom, pressing her into his thighs. "Come on, you little prick tease."

She wriggled free. "Not yet. Keep going."

They reached the top. She turned. "Just one more. You're really going to like this."

David looked up with a frown. "On the roof? It's bloody freezing outside."

"No, you'll see. There's a fire and champagne. I want us to have a drink, relax and make love. Then we'll talk."

David couldn't believe it. It sounded reconciliatory and with minimum effort from him. The Chorlton agency suddenly felt close enough to touch.

With a laugh, he picked her up and carried her to the roof terrace, pushing the door open with his knee. True to her word, it looked cosy enough for what she had in mind. He saw the fire burning in a bucket, two fold up chairs, her coat over the back of one, and two glasses and a bottle of champagne on a table by a drawstring bag. He set her down and wondered where they were going to have sex and, in passing, what was in the bag. He dropped his phone and keys next to it. The fire was warm enough for him to discard his outerwear and drop them on the other chair.

The champagne had already been poured into the glasses. He took the one she offered and drained it.

What David hadn't registered when he'd

stepped out with her was a pigeon loft on the far side of the terrace, fixed to the brick partition wall, its door wide open. He wanted Iris now but as he set down the glass and reached for her, she picked up the bag and opened it.

When she straightened, he looked at what was in her hand and after a moment of confusion, his face registered disbelief, shock then horror.

Iris circled him until he was between her and the loft. "Yes. It's real, David and it's loaded. In a minute, I want you to get in there," She nodded towards the loft, "But first I want you to take all your clothes off."

His head jerked behind him then back to her. "What?"

"You heard. Take your clothes off."

He half laughed. "What's your game, Iris? I thought we were going to do it here..." An arm waved to encompass the area around the fire. "Not there." He wafted it weakly behind him.

"You're mistaken, David. We're not having sex here, there, or anywhere. That wasn't the surprise." She raised the gun. "This was. Well, one of two. Now. Take your clothes off."

He shook his head violently, lips pressed together. She was seriously scaring him now.

Iris took a small step nearer and calmly raised the gun until it was pointing at his chest. "I'll not ask you again."

When she cocked it, David threw his palms in front of him. "No, don't shoot. I'm doing it. Look."

She watched as he took off his jumper and

267

dropped it on the floor. Then he dragged his tee shirt over his head, kicked off his shoes and shed his socks. He paused as his fingers grappled with his jeans zip and lifted his head. "Iris, please don't do this. I'm begging you."

"Get them off." Her words sent her shooting back to last Sunday, David barking the same command before ripping her clothes away. She swallowed the bile that rose in her throat.

David hopped on one leg as he struggled to get out of his jeans. He dropped his underpants, pressed his knees together and locked his hands over his genitalia. He looked a sad spectacle of a man as he blinked at Iris, his eyes beginning to swim with tears, terror in his face and compliance in the stoop of his body.

Iris thought how absurd he looked. It struck her then that the sight of him left her bereft of emotion. With a flood of joy and a lightness of being that made her catch her breath, she realised that she no longer loved him. In fact, at that moment, all she felt was contempt. "Now, get in."

David took several steps backwards and glanced behind. He was less than a foot away now. "No. You can't be serious Iris. You've finally lost your mind."

"Maybe I've just found it. Get in before I shoot you."

He shook his head.

Iris pulled the trigger.

David screamed, ducked and threw himself inside. The bullet lodged between two bricks behind him, sending a shower of mortar over him. He crouched and flung his arms protectively over his head.

With the gun still trained on him, Iris gathered up his clothes with her free hand, marched up to the door and tossed the bundle inside with a laugh. "God, you're pathetic. Put them back on." She walked back to the chairs and collected his coat, scarf and gloves, hurried back to the loft and threw them at him. "Here, you may as well have these as well."

She swung the door shut and padlocked it. David was openly sobbing now, hugging his coat tightly to his chest. Iris looked down at him. "Don't forget you've another surprise coming. I promise you'll love it."

He peered at her through the wire as she turned away. She retrieved her coat and shrugged it on then put his phone in one pocket and her gun in the other. As he watched helplessly, she collected his keys from the table and walked away.

David pushed his fingers through the wire mesh and shook it. "You're not really going to leave me here, are you?"

She glanced back, her face devoid of expression. "There's blankets and pillows in the corner plus bottled water and Gran's old commode. It evaded the house clearance. Can't think why. Oh, and I put a sleeping pill in your drink. It should keep you quiet for a few hours. I'll let the fire burn itself out."

He began pleading when she opened the door

leading back inside, shouted as her footsteps faded and cursed when he heard the front door close and the Porsche drive off.

¤

David was hoarse from calling for help but the cold wind that tunnelled through Paraffin Alley's narrow street and washed up and over the parapet caught his cries and rendered them impotent as it carried them into a cement grey sky. He was fully dressed now, coat buttoned, scarf wrapped around his neck, ears, nose and mouth. The tips of his fingers, even though they were inside fleeced leather gloves, were beginning to grow numb. He had cocooned himself within the blankets. They protected him from the worst of the cold but the ice droplets in the air were beginning to settle on the surface and would quickly soak through. David was becoming increasingly drowsy. It was the tablet that bitch had slipped him.

He cursed her for the thousandth time and curled up on the cold stone floor of the loft, a shiver accompanying every breath.

CHAPTER 36

The taxi pulled up outside Cellar Vie on the dot of eight. Eddie peered out and saw Iris silhouetted in the doorway. "Right. She's there. I'll see you back at the Grosvenor, nine thirty at the latest. Sure you've got the number? Ring me if you're going to be late. OK?"

"Will do." She leaned across the seat to kiss him. "Love you."

"Love you too."

Iris stepped forward and gave Eddie a cheery wave. She watched the taxi pull away before turning to Joanna and hugging her. "It's lovely to see you. I'm so glad you could come. Is Eddie picking you up too?"

"No. He's going to the Grosvenor to have a few drinks with Warren. I'll order a taxi to take us back there, pick him up, carry on to Didsbury where we get out, then you go onto Poynton. Is that OK?"

Warren obviously hadn't updated her. That made life easier. Iris rubbed her hands together. "That's fine. Brrr. It's freezing out here. Why aren't you wearing a coat?"

Joanna glanced down at her cashmere sweater

and trousers. "Didn't bother. This is warm enough for nipping in and out of a taxi."

Iris gave her a bright smile. "Let's get inside then."

Cellar Vie had a stylish interior, with concealed lighting, Art Nouveau artwork and walls criss-crossed with wine racks. They chose a table next to a warm radiator. Iris hung her coat on the back of her chair, smoothed down the skirt of her Biba dress and smiled brightly. "I'll get the drinks in. My treat, remember? What d'you fancy?"

Joanna thought. "Well, I like sparkling wine..."

"Me too." Iris took her purse from her bag. "I'll get a bottle of Asti Spumante." She made her way to the bar.

Joanna rested her chin in her hand and studied Iris as she waited to be served. She seemed different from the girl at the wedding reception, even taking into account the drama of the evening. She had a hard edge to her. Joanna felt ill at ease. She glanced at her watch. It was nearly quarter to eight. Thank goodness she wasn't staying long.

"Here we are." Iris arrived back at the table with two champagne flutes. The bartender followed, holding an ice bucket containing the wine. Iris thanked him and took her seat. She filled the glasses and put the bottle back.

Iris wrinkled her nose after a sip. "Oh, I love those little bubbles. The first time I had real champagne was when I first met David. He took me for a meal in a really expensive restaurant."

Joanna glimpsed a shadow scoot across her features. Iris took another sip then suddenly said, "What was he like when you were living with him?"

Joanna groaned internally. This was the line of questioning she'd been dreading. "Well, to be honest, we didn't live together long."

"But you did live with him for a while though. How long did you go out with him beforehand?"

Joanna moved in her seat, feeling exposed. She was surprised that David had told Iris anything about their relationship, or that Iris would want to know more but there again she supposed it was inevitable. Two women. One man. A shared history. She took a deep breath. "It was a bit of a whirlwind romance. We met at a party, dated for a couple of months then he asked me to move in with him so I did. We lived together for a few weeks. That was all."

"Why did you split up?" Iris reached for the bottle and replenished their glasses.

Joanna picked the simplest response. "It didn't work out."

"Obviously." This was like getting blood out of a stone. She smiled. "Come on, Joanna, you're not drinking."

Joanna reached for her glass and glanced at Iris. She was staring at her with a look that was anything but friendly. It fell away when Iris held up her own glass. "A toast. To the future."

They clinked glasses.

"So, go on then, why did you split up?" She leaned forward, her pose rigid, and fixed her

273

eyes on Joanna.

Why was this so important to her? Joanna kept her voice light. "Look, Iris, my relationship with David has nothing to do with you or yours. We're different people."

It was obvious Joanna wasn't going to elaborate. Iris traced the side of her glass, the condensation chilling her fingertip. She kept her gaze there. "He told me the other day that he still loves you."

Joanna sat back in shock. It was an accusation, spoken in a voice spiked with venom.

"Do you still love him?" Iris's eyes lifted to Joanna's. "Well, do you? Even though you're with Eddie now?"

Joanna had heard enough. "Look Iris, I didn't come here for this. I'm sorry but I think I'm going to go."

To Joanna's consternation, Iris's face crumpled and she buried it in her hands. Joanna sat for a moment, unwilling to leave her like this.

Iris sobbed fake tears and mentally kicked herself. She'd gone too far. She was ruining everything. She raised her head with a loud sniff. "Joanna, I'm sorry. I love David so much and I thought perhaps you could shed some light. You know? Help me understand why he's like he is with me. I didn't mean to upset you. Please don't go." Her voice rose as she pleaded. She was beginning to attract attention.

Joanna leaned forward. She kept her voice low and calm. "Iris, I'll stay but please, no more about David and me. It's in the past and that's where it's going to stay. If you're unhappy with him, then leave. Walk away."

Iris clamped her teeth together until her jaw ached. She would say that – she'd have a clear playing field then. Although Iris no longer loved David, it didn't alter the fact that he and Joanna had deceived her and Eddie. Miss Green Dress, all loved up at the wedding. Ooh! Eddie, it's our song. Two faced lying cow. Only days after seeing David, she was shagging him. Iris beat down rising anger.

She relaxed and gave Joanna a wan smile. "Thank you. I didn't mean to get emotional. When were you going to ring for a taxi?"

Joanna glanced at her watch. It was quarter past eight. "May as well do it now, before it gets busy. We'll pay for our part of the journey, of course."

Iris waited until the bartender directed Joanna to the pay phone then delved into her bag. She brought out a teaspoon and a small plastic bag. Inside was a Zopiclone tablet, crushed to a fine powder. She glanced around furtively, then reached for Joanna's glass, moved it to her lap and stirred in the powder before sliding it back on the table. She topped it up with Asti.

Joanna rejoined her. "They're getting busy already but I've managed to book one for nine fifteen."

"Good. Look, I'm really sorry about what happened before. Just a bit of a wobble." She upended the bottle over Joanna's glass to show it was empty. "Whoops! Shall we get another bottle? We've got time."

Joanna glanced at her watch. "OK. But let me get this."

Iris held a palm out. "Certainly not. I said tonight was my treat."

The drug took an hour to act, even less with alcohol. She had to keep Joanna awake until they got back.

¤

The taxi driver watched the two women approaching him. One was stumbling, clinging on to the other. He frowned at Iris. "She's not going to throw up is she? I'm not taking you if she is."

"No. She's on medication." Iris gave him a sweet smile. "They've reacted with the drink. She'll be fine once I get her home."

He waited until Iris settled Joanna in the back. "You're going to Poynton. Via..." He glanced at his itinerary. "...the Grosvenor Hotel and Didsbury Village?"

Iris sat forward. "Actually, there's been a change of plans. Can you take us straight to Didsbury Village?"

"Not a problem. Where do you want dropping off?"

A note of irritation crept into her voice. "Anywhere. The junction of School lane and Wilmslow Road will do. Can you hurry please."

He nodded and turned back to the front.

¤

David woke and shifted under the thick blankets. He lifted his head, remembering where he was. The bulkhead light was on. He shielded his eyes from the glare. The door from the attic opened. Iris staggered in with Joanna. David sat up. Joanna looked completely out of it, her head flopping to the side, her feet tripping over each other. He watched, open mouthed.

He found his voice when they reached him. "Joanna! Iris, what the fuck are you doing?"

Her voice was cold and flat. "I said I was bringing you a surprise. Here it is."

He shook his head in disbelief. "You're quite mad, do you realise that? First you kidnap me. Now her. Why? Just tell me why then we can sit down and talk it through and work out how to make things better."

"I don't want to make things better. I don't love you any more. Maybe I never did. Maybe it was lust but lust doesn't last, does it." She wrinkled her nose. "No, I'm wrong there. What did you say the other night? The old spark was still there? You both met up for sex? That suggests lust does last. Sometimes."

"Iris, I lied. I never had sex with her. We never even met up. I only said it to hurt you. I'm telling the truth, for fuck's sake. The one and only time I've seen her was at the reception. Please, Iris, think about what you're doing. It's not too late. Just open the door and let me out."

He rattled it loudly, "I won't say a word to anyone. I promise. We'll just forget it ever happened."

"Shut up. You're lying to save your skin. Stand back." The gun appeared. "Don't think I won't shoot you, David. Now, move away. She's had the same tablet I gave you. I can hardly hold her up."

He stepped back until he was against the wall. Joanna gently swayed as Iris took an arm away to get the key from her bag. The padlock opened with a quiet click. She removed it and cocked the revolver. "Now, push the door open then step away. No tricks."

David obeyed but as she put her hand behind Joanna to push her in, he grabbed his chance and sprang towards her. Iris panicked. Her trigger finger convulsed. The gun went off. David shrieked and threw himself to one side. This time the bullet zapped into the ground near his feet and ricocheted harmlessly away. Iris dropped the gun but recovered quickly, put both hands flat against Joanna's back and shoved her through the doorway, where she tripped over David. Her forehead smacked the wall. She collapsed like a rag doll.

Iris slammed the door and linked the padlock through the retainer. She was breathing heavily. She picked up the gun and looked at David. "You've got her now. You can do what you want with her. She's all yours. You've got all the time in the world. Consensual sex or rape? I'm not bothered. You never were. You certainly have your own definition. Do what you want with her. She's soiled goods anyway. She's nowhere near good enough for Eddie, just like you're nowhere near good enough for me. He'll never go near her again when he finds out but he'll probably pay you a visit."

She thrust the gun and the key deep into her pocket and walked off.

David grabbed on to the door and heaved himself up. "Iris, stop. You can't leave me here."

She looked back at him impassively.

He pressed his hands flat against the wire. "When are you coming back?"

"Who said I was?" She exited through the door and the bulkhead light went out, plunging the terrace back into darkness.

CHAPTER 37

Joanna was in that sweet place between sleep and wakefulness. She curled into Eddie, her leg on his thighs and her arm on his chest. She lifted her hand to his cheek. Instead of a smooth beard, she touched rough bristles. It jerked her fully awake.

She opened her eyes. David's face was looming over her. "Jesus Christ. You!" She sat up in shock, pushed their blankets back and propelled herself away from him, her heels scrabbling against the hard floor. She stopped when her back hit the wall. She gaped at him. "Where am I? What are you doing here? What's happening?"

David shuffled towards her on his hands and knees. He stopped in front of her and sat back on his heels. He kept his voice steady. "We're at Iris's house, Joanna. On the roof. This is a pigeon loft and, it's only a rough guess mind, we've been kidnapped."

His attempt to lighten the heavy atmosphere fell flat. She screwed her face towards the grey dawn filtering through the wire. "Kidnapped?

What do you mean kidnapped? Who's kidnapped us? Why would anyone...?"

"Be quiet and listen."

She covered her mouth with her hands, eyes wide.

"Iris brought me here yesterday afternoon. She locked me in at gunpoint then said to expect something else. I had no idea she meant you."

Joanna had stopped listening when he said gunpoint. She stared at him without blinking.

He caught her hands and lowered them to his knees. "Iris brought you here last night. It was late. I tried to stop her. The gun went off. Didn't you hear it?"

Joanna shook her head.

"Can't say I'm surprised. You were completely out of it. Anyway, Iris pushed you inside and you hit your head against the wall. She'd drugged you. Same as she did me." He stopped and searched her face. "Are you getting all this?"

Finally she blinked and wrenched her hands away. The cold was seeping inside her. She pulled the sleeves of her sweater over her hands and tucked them under her armpits. Her eyes were fixed on him, wide and unblinking.

"Are you listening? Joanna, can you understand me?"

Finally, she spoke hesitantly. "I was at Cellar Vie with her last night. She wanted to thank me for looking after her last Saturday." She took a deep breath and rubbed her forehead, wincing as she touched a lump.

She was talking to herself now. "I called a taxi

to go to Poynton. We were supposed to collect Eddie on the way, then go onto...Oh. Eddie will be frantic! David, what are we going to do?"

David rose to his knees to comfort her but she batted his arms away and went on, her voice rising. "I don't remember anything after that. It's like it's been erased. Oh my god. This can't be happening. Not again. Not now."

David didn't understand what she meant and he didn't care. He only wanted to know how long it would be before Iris came to her senses.

¤

The morning limped by. To pass the time and stretch her legs, Joanna paced up and down, ignoring David's eyes following her.

Everything that related to the original function of the loft had been stripped out. The construction was of hardwood bolted to the wall that separated them from the adjoining property. Joanna gathered more information as she looked around. The sides and front, including the door, was thick industrial galvanised wire, the door secured by a heavy duty padlock. The loft was solidly built, impossible to break out of.

Inside, to their right was the commode. Next to it was a toilet roll and a plastic bag, obviously for used toilet paper. They had six small bottles of water, two small pillows and the two blankets they had around them.

With endless time on their hands, they drifted in and out of conversation until it naturally turned to their relationship. Their breaths threw out pale clouds that hung in the air before melting away.

David brought up the subject. "You broke my heart when you left me."

Her retort was thrown at him. "No, I didn't. Don't confuse your heart with your ego."

David shrugged and pushed himself up against the wall, grimacing from the stiffness in his legs and back. "Can you tell me something? The truth?"

Joanna raised her eyebrows. "I don't think my honesty's ever been in doubt."

"Fair comment."

"Go on then."

"This person you're with now..."

"He's called Eddie."

"This person you're with now..." He acknowledged her twisted smile. "...When he came with you to collect your stuff that day, were you seeing him before you left me?"

"No, certainly not." Her reply was crisp.

"Well, what the fuck was he doing with you then?"

"How much of the story d'you want?"

"Enough for a satisfactory answer."

Joanna rested against the wall by David's shoulder, hugged her knees to her chest and laid her chin on the edge of the blanket.

"When I left you, I booked into a hotel. I met a very nice, very kind businessman from the States. We saw quite a lot of each other over the week I was there. No." She anticipated the look he gave her, "Not like that. He was very fatherly and felt sorry for me. I'd been made redundant just before I met you, don't forget, so I was unemployed and temporarily homeless. Eddie was with him. To cut the story short, he offered me a job in New York which I accepted. On the day we were flying out, he asked Eddie to drive me to your house to get the rest of my things."

David broke in, "So that's why you took your visa. That was for our holiday to New York."

She shrugged. "It was fortuitous."

"But you just vanished. Samantha didn't know where you were. Or so she said."

She rested her head against the hard wall, moving it side to side to let the rough brickwork pluck at her hair. "No, she didn't know. Not until later."

"So, are you still in New York?"

"No."

"Where are you living now?"

She shrugged.

"Not saying, eh?"

She didn't reply.

"OK. I get that. So there was nothing going on between you and him."

"No. I told you."

"Well, he seemed to think there was."

She turned her head a fraction.

"I was watching from the window when you left. I remember every detail. You were upset. He put his arm around you. D'you remember?"

A warm flame fanned her heart. "Yes."

"I could see his face. It was obvious, the soppy

look on it. Vomit inducing."

Joanna's face softened. That was their beginning.

"So why are you over here? Are you moving back?"

"No. I came over for Samantha's wedding and to put my flat on the market."

"Your flat?"

"Yes. The one I was living in when we met."

"I thought it was rented. So you lied to me."

"No, I never mentioned it. You made an assumption. I didn't correct you. Actually, I rented it out as soon as I moved in with you."

David glanced at her with grudging admiration. "Fair play to you."

"You and me, our relationship. It was too sudden, too fast. You never let me draw breath. I wanted the security of knowing that if it didn't work out for us, I still had a home I could eventually go back to. No doubt if I'd sold it when I moved in with you, you'd have tried to get your hands on the proceeds to further your ambitions."

"You must have had a very low opinion of me to think that."

"I'd have been right though, wouldn't I?"

David pulled down the corners of his mouth. "Probably."

There was a moment of reflection before they laughed together.

"I see you've bought premises in Didsbury Village. How've you managed to pull that off?"

His lip curled. "You're not the only one who

wants to keep things private."

"Touché. I bet you didn't come by the money honestly."

He opened his eyes wide, a picture of innocence, then shrugged to dismiss the accusation.

"Is this Iris's house?"

"It was. She inherited it. I sold it for her but she had a spare key."

"Where are we?"

"Paraffin Alley."

"So, we're still in Didsbury." Joanna stopped and cocked her head to glance at him. "This is one of the most expensive roads around here. That's why you're with her. She must be a very rich young lady."

"It fetched a good price, yes. Sold it to a builder to convert into flats. Win, win all the way."

Joanna looked hopeful. "Any chance he'll be round to do some work on it?"

David shook his head. "Not until Spring."

She slumped back. "Why has she brought me here? She said that you told her you still loved me but that's not my fault..."

"Ah. Now. it might be mine." David gave her an apologetic look. "We had a row the other night. That's when I told her. But I went a bit too far."

"How far is too far, David?"

A pause. "I embellished it a bit. I told her we'd seen each other." Another pause. "Actually, I told her we'd spent the night together." A longer pause. "In a hotel."

Joanna struggled to her feet away from him, her face pinched with anger. "Oh, you dickhead. Why the hell did you say that?"

David joined her, stretched his legs and leaned against the wall. "To upset her. It just came out in the heat of the moment. I should have known better, after her funny turns."

"What funny turns?"

"Well, these days, when she gets upset, she goes mental and generally attacks me with whatever she's got to hand. It usually doesn't last long. But this time..."

Joanna's face bleached white. "Are you telling me now that she's dangerous, that she might do something?"

He opened his arms wide, circled his eyes around the loft and back to her. "Hello?"

"David, you said she had a gun. If she means to harm us, we have to get out of here."

"No kidding."

"Will you stop being so flippant? She's your bloody girlfriend. What's she likely to do?"

"How the hell should I know? She walked out on me after that argument but she got in touch later and asked me to meet her here so we could talk. When we got up here she pulled the gun on me. The bleeding thing went off. Seems to be a habit of hers. I nearly shit myself." He pointed to the bullet casing embedded in the brickwork.

Joanna swore and covered her eyes with her hands. He noticed they were shaking. They fell into an uneasy silence. David put his fingers through the cage and rattled it manically. He began to shout for help, louder and louder until his voice cracked.

Joanna tutted. "For God's sake, shut up. You said it's an empty house. No one will think the noise is coming from up here."

David rounded on her. "You got any better ideas?"

Joanna slumped down to the ground again and spread the blanket over her. She clutched it to her chin.

He sank down beside her. "Me neither. I'm sodding freezing."

"Here." She shuffled against him and combined their blankets. They huddled together in silence for a while. Finally, she spoke, "Eddie will be worried sick."

David looked at her. "Joanna, I'm truly sorry for getting you in this mess."

She dropped her head. "So you should be."

He tucked his arm around her. "Come on, at least we can keep warm. Iris must come back today, at some point. She's not going to leave us up here another night. Well. That's if she remembers we're here."

Joanna's face turned to him slowly, a look of horror on it. "What do you mean, if she remembers?"

"Well, sometimes she doesn't."

"So we could die here and no-one would know?"

David quipped, "Well, the builders would find us eventually."

Her eyes flashed and she responded through clenched teeth. "This isn't funny. You got me into this fucking mess. You'd better think of a way out..."

David's mouth dropped open in surprise. "Joanna Brooks. You said the 'F' word!"

"I save it for special occasions. Like when I'm locked in a pigeon loft with a narcissistic sociopath whose universe revolves around himself, his money and what's in his pants."

David grinned. "I knew you still loved me."

They fell into an empty silence. After a while, Joanna looked at her watch again.

Davis glanced over. "What's the time?"

"Nine-thirty."

He nodded dismally. He watched as she curled away from him and pulled one of the pillows under her head. There was no question that this was the result of one of Iris's funny turns but why was it lasting so long this time? Had this latest switch from Jekyll to Hyde become permanent? That was a scary thought with scarier implications.

The only upside was that Joanna was with him and even their situation and her attitude couldn't crush the effect she was having on him. He was aching to hold her, to kiss her. Perhaps, in the situation they were in, she might get carried away and the lie he had told Iris would become the truth.

He stared up at the sky and the nimbostratus clouds that promised snow. His body generated a violent shiver that travelled down from his head to his feet. He turned up the collar of his coat, tightened his scarf and shuffled down next to Joanna. If he ever got his hands on Iris he would beat the shit out of her.

That's if she ever came back.

He squeezed his eyes shut against this thought and tucked his head under the blanket.

CHAPTER 38

By ten o'clock on Saturday night Eddie was beginning to fret.

He shifted on the bar stool and tapped the corner of a beer mat on the counter. "Joanna should be here by now. She promised to ring me if she was going to be late."

Warren waved a hand dismissively. "Come on Ed, lighten up. You know what women are like. Probably still flapping their gums."

Eddie got off the stool. "No. She would ring. You know what we went through before. She knows I worry."

Warren became serious. "I know, Ed but that ain't going to happen again, is it? I'm sure she's OK. They both are."

"There is something wrong, I'm telling you. I can feel it. I don't trust Iris." He strode out to the reception desk. "Still no call for me?"

The receptionist smiled patiently. "No, Mr Conlan. I said I'd come and get you."

"OK. Thank you." He walked back to the bar and shook his head at Warren's questioning look. "It's nearly ten, Warren. There's something wrong. I'm going to ring Cellar Vie."

He turned on his heels and marched back to reception. Ten minutes later, he returned, face creased with worry. "They said two women left at a quarter after nine, after ringing for a taxi."

"Description?"

"A tall blonde, a small brunette. It's them, Warren."

"You can't be sure."

"I'm telling you. They gave me the number of the cab company. I've just rung them. They confirmed a telephone booking for a fare to Poynton via the Grosvenor and Didsbury from the Cellar Vie tonight and the pick up was nine-fifteen. Jesus, Warren, what the hell's going on?"

Warren shrugged helplessly. "Maybe it wasn't them after all. Maybe they've decided to walk back for some fresh air? They could be here any minute."

The suggestion offered a grain of hope. "But Joanna didn't bring a coat or anything and it's a damn cold night. Right. I'm going to walk up there now anyway, Just in case. I might meet them if they're on foot. You stay here in case they show."

Warren nodded and patted Eddie's shoulder reassuringly but his face clouded as he watched him leave. He hadn't told him that Iris had left David and was staying here. Iris had asked him not to. But now a thought occurred to him. They would have found out anyway when the cab got here because Iris would have had to get out, so why the secrecy?

Warren was beginning to suspect that there was a side to Iris he didn't know. He was beginning to think that Eddie's gut feeling might be right.

¤

Eddie's walk to and from Cellar Vie had been fruitless, not that he'd harboured any real hope of seeing them. When he got back to the Grosvenor, Warren came clean about Iris's situation. Eddie stifled his anger. Now wasn't the time. He phoned the flat, in case Joanna had been dropped off there. Warren rang Iris's house, in case she had gone home. Both calls went through to the answerphone. They tried again, hoping that repeated ringing would produce a different result. It didn't. Eddie rang the police but, as he expected, he was told it was too soon to start worrying and to ring again after twenty four hours if she hadn't shown.

Eddie left Warren and arrived back at the flat at two thirty in the morning. He checked that Joanna wasn't there, then drove to David's house in the rental car. The Porsche was in the driveway but no amount of ringing the bell or banging the door produced anything, except irate neighbours.

He ordered Warren to ring him, whatever the time, if he heard from Iris.

Now, trapped in a vacuum of helplessness, Eddie was despairing. He was reminded, yet again, of how much he loved Joanna. He spent the night on the sofa, sleeping only for minutes at a time, praying that she would walk in at any second with a rational explanation.

At 7am, the phone rang. Eddie shot out of his seat to answer it.

"Ed, it's me." Warren's voice was cracked from lack of sleep. "I've not heard anything. I thought to ring David's real estate office when it opens. See if he's there. If he knows anything."

Eddie nodded at the phone. "Good idea. Thanks Warren. Let me know, OK?"

"Will do. What about you? Did you get any sleep? I know I didn't. Got any more ideas?"

"No to everything. I'll ring the police again."

Eddie ended the call. He stared into space for a moment then shook himself and went into the kitchen to make coffee. Such a normal task was soothing. When he walked back into the living room, he set the mug down and reached for the phone.

¤

Warren rang the estate agency and left a message asking David to ring him urgently on the number he dictated to the machine. The preset message said they opened at nine am. There was nothing else he could do until his call was returned. He showered and dressed, made a drink then, at eight-fifteen, went down for breakfast.

He was back in his room by eight forty-five. At five past nine, the phone rang. His heart jumped.

"Hello? Is that Warren?"

"Yes. Speaking."

"This is Suzanna from David Phillips Estate Agency. I'm returning your call. David's not here but I'm expecting him any minute. Can I help or do you need to speak to him personally?"

"Iris has gone missing, Suzanna. She went out for a drink last night with Joanna, a friend of mine, and they never returned. I want to know if David knows where they are."

"Oh my god. That's dreadful." There was a gasp then Suzanna's voice rose. "Have you called the police?"

"They couldn't help last night. Joanna's boyfriend's ringing them again now."

"OK. I'll get David to call you as soon as he gets here. He shouldn't be long. Let me know if there's anything I can do to help."

"Will do. Thanks, Suzanna. You're a doll."

¤

"Ed? I've just spoken to Suzanna at the real estate office. David's not there yet. She's going to get him to ring as soon as. Jesus, you don't think he's caught up in this as well? What did the police say?"

"They took a statement over the phone. Said they'd get back to me."

"Great."

"You know the drill, Warren. They won't budge from procedures. Look, I can't just hang around here waiting. I'm going to go to the agency. I'll pick you up first. Are you ready?"

"I'll be outside."

"OK. If he's still not shown, we'll go back to his house."

¤

They were back at the flat by eleven thirty. They had drawn blanks everywhere. In Bramhall, David hadn't appeared. Suzanna tried his home number and mobile phone several times. They left after eliciting her promise to ring Joanna's flat if she had any news. In Poynton, the Porsche was still in the driveway but there was still no answer from the house. David's whereabouts was becoming as much of a mystery as the two women.

Warren passed the time making tea and toast while they waited impatiently for a call back from the police. He carried the tray into the living room, set it on the coffee table and handed Eddie a mug. He took a slice of toast and said thoughtfully, "It's weird, all this. It's like they got in the cab last night and got spirited away somewhere else."

There was silence for a minute before Eddie slammed his cup down. Warren jumped.

"That's it. Jesus. Why didn't I think of it? I'm going soft. Thanks Warren." He stood and marched to the phone. Warren looked baffled as Eddie picked up one of the notes spread across the sideboard. He dialled the number and stood waiting for the connection, his foot tapping furiously. "Come on, come on, come on. Hi. I rang you last night asking about a fare from Cellar Vie in Manchester to Poynton at a quarter after nine. Is there any chance I could speak to the driver who picked them up? Is he? Do you think I could speak to him now? It's urgent." He put his hand over the mouthpiece and spoke to Warren. "He's there. The driver. He's just finished his shift. They're getting him."

Warren nodded, unclear what Eddie was doing.

Eddie waited. "Hi. Yes. You picked up two young ladies last night. One about five-six, blonde, wearing jumper and trousers. The other about five, five-two. Black coat. Ah. You remember." He fell silent, lips pressed together for a few moments as he listened. "Thank you. Thank you. You've been really helpful."

He put the receiver down and turned to Warren. "The fare was originally to come to us, then Didsbury then Poynton. Apparently the blonde was almost out of it. When he set off, the other girl told him to take them straight to Didsbury Village instead. When they got there, he dropped them off at the junction of School Lane and Wilmslow Road and headed off for another fare." Eddie remained standing. "We know they didn't come here but if Joanna wasn't able to walk far, it must have been somewhere close by."

It was Warren's turn. He threw his toast down and broke in, his voice excitedly loud. "I knew I'd been here before." He sank back on the sofa and wrinkled his face. "I came here on Monday night, to Didsbury. Iris invited me. David was away."

Eddie stared. "What are you talking about?"

"Listen." Warren was agitated. "Iris gave me the address to give the cabby. He dropped me off there. She had a key. Took me up to a flat roof."

"Warren."

"Let me finish, will you? There was a pigeon coop there. Like a cage. Massive, it was. The road was called..." He dropped his head back against the sofa and pressed his fist to his forehead as he struggled to remember.

"Come on Warren."

"It was a long road. Old terraced houses down one side. Brick wall on the other."

"The road, Warren. What was the road called? Think!"

"I'm trying to. It was something like Gasoline Alley. No."

"Petroleum Alley?"

"No." Warren jumped to his feet. "Paraffin Alley! That was it. Paraffin Alley."

Eddie grabbed the car keys. "There's an A to Z in the car. Come on."

CHAPTER 39

Iris woke suddenly. It was Sunday morning. She put her hands to her mouth, ran in the en-suite and was sick. After, she sat on the tiled floor and rested her hot cheek on the cold rim of the toilet bowl.

When the nausea passed, she walked weakly back to bed and curled up under the duvet. One eye peeked at the clock. It was nearly ten. David would be at work. He should have woken her this morning. She'd have made him some breakfast.

Iris fell asleep again. When she next woke, it was quarter past eleven. She made herself get up, took two painkillers, showered then threw on her jeans and a cowl neck jumper before making her way down stairs to the kitchen. She felt like her brain had been through a mincer. She opened the fridge to get a bottle of water. There should have been a pack of six in there. Now there wasn't. She'd only bought them the other day.

Then Iris remembered. She didn't live here any more. She'd left David. She was staying at the Grosvenor. Slowly, she sank to her knees. How could she forget that? What was happening to her?

More recollections followed, as they always did these days, marching in line, so swiftly she could hardly catch them up.

Grump's gun.

Shots.

David.

Joanna.

The pigeon loft.

Iris folded until her forehead was touching the floor. No no no no no no. She didn't. Surely she wouldn't. She gripped the fridge door, pulled herself up and stumbled into the hall, where her coat was flung over the bannister. David's mobile phone, big as a brick, was in one of the deep pockets. Grumps' gun and a padlock key were in the other. She picked the gun out carefully and examined the chamber with shaking hands. There were two bullets missing. She closed her eyes tightly.

The final memory was the wrecking ball. Her body took the full impact. She fell against the wall. David and Joanna were locked inside the pigeon loft. They had been since yesterday. It must have been freezing last night.

They might have hypothermia. They might be dead.

Iris hammered her fists against her skull. No no no no no no. She had to go back straight away. She struggled into her coat, returned the gun to her pocket, grabbed the Porsche keys from the table, ran out to the car and flung herself inside it. She remembered driving it here last night from Surprise View. She gripped the wheel and looked at the clock on the dashboard. It was half past eleven. She started the engine and the car moved forward obediently, gravel spraying like shrapnel from the back wheels as she accelerated and turned sharply out of the driveway.

¤

Joanna hadn't moved in her sleep. She had her back to David and the blankets that had been draped over them had somehow collected around him, leaving her exposed. Her sweater was covered in frost and wisps of steam were rising as it absorbed what remained of her body heat.

David woke and looked at his watch, leaned over, pulled the blankets over her and spoke softly, his lips brushing her ear, his breath a cloud. "Joanna. It's nearly eleven."

She stirred and whispered, "Is it still Sunday?"

"Yes. We dozed off again."

She turned her head slightly. It brought her mouth close to his. It took her back to the days when she would wake every morning to his kiss.

David quietened his breath, not daring to move. Their lips were almost touching and she hadn't moved away. They remained like this until he spoke, placing the warmth of his words over her mouth. "You're remembering, aren't you? How it was. How we were." His hand travelled over her hips and rested lightly on the dip of her waist.

Joanna's face creased. She pulled back and struggled to stand. Her movements were slow, hampered by a lack of coordination. She fell against the wire, shivering violently. She turned to him, her words slurred. "I think I've got hypothermia."

He grinned and arranged the blankets around his legs, tucking his arms inside. "I saw a film once about that. Two people stuck in a snow drift. They took all their clothes off and wrapped their bodies around each other for warmth. I'm game, if you are."

Joanna could feel her breath slowing. "David. If we aren't found soon, we'll die."

He studied the whiteness of her face, the blue-tinged lips. He realised she was serious. Joanna sank back down clumsily. It took her a moment to focus on her watch. Ten past eleven. Her brain was fuddled and she knew she was close to losing consciousness. If she did, she might never wake.

She curled into a ball and she spoke suddenly, voice muffled, the words bleeding into each other. "You'd better come and join me but the clothes stay on."

He needed no second bidding. He lay back down behind her and arranged the blankets around them, tucking the ends under their bodies. She pulled his arms around her. She wasn't shivering as much now. Her heart sank. That was a bad sign. In minutes, she was asleep.

He stayed alert as long as he could, savouring

her closeness, inhaling the familiar scent of her skin and hair, wishing he could turn back the clock.

¤

A car pulled up. A door opened and shut. David jerked awake and turned towards the sound before kicking the blankets away and clambering to his feet. He gasped at the ice-knifed sharpness of the air. It had to be below freezing. He grasped the wire mesh, fixed his eyes on the access door and listened intently. For a while there was nothing. Then he heard stairs creaking, hurried steps coming nearer.

Iris appeared through the door. She was panting from the exertion. All the way here she had visualised two frozen, lifeless bodies but now she saw the reality. David, on his feet facing her, hands like claws poking through the mesh, very much alive, his face more thunderous than she had ever seen it.

She let the door go and ran towards him, in floods of tears. "Oh my God, oh Jesus, David I'm so, so sorry. I don't know what…"

"Get this fucking door open, Iris." David's voice was menacing. "We're dying here. Literally dying."

Panicking, Iris felt in her pocket for the key before looking around helplessly. "I don't know what I did with it."

"Iris." His voice was thick. "You'd better find it. Now."

She walked around the terrace, looked under

the fire bucket and scoured every inch of the loft. Finally, she ran to the door and flew down each set of stairs, looking desperately from left to right, choking on sobs. When she reached the hall, she spotted it in a corner. She scooped it up, raced back up the stairs, fell out onto the terrace and ran to the loft, dragging frozen oxygen into her lungs.

She fumbled with the lock. David was shouting now, shaking the frame, cursing. Finally, the key went in, the notch turned and the padlock sprang open. She freed it and fell back as David flung the door open.

He lunged forward, grabbed her throat and towered over her, spittle flying in her face as he roared. "You sick fuck. You stupid sick fuck. I could have died of hypothermia, do you realise that? You would have had my death on your hands. I'll make sure you end up behind bars, in prison or a mental home, I don't give a shit which. Give me my keys."

Iris clawed at his hand, tears blinding her. The roaring was back in her ears and with it a hot rage, an antithesis to the glacial cold. She remembered Grumps' gun, pulled it out of her pocket, used her thumb to cock it and pushed the nozzle into David's ribs. He relinquished his hold and stepped back, hands raised. "Iris, don't. This is murder. Please, I won't tell the police. I promise. Don't hurt me."

"Shut up David. Just shut up. I'm sick of your whining. I'm sick of your abuse and I'm sick of you. I gave you a whole night with the love of your life. Did you make the most of it? Did she reject you? That wouldn't stop you, would it? I found that out the hard way. You don't say no to David Phillips."

Iris stopped to draw breath. She looked past him to Joanna. The sight caught her short. Everything drained to the pit of her stomach. Joanna hadn't woken, despite the disruption. Was she still alive? She had to be. No-one was ever supposed to get hurt.

Iris forgot David and took a step towards her.

David saw his chance. He wrenched the gun and the keys from her, made a fist and punched her in the stomach.

Iris fell to her knees.

His finger snagged the trigger. The gun went off a third time.

Joanna's body jerked, pulled upwards by a marionette's string.

CHAPTER 40

Eddie parked as soon as they turned into Paraffin Alley. "Right. Which one is it?"

Warren peered out of the windscreen. "I'm not sure. It was dark when I came and Iris was waiting at the gate."

"Shit." Eddie climbed out and looked up at the nearest house. "Come on, Warren, you must have some idea. Was it here? In the middle? The far end?"

Warren joined him and his eyes travelled down the row of terraces, a frown on his face. "It could be that one." He pointed at a house three doors down. Eddie ran to it and pushed the gate open. As he mounted the steps to the front door, there was a gunshot. He stopped and looked up and around. "Where did that come from?"

Warren had already turned to the adjacent house. He pointed. "There. Up there."

Eddie leapt from the steps to the next house. He leaned on the sill to peer in. The windows were curtain-less, the room bare.

He turned to the door and turned the knob quietly. It opened. He waved to Warren. Together they entered the hall and checked each room. They mounted the first flight of stairs, searched. Mounted the second, searched.

They stopped at the third. Warren lowered his voice. "This leads to the attic and from there there's a small flight up to a kind of vestibule. There's a door there onto the roof terrace. That's where the pigeon loft is. They've got to be there."

"OK. Let's go."

They ascended slowly, treading lightly and continued up to the roof terrace. Eddie inched open the door. He looked back at Warren, indicated silence and looked out. David was standing in the middle of the terrace, his arms hanging by his sides. A gun was dangling from one hand, a mobile phone clutched in the other. His face was turned towards the pigeon loft. In front of him, Iris was on the floor, holding her stomach and keening piteously. Eddie stared into the loft. He could make out a shape under a blanket.

He stepped out, followed by Warren, who walked straight to Iris. He crouched down and put an arm around her shoulder.

If David heard them, he didn't show it or make an attempt to move. Eddie walked up to him, plucked the revolver from his hand and applied the trigger lock. He pushed it under his belt and held out his hand. "Give me your coat."

"What?" David stared blankly at him.

"I said give me your coat."

In a daze, David took his keys from the pocket, undid the buttons and shrugged it from his shoulders. Eddie caught it, elbowed him aside and continued to the loft. He was already shouting Joanna's name. Inside, he sank down and threw the ice encrusted blanket away from her. She was unconscious, her face and lips blue.

Eddie felt for a pulse and located a weak, slow beat in her neck. He lifted her so her head was against his shoulder and noticed a dark patch on her arm. He brushed his hand along it. There was fresh blood on his fingers.

He shouted to Warren. "Get his cellphone and ring for an ambulance. Dial 999. Tell them it's an emergency." He took off his jacket, wrapped it around her and covered her with David's coat. He closed his eyes and held her as tightly as he could.

David stared down blankly as Warren grabbed his mobile. Iris lifted her head and took in the scene. Eddie holding Joanna. David, face grey, eyes unblinking with a thousand yard stare. Warren, his back to her, speaking urgently into David's phone. She was overwhelmed. All this was of her doing and hers alone. She had abducted two people without a thought of the consequences. If she'd not remembered, if Eddie and Warren hadn't found them, they would have died. She would have been a double murderer.

Now she wept, for her madness and for the pain in her head, blinding her with its magnitude. She dragged herself to her feet and swayed for a moment before stumbling to the parapet, the heels of her palms pressed against her eyes.

Iris rested her forehead against the rough brick. She couldn't go on any more. There was only this left for her. She scrambled to get a foothold on the bricks, pushing the toe of her shoe into the gaps where the pointing had crumbled away.

Only David noticed. He watched as she began climbing. What was she doing? Was she going to kill herself? His face creased. What did it matter? He was sick of her, anyway.

He shouted at her. "Go on then, Iris. Do us all a favour. Jump."

Eddie looked up. Warren spun round.

Iris had reached the top. Warren caught her by the waist as she strained to pull herself over. She cried out in frustration and her fingers scrabbled to retain their hold.

"No you don't, Iris. You don't get to do this. Not on my watch." Warren lifted her off and staggered backwards until she was left clawing the air.

Iris turned and wailed when he set her down, her hands smacking his face in frustration. "Let me go. Let me do this, please..."

Warren's arms encircled her, trapping her inside them. He held her tightly until only her shoulders were moving with silent tears. He rocked her, shushing her softly. When her body became limp, he looked down. She had passed out. Pain was ingrained on her face, lines etched into the soft skin. She looked old. Worn and defeated.

He looked at David, hatred oozing from every pore. 'You're a stinking piece of shit, do you know that?"

David gave Iris a fleeting glance before shifting his gaze to Warren. He held out his hand. "I'll have my phone back now."

Warren stared at his face. It held no expression, only an arrogance that Warren was aching to wipe off. Keeping hold of Iris, he let the mobile drop. Then he stamped on it with his heel, again and again, until it was in pieces.

David's eyes were like saucers as he stared at the shattered phone. "What did you do that for, you moron? That cost me two grand."

Warren tightened his arms around Iris. He was that close to beating the shit out of him but as a law man, he couldn't let himself.

The air shifted behind David. He turned and for the second time in his life saw Eddie's fist a second before it connected with his chin.

Warren nodded. "Thank you."

Eddie acknowledged him, stepped over David and walked back to Joanna. He knelt and gathered her in his arms again.

Warren sank down with Iris.

They waited in silence for the sound of sirens to shatter the iced stillness.

CHAPTER 41

When the ambulances arrived at the Infirmary, Eddie and Warren were directed to the waiting room. The girls were admitted for treatment. Joanna was lucky on two counts, the bullet had only caused a minor skin laceration and the hypothermia hadn't reached the critical stage.

Once she was made comfortable in a private room, Eddie was allowed to see her. Her wound had been treated and warm fluids administered directly into a vein to raise her temperature. There were hot water bottles wrapped in cloth around her and her colour was already returning to normal.

She was still unconscious. Once they were alone, Eddie pulled his chair closer, took her hand and stroked it with his thumb, planting soft kisses on her face and waiting for someone to tell him why she hadn't come round.

Dr Reynolds arrived, his white coat flapping behind him. "Quite honestly. Mr Conlan, I have no idea why. Her vital signs are functioning well. Respiration rate, oxygen saturation, systolic blood pressure, pulse rate, temperature are all normal. Of course, I can't rule out concussion. She does have a nasty bump on her forehead but not bad enough to render her unconscious for this long, if at all." Doctor Reynolds shifted his weight to his other foot. "Can I ask you a question? Has she been through any periods of great stress or emotional upheaval recently?"

Eddie smoothed his beard with one hand and the crease between his brows deepened.

"I take it that's a yes?"

He stood, walked to the window and gazed out. When he turned back to the room, he answered the Doctor's question. "Some things happened earlier this year. She was in danger and went through a rough time." He added humourlessly, "I was the cop trying to protect her."

"So why are you still with her?"

Eddie looked back at Joanna. "We fell in love."

They were silent for a minute. Dr Reynolds spoke again. "I'm not moving her to the main ward. I want her to have peace and quiet. Then we'll wait."

Eddie frowned. "What do you mean?"

"I think she's not ready to face the world just yet. I think what's happened now has triggered memories of whatever she went through before. I think her brain needs to process everything."

Eddie nodded. That made sense. He walked back to the bed, sat down and held her hand again. "Is there anything I can do?"

"Talk to her, play some of her favourite music, maybe. That sometimes helps."

Outside, Warren was standing with a pretty

staff nurse. They had listened while Eddie was talking and now she looked at Warren. "That is so romantic."

Warren flexed his arms. "I was there, you know, during the troubles."

"You were? How exciting. How come?"

"I'm a Deputy in South Dakota, USA."

Her eyes travelled over his physique. "Wow. Are you really? I bet you look great in your uniform."

Warren gave her a cheeky grin. "I bet you look great out of yours."

Eddie's voice interrupted him. "Warren, can I have a word?"

He winked at her and disappeared into the room.

"Warren, would you do me a favour, go to the apartment and pick up Joanna's cassette player and tapes?"

"Sure. Any particular ones?"

"She only packed a few. You may as well bring them all. They're on the breakfast bar. Here..." He tossed him the keys.

Doctor Reynolds broke in. "Right, better get on with my rounds. I'll pop in first thing in the morning."

Eddie nodded and thanked him. When he left, Warren walked to the opposite side of the bed and picked up Joanna's other hand.

Eddie looked at him. "Warren, what're you doing?"

"Just thought we could hold one each." He grinned sheepishly and gently laid it back down.

"Bad idea?"

"Warren."

"OK. I'm gone already."

Eddie shook his head and leaned over Joanna to kiss her brow. "This is the man you kissed. Do you remember, sweetheart? So you could pass him that message without detection?"

He searched her face. "When they brought you back to the cellar I did this..." He gently pressed his mouth on hers.."...and I said, now I'm the last man you kissed. Can we keep it that way?"

Eddie caught his breath. Had her expression changed? A tiny inflection of a smile? He moved close to her ear. "Joanna, sweetheart, if you can hear me, squeeze my hand." He looked down, holding his breath. Nothing. Looking back at her face, it was as it had been before. He must have imagined it.

He dropped his head and closed his eyes. He wouldn't move from here until she came back to him. He would stay here forever if he had to.

¤

Trish looked up at Doctor Reynolds. "So, what happens now?"

The doctor glanced down at the annotated notes he had been scribbling on his clipboard. "I'm sending her for an MRI scan."

"What's that?"

"It's a brand new and incredible piece of equipment. We only acquired it this year. Simply put, it's a machine that uses magnetic fields and radio waves to produce detailed images of the inside of the body. In Iris's case, the brain. It shows any abnormalities. Like a tumour."

Trish's face fell. "A tumour? Why do you think that?"

"I rang her GP earlier. Asked him about her medical history. That didn't raise any red flags but then he told me that during her last appointment with him, some weeks ago, she'd mentioned stress headaches and he'd been struck by her aggressive behaviour, quite at odds with the Iris he'd known since she was born. I suspect she might have a brain tumour and a scan will confirm if I'm right."

Trish looked at Iris, who lay lifeless on the bed. "How long will it take?"

"Between ten and twenty minutes."

Trish straightened and pressed her lips together. "If the results show she has, I hope it's not too late." She broke off.

"If the MRI detects the presence of a tumour, she'll be operated on immediately by our neurologist and his team. Don't worry. He's one of the best. She'll be in the safest possible hands."

Dr Reynolds smiled and patted her shoulder on his way out. Trish's face crumpled. She'd known nothing about this. Poor lamb. What a dreadful time she'd been having, what pain must she have been in?

She looked down at Iris's face, lined and troubled even as she lay unconscious. David Phillips hadn't helped things. His treatment of her had been despicable. Iris had gone from a sheltered life into the arms of a ruthless predator who had stolen her money, her innocence and her trust to further his own agenda.

Trish desired, more than anything else, that one day karma would visit him.

¤

Eddie stayed by Joanna's bedside for the rest of the afternoon, evening and through the night. He played music, talked to her and told her repeatedly how much he loved her.

Warren had stayed at the hospital too. Trish warmed straight away to the handsome young American. He had a cheeky smile, an honest face and a sincerity that she knew was genuine.

¤

The MRI scan revealed a large tumour pressing on Iris's frontal lobe. She was rushed into surgery for a craniotomy. Five hours later she was wheeled back to her room, where an anxious Trish was waiting. Mr Monroe, the neurologist, came with her. He told Trish that he had removed the whole tumour. A sample had already been sent by courier for a biopsy. The results would come through in two to three days.

When Mr Monroe left, Trish felt more cheerful. Warren was at the canteen and returned fifteen minutes later with paper cups of tea and pre-packed sandwiches. Trish took the tray so he could sit with Iris but he stopped short when he saw her. Half her head was shaved and a half moon flap of skin was stapled to the side of her scalp. He turned to Trish, distraught.

She smiled. "Warren, it's OK. The operation went well. They got all the tumour out. Look at her."

Iris was sleeping soundly. Warren saw the difference in her face. It was soft in repose, unlined, free from pain.

"They'll know in a few days whether it's malignant or benign. She'll be under for a few hours yet. Mr Monroe will be back in the morning to assess her." Trish stretched painfully and adjusted herself in the chair. "After that, we wait."

"I've got another week before I go home. I'll help you look after her."

"You're a good lad, Warren. Thank you for caring." Her chin wobbled and she turned quickly to find a tissue.

He felt awkward. Such events and depths of emotion were new to him. He patted Trish on her arm and said in a falsetto voice, "There, there, dear. Don't cry."

It sounded silly to his ears. He glanced at her. She glanced back. Their mouths twitched and they laughed together quietly.

CHAPTER 42

As dawn approached and the indigo sky was washed though with magenta, Eddie woke, stretched, leaned forward, kissed Joanna and whispered, "Good morning, sweetheart. Are you going to come back to me today?"

It had been a long night. He had kept vigil by her bedside throughout. Yawning, he lowered his head to rub the back of his neck.

"Eddie..."

His head shot up. She was awake. He wrapped his arms around her carefully, eager to feel her against him. "Oh sweetheart, I've missed you."

Joanna rested her head into his neck and breathed slowly and gently as she tried to place herself. "What am I doing here? Last I remember, I was locked in that place with David." She started to put her arm around his neck but winced and noticed the bandage on her upper arm.

"Careful. It's a gunshot wound but it's just a nick. It's not serious."

Joanna lay her head on his chest and took a few deep breaths. "I lost it a bit when David told me Iris had a gun. You know how I am about them after..."

He smiled and caught her hands. "Shhh. I know, sweetheart. Honestly, it's a flesh wound. There are no internal injuries. We heard the shot as we arrived. When we got up there, David was holding the gun. I think it fired accidentally. It's thanks to Warren we found you. Iris hasn't fared too well though. She was admitted with you yesterday."

Joanna's brows creased. "Yesterday?"

"Yes. You've been unconscious since we found you early in the afternoon. As well as your arm, you were suffering from hypothermia and shock."

"You're joking. Stupid remark. Of course you aren't. So it's Monday." Her brows rose. "Sorry? What's wrong with Iris?"

"They whisked her away for an emergency operation to remove a brain tumour. That's all Warren could tell me last night."

"That's dreadful. The poor girl. Maybe that affected her behaviour."

They were silent for a minute, then Joanna looked at him. "David?"

"He's alright, apart from his jaw."

"What happened?"

"I hit him."

"You hit him."

"He was being a prick."

"Fair enough."

"He came round and stormed off before the ambulances arrived."

She nodded, inhaled to speak, thought better

of it, closed her mouth for a moment then opened it again. Her words caught in her throat. "What frightened me most, up there, was that I was never going to see you again." Her voice broke. "After everything we'd already been through, it would have been so cruel."

Eddie pulled her to him. "Oh, sweetheart. Don't you think I was feeling the same? I love you. You're my life."

Joanna burst into noisy tears. Eddie reached for a box of tissues.

She scooped up a handful, pressed them against her eyes, blew her nose and smiled. "But we made it. Once again."

Then they were kissing hungrily.

¤

Trish woke with a start and looked at her watch. It was nearly eight. She glanced at Warren, gently snoring as he balanced on a chair, his torso spread across the foot of the bed. Iris was still asleep, her arms resting on top of the covers. Trish inhaled quickly and hissed at him. The fingers of Iris's left hand were twitching. Warren rubbed his eyelids open, blinked to clear his vision and looked at Iris. Her eyes were open and searching the ceiling in confusion. Slowly her gaze lowered. She could see she was in a bed but the room was strange and smelt of floor cleaner and antiseptic. Tubes and wires were protruding from her. She moved her eyes to the right. Trish was there, tears pouring down her face. She moved them to the left. Warren was there, looking equally emotional.

She must have passed away. They were mourning her. She glimpsed something in her memory, tucked behind a curtain of gauze. A wall. Rough brick, ice cold wind. Did she jump to her death? Her throat was sore, dry. Her fingers clawed the sheet and she turned to Trish in panic.

"Iris, it's alright. You're in hospital. You're safe." Trish leaned over and hugged her gently. She sank back in her chair and took her hand. "Warren rang me and told me everything that happened. You were admitted yesterday."

Memories were limping back, battle weary and slow. She looked at Trish in horror. It was hard to select the words to make a question. When she spoke them, they fell into each other. "What have I done?"

"Iris, don't speak, please, lovey. Just listen. You've been very ill for a long time. They found a tumour on your brain. You were rushed into theatre yesterday evening. They removed it." She looked into Iris's face to make sure she understood.

"Joanna?"

Trish gripped her hand. "Joanna's safe. She's in this hospital too. Eddie's with her."

Iris exhaled in relief then formed another word. "David?"

"David? Oh, he's alright. Iris, there's nothing to worry about there. All you need to do now is get well. The neurologist will be in to see you this morning. Until then, rest. Sleep if you want to."

Iris felt a soft calmness after Trish's assurances. She looked over to Warren and smiled. He moved up the bed and bent to kiss her forehead."Hi, babe."

She tried to chuckle. It almost worked.

He grinned. "You had us worried there for a while."

She closed her eyes, a smile floating on her face.

Trish and Warren exchanged looks of relief. Iris was responsive. She recognised them. He threw out a breath and said, "I'm starved, Trish. I'll nip down and get us a brew and a couple of bacon sarnies."

Trish lifted her eyebrows.

He shrugged modestly. "Well, you start to pick up the language after a couple of weeks."

¤

The neurologist was a tall Irishman with beetling brows and striking blue eyes. He strolled in, hands shoved casually in the pockets of his white coat. "Well, pleased to meet you again, Iris. Can you describe how you're feeling?"

She cleared her throat to reply. How did she feel? Weighed down by guilt for what she had done. Ashamed and alarmed by the depth and ferocity of her behaviour. She breathed in then spoke painfully slowly, enunciating each word and paraphrasing to save her strength.

Mr Monroe nodded slowly as she spoke. When she finished, he took his hands from his pockets and folded his arms. "Well, we got all the tumour out, I'm pleased to say. Frontal lobe tumours cause behavioural and emotional problems – it can make you think and act in all sorts of ways, completely alien to your normal self."

Iris glanced at Trish and Warren with a wan smile.

"There can be physical changes too." He went on, "but from what your friends here told me, they saw nothing that signalled that. So," He hesitated then continued, "If you did certain things that were, let's say, out of the ordinary, a little worrying even, I hope you understand why and not beat yourself up. You were having bad headaches though, I understand? How are they now?"

She blinked. That was why she felt different. "I've not got one." Her face broke into a happy smile.

Mr Monroe beamed. "Good. Delighted to hear it. Ditch the painkillers. They're no good for you if you eat them like Smarties. Now, you're slurring but that's normal – if it doesn't improve, we can arrange for you to see a speech therapist."

Iris relaxed against the pillows as he continued with a sensory assessment. Her fingers and feet and eyes responded well to stimuli. After that, he went through the hospital aftercare and a list of dos and don'ts for her convalescence.

Finally, he stood and shook her hand. "Well, Iris. Once we're satisfied with your progress, you can go home. Is there someone who can be with you?"

Trish lifted her hand. "That's all taken care of, Mr Monroe. She's moving in with me. I'm retired so I'll be there to look after her."

Warren piped up. "I'm helping too."

"Well, that's sorted. I'll leave you now to get some breakfast. You must be hungry."

Iris looked up at him, her voice tremulous. "Thank you Mr Monroe, for saving my life."

"Well, make sure you live your best one. With friends like yours, I think you will." Mr Monroe smiled at each in turn, winked at Iris and marched out.

A tear rolled down Iris's cheek from eyes that were growing heavy. As they closed, she whispered, "He's right. Thank you both."

Trish arranged the blanket around her and within seconds she was asleep. Trish flattened her hands on the bed and looked over at Warren. "One day, I hope she meets a wonderful man who'll fall in love with her, because she's Iris."

Warren nodded. "I'm sure that'll happen but for now, I hope she's done with David Philips."

Trish's face clouded. "I'll not let him near her, if he tries. You know, Warren, I hate that man with every fibre of my being for what he did to her. I wish he would get his comeuppance."

Warren smiled. Maybe he would.

¤

Dr Reynolds clapped his hands and rubbed them together briskly after examining Joanna. "Well, young lady, It's looking good. How are you feeling?"

"I feel fine, Doctor. I don't know what else to say. Apart from a bit of pain in my arm, I feel great, like I've had the best night's sleep ever."

"Good. Good." He grinned and landed his hands on his hips. "I see no reason to keep you any longer. You can go home this afternoon. The nurse will change your dressing before you go."

"Oh, that's great. Thank you Dr Reynolds."

As soon as he left, Joanna swung her legs onto the floor. Eddie rushed round the bed. "Careful. Don't stand too quickly, sweetheart. Head and shoulders last. Here." He placed his hands on her waist and she gripped his shoulders. When she was upright, he pulled her into an embrace and gently kissed her. As she sank into it, there was a cough behind them.

Warren walked in, a wide smile on his face. "Joanna! You're awake."

"Come on in Warren. Don't bother to knock."

He grinned at Eddie. "Sorry Ed. Old habits. Thought you'd like to hear the good news about Iris."

Joanna smiled in relief when he told them. "Oh, thank goodness."

Eddie helped her back into bed and she pulled the covers over her knees. "Warren, I'm being discharged this afternoon but I'd like to see Iris before we go. I mean, if she wants me to? I know her opinion of me. There's no love lost there."

"I can ask her, for sure but it was the tumour that made her behave like she did. Honest, Joanna, she's really the sweetest girl you could meet."

Eddie stepped in. "Joanna, I'm going to head back to the flat and pick up some things for you. If Iris wants to see you, you can go when we're on our way out. How does that sound?"

Joanna nodded. "Thanks, Eddie. Can you bring my jeans and the Arran jumper? It's the warmest one I brought. And my flat shoes?"

He nodded and reached for his car keys and jacket.

¤

"No. She must hate me." Iris looked like a rabbit caught in headlights.

Warren sat on the side of the bed and shook his head. He reached for her hand and pressed it between his. "Iris, my little honeypot, listen."

She pressed her lips together anxiously.

"I know Joanna well. She's not going to do or say anything to upset you. She's not like that. Anyway, she's fine. Well, apart from a gunshot wound, being drugged, locked up and suffering from hypothermia and shock."

Trish rolled her eyes. "Oh, Warren. For goodness sake!"

"No. Truth." Iris turned her head to her friend. "No more lies. Yes. OK."

Warren placed her hand back down, stood to

attention and saluted. "Right Ma'am. I'll take that message back to her."

Iris nodded.

Warren clicked his heels and made his way along the corridor and back down the stairs to Joanna's room. He remembered to knock. The room was empty. He hung around and eventually she appeared in her hospital gown, rubbing her wet hair with a towel.

She smiled brightly. "Hi Warren. Just been for a shower."

Warren marched up and gave her a hug. "Ah. My lovely lady's looking much better."

Joanna returned his hug with her good arm. "Thank you. OK. You can let me go when you're ready." After a few moments, she added. "Actually, now would be a good time."

She sat on the bed while Warren took the chair. "So what did Iris say?"

"She's worried about what you'll say."

"I'm not going to say anything. Iris was ill. She wasn't in control of her actions."

Warren held his hand up to stop her. "Let me finish. But she's said she'll see you."

Joanna sat back with a satisfied nod.

Warren kept Joanna company until Eddie returned, carrying a holdall. He set it on the bed and turned to Warren. "Can you go back and tell her Joanna will see her in a half hour?"

Warren rolled his eyes. "I feel like one of Iris's pigeons. Why don't you just strap a note to my ankle?"

They waited until he left then Joanna dressed

and packed the clothes she had worn on admission together with her music. Task completed, she turned to Eddie. "I discovered why Iris hated me so much. She found out I was David's ex and he'd told her that we'd met up and had sex a couple of days after Samantha's wedding."

Eddie's brows lifted. "He did what?"

Her jaw set. "He told her a pack of lies about us and she believed every word."

Eddie crossed his arms and frowned. "Joanna, while we're on the subject, can I ask you something that's been bothering me?"

"Of course. What is it?"

"While you were locked in with him, did he do anything to you? Don't be embarrassed to tell me. I need to know if he assaulted you. Sexually or physically."

Joanna rested her arms on his chest. "No. We had to huddle up together because of the cold but no, he didn't do anything."

Eddie's face relaxed.

"You're still the last man I kissed, so let's keep it that way."

His eyes widened. "You heard me last night?"

"From a galaxy far, far away." She tipped her head to one side. "Actually, there's something else I've been expecting you to say..."

Eddie thought for a minute then his face cleared and he grinned. "Ah. That. OK." He wrapped his arms around her and tutted. "Honestly, Joanna, I only have to turn my back for a minute and you get into trouble."

He felt the soft breath of her laugh on his neck. He rested his cheek on her head and closed his eyes. "We've come a long way since then, haven't we?"

Another warm breath, a soft kiss. "And we've got a lifetime yet."

CHAPTER 43

Joanna knocked on the door, opened it tentatively and poked her head round.

Iris's eyes widened. She gave her a hesitant smile. "Joanna. Come in."

Joanna stepped inside and shut the door quietly behind her. When she turned back, she noticed an attractive older lady, with bright shrewd eyes and a welcoming smile, sitting by the bed.

She stood to shake Joanna's hand. "Pleased to meet you, Joanna. I'm Trish, Iris's friend."

"Best friend." Iris corrected. "Joanna, how are you? I'm so..."

"Iris, How are you? I'm so..."

They spoke at the same time, words colliding. Iris's face began to crumple. "So sorry."

Trish placed a soothing hand on her arm.

Joanna sat down and took a deep breath. "I'm absolutely fine, Iris. I've been discharged and we're on our way home so I won't keep you long. I wanted to see you, to tell you how glad I am that your operation was a success." Impulsively, she leaned over the bed and wrapped her arms around her. She felt Iris lean into her, a passive signal to continue. "I'm so very sorry for everything you've had to go through, with your illness, with David, with me showing up and I know it was the tumour that made you act like you did."

Iris pulled away and looked up at her. Tears were rolling down her cheeks. "You. Always so kind." She was too emotional to say more.

"Iris," Joanna sat back in her seat and took her hand. "In case you still believe what David said, I need to set the record straight. You asked me at the Cellar Vie why I left David. It was because he was violent."

Iris's eyes were big in her face. "You too?"

"Yes. And another thing. The one and only time I saw him was at the wedding, Well, apart from..." She saw remorse crowding into Iris's face and hurried on. "I could never be unfaithful to Eddie. I love him too much. David's a cruel and selfish man. He's not capable of real love. He certainly didn't love me. I hope you believe me. I hope that you've finished with him and never let take him back, not even if he begs you."

Trish spoke vehemently. "Just let him even try. I'm still furious he got his hands on so much of her inheritance."

Iris frowned. "Too late, Trish. Have to move on. Joanna?"

"Yes?"

"You going to the police?"

"No, of course not!"

Her relief was only temporary. The frown

became deeper and infused with fear. "David will."

Joanna shook her head with a smile. "Ah, but no-one knows he was there. When the ambulances arrived, there was only us. You, me, Eddie and Warren. David can't prove anything else."

Iris blinked and understood. "After everything, you'd protect me?"

"Yes."

Iris sank into the pillows, overwhelmed with gratitude. "Thank you."

There was a knock. Eddie's face appeared, "OK to come in?"

Trish stood, beckoned him over and shook his hand. "I'm Trish. Lovely to meet you, Eddie."

"And you, Trish. So," He turned to Iris, "How are you feeling?"

She smiled from her pillows. "OK, Eddie. I'm sorry."

Joanna scolded her gently, a smile softening her words. "Now then. It's done. Over with."

Iris nodded slowly. The smile sat comfortably on her face.

Another knock sounded. Trish chuckled. "It's like Piccadilly Station in here. Come in."

There was silence followed by another knock.

Trish called out, louder this time. "Come in!"

Silence. Knock.

Joanna walked over and opened the door.

Warren stood there with a wide grin. "Can I come in ??"

"Warren, you idiot."

332

He walked in. "Sorry, Trish. I have to knock and wait to be invited in these days." He switched his gaze to Iris, winked and jerked his thumb at Eddie and Joanna. "Because these two are always at it."

Eddie ignored him. "Look, it's getting a bit crowded in here now. I'm mindful that Iris needs peace and quiet. We'd better get going, sweetheart." He put his arm around Joanna. "I want to get you home and back into bed as soon as possible."

Warren tutted and shook his head at Iris. "See what I mean? Like bloody rabbits."

Iris burst into laughter and slapped him playfully. "Warren!"

Trish looked at her happily. She was back.

Sweet, adorable and wonderfully childlike Iris Ferguson was back.

CHAPTER 44

David arrived at the shop at nine-thirty on Monday morning. Suzanna paused from decorating a Christmas tree in the corner of the room and looked at him. "There you are. The Scarlet Pimple returns. Has Iris turned up? I got a call saying she was missing. Then you vanished too. I left you countless messages to call me back. I was getting worried. Where the hell were you?"

David rolled his eyes as he hung his coat up. "Make me a coffee, Suze. You wouldn't believe what I've been through this weekend."

Suzanna put another bauble on the tree and studied it for a minute. She moved it to another branch.

"Coffee? Hello?"

She walked to the kettle. "It's a good thing you came in. I was going to cancel your viewings for today."

David frowned. "Why? You could have done them."

"What?" She turned, astounded and dropped the milk jug back on the tray.

"Hey, watch it. That's bloody Denby."

Suzanna snapped, "Have you seen my schedule for this week? I've got enough to do without picking up your slack."

"I see you've got time to put a sodding Christmas tree up."

"Christmas is only twelve days away. The tree goes up and I want some petty cash for new decs. I'll nip out for them at lunch."

"Fuck Christmas."

"I beg your pardon?"

"Suzanna, have you not been listening? I have been through hell. I'm lucky to be alive."

"Well tell me where you've been then. I've had people asking for you and looking for Iris. Two Americans. Both quite fit actually. Not wanted by the FBI, are you?"

He took the mug she held out and sat at his desk. "Very funny." He flipped his mouse mat clear of bits and laid it back down. "I," He announced dramatically, "Have been locked in a pigeon coop for twenty four hours."

Suzanna's mug paused, on its way to her mouth. She stared at him for a moment. Then she burst out laughing.

David stared back, his eyebrows lifted. "I'm not joking."

She leaned over the desk, helpless, one hand slapping the surface.

David waited.

She sat up and wiped under her eyes carefully. "Oh, David, you're hilarious."

He folded his arms and sat back, eyes not leaving her face. When she noticed his expression, she stopped and blinked. "You're serious?"

He nodded slowly. She shook her head and her mouth fell open. Then she dissolved into laughter again.

"You don't believe me."

She struggled to speak and shook her head instead.

"OK. Whatever. But you can stuff your new decorations."

¤

At 3.30pm, David returned from an accompanied viewing in a bad mood. It was another old fart heading for an old folks' home. Why did they always follow an inch behind him throughout, making constant interruptions to point out irrelevant features they thought special and inserting useless prattle into his slick narrative. It was so irritating.

David threw his briefcase on the floor and shook off his mac. He'd lost his cashmere Crombie coat to that American bastard, who'd even managed to deck him a second time. Cost a bloody fortune, that coat did. He'd never see it again now.

Suzanna was on the phone. He glanced at the Christmas tree with grudging admiration. She'd bought new decorations after all. It looked good but he wouldn't have much in the way of Christmas spirits this year, unless it was single malt. He still needed the money for Chorlton and could only think of two possible ways to get it. He could either worm his way back into Iris's life or threaten her with a civil lawsuit and claim compensation. From where he stood, the second was the more realistic option. He thought it fair, after everything she'd put him through.

Feeling more cheerful, he sat at his desk and signed Suzanna's petty cash claim. He didn't look up when the door chimed.

"David." A man's voice lifted his eyes.

His face collapsed when he recognised him. Warren had an easy gait as he walked past Suzanna. He stopped in front of David's desk.

Suzanna smiled at him and put her hand over the mouthpiece to address David. "This is one of the gentlemen who were looking for you on Sunday."

David sat up straight. He felt fear trickling down his back but kept his face expressionless. "What do you want?"

"To give you a piece of advice. Iris is alright, by the way. I'm sure you were as worried about her as we were."

"Should I be? She locked me up in that stinking pigeon coop. I could have died of hypothermia, or been shot by the mad bitch."

Suzanna put her caller on hold to listen. She kept the phone to her ear and her face turned away.

Warren moved until his legs were touching the desk. Then he leaned over and rested his arms on the top of David's monitor, hands idling in front of the screen. "Iris had a brain tumour. She was rushed into theatre last night, where they removed it. They pretty much got it in the nick of time."

"Is that supposed to excuse what she did to me?"

Warren exhaled loudly through his nose, righted himself and walked round the desk. David shrank back as he reached him. Warren grabbed the arms of the chair, spun it to face him and looked into David's face. "I'm going to tell you a couple of things and you'd better listen. Right?"

David nodded, sweat beading on his brow.

"One, Iris didn't kidnap you. You invented the story to get back at her for dumping you. Me, Eddie, Joanna, we'll all vouch for that if anyone asks. Right?"

David nodded again.

"Two. I've given Iris the direct line number to the Detective Inspector at the CID that I've been working with. If you go anywhere near her again, she'll ring them and they'll drag you in like a shot. I've told them about some of your shady business dealings, including the theft of two large sums of money from Iris. Now, she says she doesn't want to take the matter further but if you try and get in touch with her, she will. As for the rest of your activities, that's up to them to investigate."

David didn't protest.

Warren released the chair arms. He'd said what he'd come to say but he wasn't quite ready to go. In one movement, he grabbed a handful of David's shirt and pulled him forward until their noses were touching. "I'm this close to punching your lights out. You're a cowardly piece of shit who gets his rocks off bullying and abusing women. So stay away from her. Right?"

David's expression stuttered for a moment then, in horror, his gaze dropped to his trousers. Warren looked down at a dark patch spreading over David's crotch. He pushed him away and straightened up. "I think I'm done here." He turned to look at Suzanna, winked, walked back to the door and left.

By the time she came off the phone, David had vanished inside the staff toilet. Suzanna found herself grinning. David Phillips was finally getting back some of what he had dished out and she was glad she had been there to see it.

CHAPTER 45

Trish was out of the room when Warren arrived back at the hospital. Iris's face lit up when she saw him.

He marched over and kissed her lightly on the lips. "How's my girl?"

"Seen three therapists." She chuckled. "So much fuss."

Warren fell into the chair next to her. Trish had told him that the success of the operation had been such that Mr Munro was cautiously optimistic that there would be no long term cognitive impairment. Apart from the slur and her monosyllabic speech, Warren thought she seemed OK. "Well, you deserve a fuss, after what you've been through. Now, you don't have to worry about David. He'll not be taking any action against you and he's not going to get in touch with you again."

"Why?" She turned onto her side and rested her arm on his.

He stroked it gently. "Let's just say we've had a little chat and he's agreed that it's not in his best interests."

Her eyes widened. "Honestly?"

"Honestly."

She breathed out a long sigh of relief and closed her eyes. "Thank you, Warren."

After a few moments, he realised she'd fallen asleep, a little smile warming her face.

¤

It was five o'clock when David locked up. Suzanna had already gone. He collected the Porsche from behind the shop, switched the lights on, executed a perfect three point turn and guided it smoothly through the entry and sharp left into the rush hour traffic. The journey would take him past the Hare and Hounds. When he drew near, he flicked the indicator and turned into the car park.

Inside the pub a log fire burned in the grate, the cheerful flames warming the room and lighting up lacquered oak walls and beams. It was quiet, being early Monday evening. He ordered a double scotch and dropped into a soft armchair by the fire. He looked down at the new trousers he'd hastily bought after Warren's appearance. They were not something he'd normally dream of wearing but there was only one menswear shop in Bramhall and choice was limited. He wriggled in his seat and pulled at his crotch. His new underwear was a size too small and in danger of cutting off his blood supply.

He was angry that Suzanna had refused to be drawn into what had happened at the shop and refused to accompany him to the police station to report Warren. She insisted that because of the phone call she'd been on at the time, she'd heard none of the conversation.

He stared into the fire miserably and stretched his long legs in front of it. What a crap day. Absolute bleeding crap.

By six-thirty, David had downed another four doubles. He decided it was time to leave. He stood and made his way carefully through the pub. Outside, the ice cold air snapped at his face. When he reached the car, he fell inside and turned on the heating. The efficient system soon had hot air blowing through the vents. He began to feel as mellow as the single malt in his bloodstream.

On reflection, life didn't seem so bad after all. So what, if his plans for the Chorlton shop had to be shelved? It was only a temporary glitch. He still had Didsbury and of course Bramhall. He was sure another opportunity would present itself. There must be more rich and gullible females like Iris knocking around. He had the looks and the charm to be a Lothario. A damn successful one too. He could easily make up the money he needed. And more besides.

He laughed and pulled back into the main road. He was hungry. He would call into the Chinese takeaway on his way home. There was a menu in the glove compartment. He leaned across, opened it, rummaged inside and turned it the right way as he straightened up.

He looked through the windscreen. The traffic lights ahead were on red. The tail lights of the cars in front showed their drivers were already breaking.

He was approaching too fast. He glanced at the speedometer. He was doing forty.

The next second slowed and stretched. His foot slammed the brake pedal to the floor. His hands spun the wheel anticlockwise. The tyres skated on black ice. A tree loomed in front of him.

The impact crumpled the bonnet like paper and it buckled against the windscreen, obliterating his view. The force threw him forward then kicked him back as the seat belt locked.

All of a sudden there was noise around him. Too much noise and voices. Too many voices. People shouting. Horns blaring. Somebody screaming.

What was all the fuss about? He couldn't hear himself think. Why couldn't they all go away and leave him alone?

Then there was blackness and the noise stopped and everything was still and he didn't have to think at all and there was a glorious, peaceful silence.

CHAPTER 46

The rental car was nearing Manchester Airport. Joanna's suitcases contained a beautiful china tea set for her tea room, spotted in a Didsbury charity shop. They had selected an estate agent and her flat would be on the market next week. The agent was doing accompanied viewings only and would keep her informed by telephone. She was looking forward to going back. She felt a twinge of nostalgia at leaving her city and her country again but her heart and her future were with Eddie in South Dakota. Added to that, she was looking forward to seeing John and Laura, the dogs, and her tea room. Everything she loved was there, waiting for her and Eddie's return.

Warren had phoned them yesterday evening with good news. The hospital had received the results of the biopsy. Iris's tumour was benign. She had been discharged and had moved in with Trish that evening. On Trish's insistence, Warren checked out of the Grosvenor and was staying with them until his flight on Friday.

He extended an invitation from Trish for them to call in on the way to the airport. They arrived mid-morning with flowers, magazines and chocolates. Trish showed them through to a warm and cosy living room, where Iris was tucked up on the sofa. She was delighted to see them. She had colour in her cheeks and was wearing a contented smile. Warren was busy decorating a Christmas tree in the bay window.

They stayed long enough for a cup of tea and to share emotional hugs with Iris and Trish. When it was time to leave, Warren walked them to the door and grinned broadly at them. "Right you two, behave yourselves 'til I get back. Give my regards to your folks."

Eddie's opinion of Warren had risen tenfold since they'd been in England. The unwavering loyalty and friendship he'd shown had made a big impression on Eddie. He shook Warren's hand warmly. "Will do. Enjoy what's left of your week, such as it is."

Joanna smiled and threw her arms around him. "You've been brilliant, Warren. So good with Iris and everything. You're a sweetheart. We'll see you when you get home."

"You surely will. And I promise I'll knock. Maybe."

¤

It was surprisingly quiet at the airport. The check-in was quick, the queue at Passport Control was short, their flight was on time and before they knew it, they were on the plane, strapped into their seats and waiting for it to taxi to the runway for the first leg of their journey home.

Joanna put her head on Eddie's shoulder and spoke softly. "The last time we flew from here was under such different circumstances. Was it only eight months ago?"

Eddie smiled and rested his cheek against her head. "We didn't have a clue what we were heading into. Well, you didn't."

She lifted her head. "Maybe one day, we should write a book about everything that happened to us."

"Maybe we will. In the meantime, there's something I've been meaning to ask you."

"What's that?"

"If you'll marry me."

Joanna broke into a smile. "Do you want to know now?"

"Yes please."

Her kiss was the answer he wanted.

CHAPTER 47

Suzanna couldn't believe her eyes when David walked into the shop on Friday morning. She stared as he carefully removed his coat and gloves and walked slowly to his desk. "I thought you weren't coming in this week. Why aren't you at home, recuperating?"

He placed his briefcase on the desk, opened it and removed a sheath of papers. "Bored out of my tits. Anyway, they said I could come back when I felt ready."

Suzanna rolled her chair away and looked at him."So, how long have you got to wear that surgical collar?"

"Ten days all together. Then it has to come off." He sat down carefully and moved his body to the side to answer her. "It's not too bad. Quite comfortable, actually. I'm in more pain from the seat belt. Bruised ribs. Bloody sore."

"You didn't say much when I picked you up from the hospital. Did the police speak to you?"

David smirked. "Yeah, but there wasn't a lot to say. I wasn't conscious when I was brought in so, thankfully, they couldn't breathalyse me. I was well over the limit. The doctor wouldn't give them permission to do a blood test either. I've been charged with speeding and been given a fine and three points so I got away lightly."

Suzanna looked at him angrily. "If I'd known you'd been drinking you'd have made your own way home. David, you idiot, you could have killed somebody."

"Yeah, alright. But I didn't. Even the tree's only suffered minor injuries. Gutted that the Porsche is a write off. It was towed to the Police compound. That's going to cost me. Storage and disposal. First though, the insurance assessor's got to go and check it out. Which brings me to another reason I've come in today. I've got the insurance claim form. Will you fill it out for me? I'll sign it. Want to send it off as soon as possible. It's new for old so I'll get twenty-five thousand quid back. Brilliant, eh? So I can go ahead with the Chorlton shop after all, as soon as the payment comes through."

"Why can't you complete the form?"

"Can't use my right hand. I twisted it on the steering wheel."

Suzanna couldn't resist a snigger. "That's you stuffed, now Iris has dumped you."

"Oh, very funny. Listen, I won't go short, don't you worry."

"Well, come on then. I managed to cover some of your viewings but I had to cancel the rest and the valuations too, obviously. I've put a list on your desk with contact numbers."

"Cheers. I'll go through them now."

She took the claim forms from him and laid

them out on the desk to examine them.

The room fell silent. Suzanna read the letter and turned to the policy document. She looked over at David. "I think you should know..."

He snapped, "Suze, I'm not interested. Just fill it in. I'll manage the signature."

"But you..."

"Suze. Stop mithering. Just fill it in."

She exhaled noisily. "David. Will you listen? This form's not..."

"Suzanna. Can't you see I'm busy?" His face was pale and pinched. He had shadows under his eyes and his forehead was more creased than she'd ever seen. At that moment, Suzanna glimpsed what David would look like when he was old. He continued, turning to face her, his voice becoming strident. "You're only filling in a bloody form. If you interrupt once more, you're sacked. Right?"

She sat back, shocked and angered by his venom. She'd done everything he'd asked of her this week and more besides, and not just this week. Every week. She was sick of it.

David turned back to his desk, muttering angrily. He picked up the phone with his left hand, clamped it between his right ear and shoulder and began to dial.

Suzanna pressed her lips together and chewed the inside of her mouth. The only thing keeping her here was his promise to make her manager when he took charge of the Didsbury shop. After these last few weeks though, she was beginning to think that she didn't want to work for him at all. A friend, who had recently opened an estate agency near Suzanna's home, had been asking her to join her as an equal partner but Suzanna kept refusing, partly through a sense of loyalty to David and partly because she was scared of the venture failing.

Now she was finding the prospect increasingly attractive. An opportunity, not a risk. She was brilliant at her job. She had integrity and a flair for marketing and PR. Perhaps she would take a bottle of wine round to her friend tonight and do some serious talking.

When she focussed on the letter again, she re-read it with a growing smile, extracted the claim form, took the top off a black Biro and began to complete it.

CHAPTER 48

By Friday, the week after Warren flew home, Trish and Iris had settled into a comfortable way of life. Trish looked after her without making a fuss and Iris let her without making demands.

After breakfast that morning, the post arrived. Trish brought it into the living room, leafing through as she entered. "Christmas card. Christmas card. Oh, I love this time of year. Such a change from buff windows and typed addresses and franking. Oh. Spoke too soon. There's one for you, Iris."

Iris looked at it in surprise. "It's been redirected."

"Sorry. I forgot to tell you. I had a redirection order done before you were discharged. I didn't want to risk hospital letters or anything important going to David's – or Paraffin Alley."

Iris smiled warmly, "You think of everything." She turned it over and looked at the address on the flap. "It's from an insurance company."

Trish sat and put the rest of the post on her knee. "Well, open it then."

Iris pulled out a wad of official looking papers.

As she unfolded them and read the letter on the top, her eyes widened and she inhaled sharply.

Trish paused from opening the first card. "What's wrong?"

She scrolled down the page. "David's crashed the Porsche. They've said he's not the registered owner and they've sent me a new claim form."

Trish frowned. "Why?"

Iris looked up. "Because I am, apparently."

"You?"

"Yes. Well, I bought it for him."

Trish's forehead creased and she looked at Iris with astonishment. "I'm sorry? You bought David a Porsche? Iris, what on earth possessed you?"

She shrugged, embarrassed. "He said he'd always wanted one. He was so good after Gran died. I bought it with the auction proceeds." She looked at Trish glumly. "I know. I'm stupid."

Trish threw the cards down and moved to the sofa with a deep sigh. "Oh, Iris. He really did see you coming."

Iris sighed. "I know, Trish but I was so in love with him." Her shoulders caved. "I wanted him to love me too."

Trish held her hand out. "Can I see?" She began to sift carefully through the papers. That done, she returned to the covering letter.

Iris watched her silently, wondering at her serious face.

Finally, Trish drew her eyes away and let them fall on Iris. A smile began to tug at her lips. "What it is, Iris, you paid for the car so it belongs to you. The DVLC registers the keeper of a car, not its owner."

Iris nodded slowly.

"When you bought the Porsche, you took out comprehensive insurance. David was down as the named driver."

"But it was a present for him."

"That's academic. It's still your car, Iris. Only you, as the registered owner, are entitled to claim. The assessor's been to see it, he's confirmed it's a write off and you now need to complete the new form they've sent and they will pay you, new for old." She grinned, "Twenty-five thousand pounds."

Iris's expression changed from incomprehension to surprise then delight. "Twenty-five thousand pounds?"

Trish nodded and laughed happily. "I would say that's adequate compensation for the money he's stolen from you."

Iris began to laugh with her. "I think you're right. Oh, Trish. This is fantastic."

"How about celebrating? Hot chocolate and a mince pie with brandy butter?"

Iris sighed. "Heavenly. I can't wait to tell Warren when he rings." She chuckled. "Not about the hot chocolate and mince pie with brandy butter. I mean the money."

"He'll be over the moon, bless him. I'm glad you're keeping in touch. He's such a nice lad."

Iris's smile fell. "But what's David going to do..."

"He won't do anything, Warren's made quite

sure of that, but I'd love to be a fly on the wall when he finds out."

Trish put the Christmas tree lights on, turned the fire up and sat down. They'd had lunch and Iris had showered after, changed into jeans and a comfortable jumper and brewed a pot of tea.

As they sat together on the sofa, clutching mugs and gazing into the fire, Trish took a deep breath. "Iris, I've got something to ask you. You don't have to decide now, but at least think about it?"

Iris nodded.

"What it is, I've got a cottage in Devon. We inherited it from my husband's parents. We'd always intended to retire there but, of course, he died." She pressed her lips together for a moment before continuing. "I was thinking about moving there. I've discussed it with my son and he's all for it. It's in a beautiful spot, by the sea, in a lovely little village. He wants to buy this house because he and my daughter-in-law love the area and it's convenient for transport links."

Iris blinked. Was she going to be left alone? She wasn't ready yet to step out from the safety of Trish's umbrella.

Trish went on, "I'd like you to move down with me and stay until you're fully recovered. It's the perfect place to convalesce. Then, when you feel ready, you can decide what you want to do with your future. Anyway, give it some thought."

Iris's face lit up. "I don't need to. I can think of nothing better."

Trish was moved to see the pleasure on her face, the sparkle in her eyes. She put an arm around Iris's shoulder and squeezed it gently. "Well, that's settled then. In the new year, we'll make our plans. Yes?"

"Oh, most definitely, yes."

"Lovely! Right, young lady, we got some forms to fill in."

CHAPTER 49

Bill Byrne was in a state of agitation when he pulled up outside 8 Paraffin Alley. He had contacted Suzanna to collect the keys, only to find out that David hadn't changed the locks. Luckily, Bill still had the original ones but he was less than impressed with David's lack of diligence. Bill had promised him exclusivity on all the apartments, for marketing and sales, and David would earn a very generous commission over the next few years. In return Bill didn't expect one hundred percent commitment, he demanded it.

As soon as he climbed out of his car, the door of number six opened and an elderly man hurried down the steps towards him. Bill issued a greeting but it was brushed away impatiently. "This is your place now, am I right?"

Bill nodded. "Is there a problem?"

"I'll say there's a problem. What a disturbance last weekend. Cars, people going in and out, screams, I even heard gunshots."

Bill frowned. "What are you talking about?"

The man pushed on. "Then bloody ambulances turning up, all sirens and flashing lights. I tell you, It was bloody mayhem. We don't expect that sort of thing around here. This is a respectable road. What sort of business are you running? Is it one of them illegal raves? Are they doing drugs? It better not be a knocking shop. I'll not stand for it, I'll tell you that for nowt."

Bill opened his mouth to reply but the door of number ten opened. An old woman emerged and began to walk down the steps. She was slow on her feet and they waited until she joined them.

She eyed Bill suspiciously. "This is your place now?"

Bill was trapped in a pincer movement. He stepped back to keep them both in his sights. "Yes. Are you complaining about the noise too?"

The man nudged him. "She wouldn't have heard anything. Deaf as a post. You'll have to shout."

She saved Bill the bother. "Well, there were people turning up in cars last week, one came and went a few times on Saturday and another turned up on Sunday. They all went into number eight. I went and had a look. They didn't have parking permits. Disgraceful. Stopping legitimate visitors. I was so cross."

Bill was becoming more and more perplexed. The man broke in. "One of the cars was a black Porsche. A right flashy job."

Bill's eyes narrowed. He knew only one man with a black Porsche who would have a reason to be at 8 Paraffin Alley.

The woman spoke again. "Little Iris was

waiting for a chap who pulled up in a fancy black car. He went inside with her then she came out after a bit, got in his car and drove off."

The man looked surprised and shouted in her ear, "Little Iris? What was she doing here?"

"Oh, she's been here a few times. Lets herself in, stays a few hours, then goes."

"Has she? How does she look? She took it hard when Dorothea died."

"No she didn't. The old cow made her life miserable. Dorothea's passing was the best thing that could have happened."

Bill looked from one to the other in confusion. "Who the hell's Iris?"

"What?"

He shouted it.

The woman pursed her lips. "Iris used to live here. Iris Ferguson. When her grandmother Dorothea died, she sold the house. To you, apparently."

Apparently not, Bill thought, judging by the constant stream of human traffic. He held his hands up to both neighbours. "Look, I'm sorry for any distress this has caused you. I think I know who's at the bottom of it and that person will be dealt with severely. I promise you. Nothing like this will ever happen again."

The man sniffed. "It better not. If there's any more of it, I'll call the police. What's more, I'll raise an objection to any planning applications and I'll make sure the rest of the street does as well."

Bill baulked and shook his head vigorously. "That won't be necessary. Perhaps I can offer you a little something by way of compensation?"

The man perked up. "Well, Very thoughtful of you, I must say. I'm partial to a drop of Lambs Navy, myself. Can't afford it these days, not on an army pension."

Bill turned to the old lady.

The old man broke in. "Don't worry about her. She's sound. Tell you what. Drop off half a dozen bottles to me by this evening and I'll say no more about it."

Bill kept his temper in check. The old soldier was playing him like a fiddle but he'd let him get away with it.

David Phillips wasn't going to be as lucky.

CHAPTER 50

"You had a call from Bill Byrne yesterday." Suzanna turned to her notepad.

"Give me a minute, I want to ring the insurance people. Not heard about my claim."

Suzanna nodded, concealing a smile. This was one conversation she very much wanted to hear. She watched as David dialled, his foot tapping impatiently on the carpet. He rubbed the back of his neck gently and began speaking in a soft, honeyed voice.

Suzanna rolled her eyes. Obviously talking to a woman. She waited and was rewarded by a sudden change of tone.

"What do you mean, I can't claim. It's my car. It was a present from an ex-girlfriend."

She could see the side of his face turn a blotchy red. Looked like his blood pressure was up.

"But I've just told you. It was a present. It's my car. My claim. Let me speak to your manager. Oh. You are. Well then, put me through someone who knows what they're talking about. Preferably a man."

Suzanna threw out a breath and rolled her eyes expressively.

After another conversation, David slammed the receiver back in its cradle. He turned to Suzanna. "I can't claim. The stupid bitch said it's Iris's car. Her insurance. You filled the forms in. Didn't you notice?"

Suzanna shook her head innocently. "No. Didn't you?"

"No. She told me to take it up with Iris. Fat chance of that."

Suzanna shrugged philosophically. "Well, there's nothing you can do but move on. You've still got the pool cars. Look at it this way. The Porsche didn't cost you anything so you've not lost anything."

"Except the Chorlton shop." He looked crestfallen.

"Oh. Don't forget Bill." She ripped the relevant page from her pad and waved it around.

David grabbed it from her, walked back to his desk and sat down to read it. When he finished, he stared at Suzanna, his eyes blazing. "I don't believe it. Is this a joke?"

"No."

He sat up and read it out loud. "Bill rang. He's dispensed with your services, using another agency to market the Paraffin Alley apartments." He glanced up, his face contorted. "I don't believe this." He read on. "Ditto the new block in Chorlton." He turned to Suzanna. "Get him on the phone now. He can't do this to me. Paraffin Alley's the bedrock of my Didsbury shop. Not to mention the Chorlton apartments."

She shook her head. "I suggested last night

361

that you ring him but he was adamant that he had nothing more to add."

"No. I'm not having this." He reached for the phone. On connection, he spoke angrily into it. "I want to speak to Bill. Well, where is he then? It's David Phillips. What do you mean, he told you yesterday? I got a message. Not good enough. I want to speak to him. Now."

He fell silent and pulsed a finger manically on the desktop. After a few moments, he brought the receiver quickly back to his mouth. "Bill. What's going on?"

David's eyes closed and his head dropped like a weight into his hand. Several times he opened his mouth to speak but it was obvious he was listening to a diatribe that was in full swing.

Eventually David spoke. "I swear, Bill, it wasn't my fault. I'll make good. Honest. I'm depending on the flats to make the Didsbury agency viable."

Bill cut him off. David slammed the receiver into the cradle.

Suzanna flinched. "Ouch. He obviously isn't taking you back on, then?"

David turned slowly to her. On a face that had paled to ash grey, two red spots of anger burned. "What?"

"Bill. Not giving you a second chance. What have you done to upset him?"

"Let's just say that you won't be promoted to manager of this shop any time soon."

"What the hell have you done, David? It's to do with Iris, isn't it? Surprise View? The two men who came here?"

David stood and walked over. Her reflexes pushed her chair away. "D'you know something, Suzanna? I'm sick of you sticking your nose in my affairs. You think I'm a joke, don't you? Always taking the piss. Well, try it one more time and I'll kick your skinny black arse out the door."

His timing couldn't have been better. Suzanna had planned to tell him today anyway. She kept her temper in check, reached into her handbag and handed him an envelope.

He looked at it blankly.

"It's my letter of resignation."

"What?"

"My resignation. I'm owed a month's leave so," She glanced at the calendar, "as from now, I no longer work for you. I'm going into partnership with a friend in her estate agency."

David's mouth hung open.

"I'm sure you'll find someone else soon to replace me."

She gathered her things from the desk and walked to the door, where she slipped her coat on and buttoned it. She opened the door and stopped briefly to look at him. He was standing like a lost child in the centre of the room, still clutching her letter. For a fleeting moment, she felt pity.

He blinked and looked past her. She followed his gaze. An attractive middle aged woman, beautifully dressed and wearing expensive jewellery, was waiting to pass her.

Suzanna stepped aside and watched as she walked into the shop.

She addressed David as she approached. "Good morning. I hope you can help me. I've recently divorced and been given the house as part of the settlement. It's a substantial property in Prestbury, far too big for me, so I want to sell it and buy something more bijou."

David's face changed in an instant. Prestbury in Cheshire. Stockbroker belt. Millionaires' paradise. He gave her a brilliant smile, placed his hand gently on the small of her back and walked her to his desk.

She took the seat he indicated. He took the chair opposite. "My name's David Phillips. I own this agency – but please, call me David."

"Thank you David. I'm Miranda."

"Miranda. What a beautiful name." Ocean blue eyes filled her vision.

Suzanna stifled a laugh. David's charm was in overdrive and seemed to be working.

"Would you like me to come and value the property, Miranda?"

"Yes, please, David. Any time's convenient for me. Morning, noon or night."

David reached for his Filofax and opened it. "Well, luckily enough, I can do it this afternoon, then work out the valuation back at the office. I'll have the figures by this evening. We could discuss the way forward. Over dinner perhaps?"

Suzanna chuckled as she walked away.

David Phillips was going to be fine.

PART FOUR
DEVON, ENGLAND

CHAPTER 51

By May the following year, Iris had lived with Trish in Devon for three months. With her friend's care and the beauty of their surroundings aiding her convalescence, Iris had made a full recovery. In March, she felt well enough to volunteer two days a week at a cat sanctuary not far from the cottage. By April, she felt able to increase this to four.

One day, her shift finished, Iris made her way to the sanctuary office. Andrew, the manager, was perched on his desk, arms crossed, engaged in conversation with another man, who had his back to her. Andrew was laughing, wiping his eyes.

Iris hovered in the doorway as the other man began speaking again. He had a nice voice, deep and warm. She wondered what sort of face would match it. She waited for the right moment to interrupt.

The man started telling Andrew a joke. "So anyway, I was having dinner with a chess champion the other day and there was a chequered cloth on the table. It took him two hours to pass the salt."

Iris exploded into laughter and both men turned to her. She touched her mouth. "Sorry, I didn't mean to eavesdrop."

Andrew beckoned her forward. "Iris, come in, come in."

She walked shyly over. "I'm just coming to tell you that I've finished the morning feed, all the litter trays are done, fresh water, floors swept and mopped. Is there anything else before I go?

"Yes. Meet our new vet, Mr O'Malley."

With one look, Iris registered everything about him. Medium height, medium build. Sandy hair, sandy eyes. His age. How his eyes twinkled, how the corners crinkled and how the lines around his mouth deepened when he smiled at her. How his face was kind and open.

He held out his hand and she shook it. "Hi, Iris. Pleased to meet you. I'm Tom."

Andrew started to whistle a tune.

Tom rolled his eyes. "Go on, Andy. Get it over with."

"Thank you." Andrew stood, began to waltz around Iris and broke into a song. She clasped her hands under her chin and giggled.

"I'm Abraham deLacey, Giuseppe Casey, Thomas O'Malley, O'Malley the local vet."

Iris clapped in delight. "Thomas O'Malley. How wonderful!"

She realised Tom was staring at her. She couldn't help but stare back.

Andrew stood to the side, eyes travelling from one to the other, an amused look on his face.

"Right. Enough frivolity. We're not here to enjoy ourselves. Iris, love, many, many thanks. Get yourself off home now. See you tomorrow."

¤

Tom called in the next morning. He parked near the office and strolled over to the sanctuary building and into reception. Iris was sitting behind the desk, a tiny tabby kitten swaddled in a cloth on her lap. She was feeding it a pipette of kitten milk and, so immersed in her task, she didn't notice his entrance.

"Iris."

She looked up and smiled with pleasure. "Oh. Hello, Tom."

"I'm just off on my rounds. Thought I'd pop in. We didn't get a proper chance to say hello yesterday."

Iris's smile widened. She finished feeding the kitten and placed him gently on a heated pad in the basket by her feet. She straightened up with another, this one pure black.

Tom's mouth dropped open in mock surprise. "How on earth did you do that?"

She looked at him, back at the kitten then collapsed into laughter.

Tom walked to her side of the desk and looked down at the five kittens curled together in the basket. "Ah. There's more than one. Clever."

Iris looked down and back at him, still laughing. "You are silly."

He grinned. "You've got your work cut out there. Do you want some help?"

367

He pulled a chair over and joined her. "Who's next?"

Iris prepared a pipette for him. "The ginger one."

They sat together, completely at ease, singing along to records on the radio, chatting, Iris laughing at his jokes. He didn't ask personal questions, apart from how long she'd been volunteering and Iris didn't offer any other information other than her love of animals and her dream that one day she'd work with them. It was a treat to be with someone who had no agenda other than sharing her company.

¤

Over the next month, Tom popped in whenever he could. Iris would make tea and sometimes brought in scones she'd baked that morning. Never with cherries though. They chatted as if they'd known each other for years, their conversations punctuated with smiles and laughter. She found out that he was her age, single and had moved from Lytham St Annes in Lancashire six months ago into the big rambling house his late grandparents had left him just outside the village. He told her he was setting up a small animal practice and intended to convert the ground floor into a waiting room, treatment room and surgery. He was concentrating on providing affordable pet care for low income families and pensioners.

Tom confessed that he wasn't rich by any means but he absolutely loved what he was doing and he was happy. That, he felt, was a life well spent. Sometime in the future, when he was fully established, he wanted to take somebody on to cover reception during clinic hours and assist him at other times. The applicant would receive training for both.

Tom had looked at her pointedly until she took his cue and said she would like to work with him, if he thought she'd be suitable. To her delight, he had winked and said she was perfect for him, at which she had blushed and felt her heart flip.

¤

It was a beautiful summer day when she finally told him about herself. They both had a free afternoon and had decided to go for a walk along the beach.

Iris picked up shells as they strolled and they admired the beauty, colour, texture and shape of each one as it lay in the palm of her hand. Tom listened raptly as she walked him through her life, the wonderful early years with her parents and her grandfather, the wilderness years after their deaths, her grandmother's fatal accident.

She told him about Paraffin Alley and how Grumps had called their house 'Surprise View' because it faced an eight foot brick wall.

"Go on. There was no view – that was the surprise!" Tom bent double, laughing.

Then she found the courage to tell him about David, about Joanna, about her tumour, about the terrible things she had done as it grew inside her brain. How it had transformed her into a violent woman, fuelled by fear, anger and jealousy.

This was the defining moment of their friendship. Would he walk away? She braced herself as she waited for his reaction. To her astonishment and joy, he stopped, pulled her into a hug and told her she was the bravest, most wonderful person he had ever known. They stayed in each other's arms, scarcely breathing, knowing that something special was happening. Their embrace became a kiss, wrapped in warmth and passion.

When they continued, Tom caught hold of her hand and they strolled in silence, enjoying the new depth of feeling between them.

Finally, he spoke. "So where does Iris Ferguson go from here?"

She stared out to sea, blinking at the sun as it sparkled on the surface. "I don't know, Tom. I really don't know. I'm thirty and I know nothing about the world. I'm scared of what the future might hold for me." She turned to him. "I'm frightened I'll get things wrong again. I need a leap of faith."

Tom stopped and regarded her. His face was serious but held a gentleness that tugged at her heart. "Would you make that leap if you knew I was there to catch you?" His face broke into a grin. "And if you trusted me not to drop you?"

Iris laughed as she jumped into his arms.

And he didn't.

ABOUT THE AUTHOR

Cathie Melling was born in Harrogate, brought up in Manchester and now lives in with her husband in Lytham St Annes in Lancashire.

She had many short stories featured on BBC regional radio earlier in her writing career. 8 Paraffin Alley is her second novel.

Printed in Great Britain
by Amazon

24251970R00205